18 BUZZY LANE

A Casey Quinby Mystery

18 Buzzy Lane

By Judi Ciance

judiciance@gmail.com
judiciance.com
Published: October, 2016

ISBN-13:978-1537463537
ISBN-10:1537463535

Also in the Casey Quinby Mystery Series:

Empty Rocker (November 2012)
Paint Her Dead (October 2013)
Caught With A Quahog (October 2014)
A Tale of Two Lobsters (October 2015)

Dedication

To My Husband
Paul Ciance
*His encouragement to continue,
his patience to listen and
his help in keeping me in line
are why Casey is back on the scene.*

and also,

*To my special friend
Dell French
Who is now watching over me
and my endeavors to become
the best I can be.
Miss you, Dell.*

Acknowledgements

This author wants to thank Beverly Blackwell and Judy Pinkham. Because of their support, expertise, and guidance, I was able to bring the reader yet another suspenseful and absorbing case in the exploits of Casey Quinby.

I also thank my critique groups for keeping me on track and helping me develop more as a writer. David, Ray, Dallas and Mark ... you guys are the best.

18

BUZZY LANE

Enjoy

A Casey Quinby Mystery

By

Judi Ciance

*To Sally
Casey's back to work!
Judi Ciance
January 31, 2017*

Chapter 1

A month passed before I returned to my office in Barnstable Village. I figured my first case as a PI would be to follow a cheating spouse, search for a missing person or investigate a probate matter—boring. It turned into a murder investigation with me right in the middle. I almost died.

For just a minute, I wondered if leaving the Tribune had been smart. My old boss, Chuck Young, assured me if I wanted to come back to the newspaper as the head investigative reporter, my door key would still fit. I banished the thought.

Then there was Sam, my significant other. I promised him that I'd ease back into my new career with light duty cases. Of course I crossed my fingers behind my back. But then, he knew that—after all, he was a seasoned police detective.

I walked over to my front window. People living on Cape Cod craved the sand and beach— for me, it was the view of the District Court to the left, Superior Court to the right, and the District Attorney's Office straight across the street.

I was content in my new profession. I was ready to unleash my inner Sherlock—again.

My mind was still in dream mode when I turned to walk back to my desk. The sudden knock on the front door startled me straight off the floor. I spun around. The sun streamed through the window so brightly that I couldn't make out if the knocker was a man or a woman. I took a deep breath to calm my racing heart, walked over, unlocked and opened the door.

An old man carrying a Macy's shopping bag with something inside wrapped in a bright pink towel occupied my welcome mat.

"Can I help you?"

He looked up at my shingle. "If you're Casey Quinby, Private Investigator, you can."

Chapter 2

Boston - Tuesday

The eight a.m. traffic on Route 3 heading into Boston from Cape Cod was filled with its normal heavy-duty horn honking. "Remind me why I agreed to take this case." The sun was blinding. I started to reach into the console between the front seats when a finger-slinging asshole cut me off. I needed both hands back on the wheel. "Do me a favor and find my sunglasses before we get into an accident."

Marnie fumbled through a bunch of crumpled up old receipts and empty gum wrappers. "Not here." She reached in her purse. "Take mine."

"Thanks. If there's not an accident or jam, we should be in the North End by nine-thirty. We're not meeting Maloney's father until eleven, so we'll swing by Quincy Market and I'll grab a new pair."

"Before we get to Boston, fill me in on what's going on."

"Patrick O'Malley, my mystery visitor, is from South Boston. He's a friend of Big M's. I'm not really sure why he made the trip to the Cape, except he said he wanted to meet me. Believe me, he didn't say much more. He had a Macy's bag with him. In the bag was a pink towel with something wrapped up in it. He didn't take the towel out of the bag, just moved it a little, so I could make out what he was concealing. It was a Raggedy Ann doll."

"Who did the doll belong to?"

"He said he and his wife had given it to their granddaughter who died twenty-five years ago in a house fire in Sandwich. The baby was only one month old. Patrick called Big M, told him he

3

was in my office, then handed me the phone. I had no idea what I was agreeing to, but took the case because Big M asked me to. Nothing else was said. Patrick thanked me, shook my hand and said he'd talk to me after I met with Big M." The North End exit was just ahead, so I eased into the right lane.

"Why didn't Big M want us to meet him at the police station in Southie?"

"I'm not really sure, but he was emphatic we didn't. The directions he dictated over the phone are in my purse. He said to leave my car in the same police lot we used the day we came up with Sam and Maloney, then walk up Hanover Street, cross over the Rose Fitzgerald Kennedy Greenway and go down two blocks to the Marriott Custom House. He's going to meet us in front of the hotel."

Chapter 3

"So much for a short-cut. I'll never again ask a stranger in an unfamiliar place for directions, especially when the first turn leads into an alleyway. Even on television, alleyways have dumpsters, doorways, windows, fire escape ladders and sometimes small balconies. This is barely wide enough for us to walk through single file. God forbid if we cross paths with a rat."

"Stop your bitching. One of these days I'll introduce you to New York City. In the Big Apple, buildings are butted up against each other, so you have to walk a couple blocks just to get to the other side. This is nothing."

"This is a first and a last. I see light behind us and in front of us, but this dark spot in the middle just isn't cutting it." I picked up the pace.

Strange looks followed us as we emerged from the 'crack' between the two buildings. I looked up at the business signs that framed the end of the alley. The one to the right was barely readable, the paint and logo faded with age and worn by the elements. In its day, it was a fur warehouse. The windows were frosted on the inside and layered with soot and dirt on the outside—an indication the business was defunct.

Marnie studied the building to our left. "These are some old structures. This one's divided into a few establishments—and not all commercial."

I walked past her, my eyes moving as fast as my feet. "The second one looks like a private association." The sign was lettered

5

by an amateur—SICILIAN AMERICAN CLUB—Members Only. "There's even a little window, eye level." I laughed. "Did you ever see the movie, *Public Enemy*, with James Cagney? To get into the Private Club he had to knock, wait for somebody to slide the window covering open and approve him for entry."

Marnie shook her head. "You've got a vivid imagination."

"I wonder if there's anyone inside. Maybe I should play Cagney and knock."

"Don't be a jerk. There's a bench across the street. Let's sit, regroup and figure out which way we go from here." Marnie didn't wait for a reply.

She was standing on the center island when I turned around. I held my hands up like a megaphone. "Where's your sense of adventure?" I looked down the street before I crossed. "Wait for me."

"If we're going to spend time in Boston, you can't be running solo. You don't know the city. I'm sure it's a fun, exciting place on an ordinary day, but you're here on business. And, Casey Quinby, if I know you, nothing is going to be ordinary."

"Let's get a coffee and go over the basics before we meet with Big M. It looks like there's some people traffic down the street." I stood and waited for Marnie's response.

"Yeah, sure."

Two blocks down and around the corner we found a Dunkin Donuts. "Well, damn, if we hadn't taken that so-called short-cut, I'd already be enjoying a cup of French Vanilla. Want one?"

"You buying?"

"Yep. I'll hit you up later when it's not just a cup of joe."

We got our coffee and found a two-seater high top in the corner.

"I still don't understand why we couldn't meet him in Southie"

"I don't know." I shrugged. "Did Maloney say anything to you about us meeting his father?"

"Nothing. I asked, but he said he really wasn't sure what was going on, and if and/or when Big M wanted him to know, he'd tell him." Marnie shook her head. "What did Sam say?"

"He didn't seem too concerned because whatever it was came from Big M. Still, it's unlike Sam not to give me all sorts of instructions before I'm about to embark on a case. I'm sure Big M filled Sam in on why we're here. You know—from one cop to another." I took a drink. "It's all pretty strange."

"How did Big M get involved?"

"The old man, Patrick O'Malley, said he was a friend of Big M's who told him to talk to me. I guess I should be flattered."

"I'm more confused than ever. Didn't this Patrick man detail the whole story?"

"No, he said he'd rather I got everything from Big M. I have to admit, I'm baffled, but we should know something soon enough."

Chapter 4

As we rounded the corner from Commercial onto State Street, Big M came into view. He was standing in front of the Custom House.

"Morning ladies." He gave us both a hug.

"And, good morning to you, too." I looked around trying to figure out where we were going to hold our meeting.

"A friend of mine owns the Black Rose Pub." He turned slightly to the left and pointed to a building we'd just walked by. "He's got a small meeting room in the back. It's empty today, so we'll meet there, then have lunch."

"You lead. We'll follow." I looked up over the door. "*Lobsters Love Guinness*. Love the flag. I want one."

"You and a thousand others. He'd make a fortune if he sold them."

Big M obviously knew the hostess. She kissed him on the cheek, then directed us to the backroom. "I grew up, then worked with her father, Jim Kelly, in Southie. In fact, he's going to stop by. I want you both to meet him."

"Is there a reason for the introduction?"

"First, I want Jim to meet Rusty's better half. My son did good." He smiled at Marnie. "Our kids grew up to together. But, most important, you're going to find him helpful in your new case."

I shrugged and turned my palms toward the ceiling in a questioning manner. "Since I have no idea what my new case actually is, anything he tells me will be helpful."

Big M checked his watch. "He won't be here for another hour, so we'll get started."

I pulled a notepad from my briefcase. "Tell me about Patrick O'Malley. The only thing I know is his granddaughter died in a fire in Sandwich twenty-five years ago. When he showed up at my office he was carrying a Macy's bag with a Raggedy Ann doll wrapped in a pink towel. I started to ask questions, but was told he'd rather I talk to you. It was bizarre—yet intriguing."

Big M leaned forward and rested his arms on the table. "Twenty-five years ago, Patrick and Mary O'Malley buried their only daughter and son-in-law, Megan and Charlie Davis, along with an empty casket for baby Carleen. The baby's remains were never found. It was determined that the child, being so small and the fire so intense, was burned beyond cremation. The fire marshal reported the cause as a wood burning stove improperly installed in the family room. Further documentation stated that the fire got away from the stove, traveled through the rest of the house, then worked its way into the garage where Patrick's son-in-law stored containers of gasoline for his toys. The rest is history."

"At this point, all I'm hearing is a fire story with a tragic ending. Obviously, there's more. Are the O'Malleys from the Cape?"

"No, they're from South Boston—friends who are like family. Pat and my father did the Southie St. Patrick's Day parade together. You don't get much closer than that."

"So, the daughter and son-in-law lived on the Cape?"

"Yep, for about four years. They built a house on four acres, between two cranberry bogs in Sandwich. Their closest neighbors either weren't year-round or were so far away, that when the fire started, nobody noticed."

"If the three occupants of the house died in the fire, then where does Casey fit into the equation? What's she being hired to do?" Marnie took the words right out of my mouth.

"I guess I'm still not seeing the complete picture," I said.

9

"Before we go any further, let's order lunch. I recommend the fish and chips—best around."

"This is your neck of the woods. I'm in."

"Me, too," said Marnie. "And a Diet Coke, please."

When Big M walked to the bar to order, I turned to Marnie. "There's a hell of a lot more to this story. I'm interested, but Sam's not going to be happy even though he's the one who encouraged me to talk to Big M."

"All the details are probably why Maloney wouldn't talk about it either."

"Foods ordered." Big M resumed his position behind the table facing the door. "Back to Patrick O'Malley."

I nodded in agreement.

"After what was called 'a thorough investigation' by both the police and fire departments, it was ruled an accident and the case was closed. Pat never thought the fire was an accident, but he had no proof otherwise. For years, he tried to come up with something to make them reopen it, but no dice. He found nothing. Nothing, until now."

My puzzled expression screamed fifty questions.

"Pat came to me last week, not at the station—at my house. He showed me the same Macy's bag and its contents that he showed you. The only difference was I got an explanation."

"And?"

"You already know the doll was a gift from the grandparents, Patrick and Mary. What you didn't know is that baby Carleen had it in her crib with her every night—Megan made sure of it. Megan O'Malley Davis was a Southie girl. She didn't want to move to the Cape. It was her husband, Charlie Davis, who made the decision to relocate. Megan's parents weren't happy. The Raggedy Ann doll was the O'Malley's tie to Carleen."

I put my elbow on the table and my chin in the palm of my hand. My eyes studied each move on Big M's face, as I absorbed every word he said.

"When did Raggedy Ann reappear?"

"A week ago last Saturday, he went outside at seven a.m. to get the newspaper and the bag was on the front stoop," said Big M.

I freed my chin and leaned closer. "Do the O'Malleys think Carleen is still alive?"

Chapter 5

The server had just cleared our table when Jim Kelly walked in. "We were getting ready to order coffee," said Big M.

Jim looked at the server. "Make mine Irish."

"That kind of a day?"

"Nope, it's after twelve o'clock."

"I'll never understand Irish humor," I said.

"Jim, I'd like you to meet Casey Quinby, the PI Patrick hired to look into his granddaughter's case, and her friend, Marnie, Rusty's better half. Marnie is an Assistant District Attorney out of Barnstable."

Jim shook hands with both of us, then took a seat beside Big M. "Your son inherited your good taste." He gave Marnie a nod of approval. "Did you fill them in on Patrick's backstory and current story?"

"I gave them the overall version without going into the reason behind the O'Malleys suspicions regarding the fire."

"I'm going to back up and give you some history on Megan and Charlie Davis. Big M and I grew up down the street from Megan. She was six years younger than us. Our families were very close. That's how it used to be in Southie back then. Things have changed, but that's a different story. Charlie wasn't a native to Southie. He came from Dorchester—the same neighborhood as Mark Wahlberg. They weren't really friends, more like associates. They both ran the streets and got in trouble. Charlie didn't get caught or, should I say, didn't get charged. Mark did, but he straightened himself out and, from what I understand, Charlie didn't."

"When did Charlie come into Megan's world?" I asked.

"She was only seventeen. Patrick was furious. But, the more he tried to break Megan and Charlie up, the more she gravitated towards him." Jim shook his head. "It wasn't a pretty picture. It's every South Boston's Irish family's dream to have their daughter marry a Southie and stay in the neighborhood."

Big M took a deep breath then continued where Jim left off. "Patrick practically disowned his daughter for her involvement with Charlie. Although he denied it, we're positive it was Pat who spread rumors tying Charlie to drugs. There was no big wedding. Pat and Mary only started talking to Megan again, when they found out she was pregnant."

"Was anything ever proven to substantiate the drug claims?" I asked.

"Nothing."

Marnie looked at Big M. "Did you see anything that would authenticate a drug connection? Sometimes what parents think and what a person's peers see, are very different."

"We didn't like Charlie. He didn't fit in, but we were Southie boys, and he was messin' with one of our girls. Having said that, I don't recall seeing anything that would associate Charlie with drugs."

"I have a question and you have an answer." I looked only at Big M. "Why didn't we meet at the precinct in South Boston?"

"This case has been a sore subject for twenty-five years. Patrick didn't understand, or didn't want to understand, why the South Boston precinct couldn't handle the investigation. No matter what we tried to tell him about jurisdiction, he wouldn't accept any of it. He claimed the probe done on the Cape was inadequate and he let them know about it. Several times he was escorted out of the Sandwich PD. One of the times I drove down there to bring him home."

"There were about four years where we didn't see much of Pat. He just couldn't accept the loss of his daughter and granddaughter." Jim took a deep breath. "I don't know how I'd handle it myself."

"He finally started to come around. He never talked about Megan and Carleen, but he got his life together as best he could." Big M held his cup up to catch the attention of a passing server. "Anyone else?"

Marnie and I got a fresh cup. Jim was still nursing his Irish special.

"First I've got to get things in somewhat of an order. I won't have any trouble getting reports from the Sandwich PD and fire departments. I'll also check with the Mid Cape Medical Examiner, Ernie Mullins. I've worked many cases with him, so since it's a closed case, I'm sure it won't be a problem getting copies of his reports."

"Remember, this goes back twenty-five years," said Big M.

"Ernie keeps everything—maybe not hard copies, but it's all scanned into his computer and backed-up on discs."

"Since this wasn't our case, we have nothing in the archives relating to it." Big M shrugged. "And, at this point, I don't want my boss to know I'm semi-involved in maybe reopening it."

"I understand, but there are things I'll need your help on."

"I assumed that." Big M glanced at Jim. "I said you might find Jim helpful? Well, this is what I was referring to. Jim owns a neighborhood bar in Southie. He's got contacts that may be able to furnish interesting information."

"I welcome any help I can get, but I need to be the one who decides what I need." It seemed forever before anyone spoke.

Jim sat back in his chair and folded his arms over his chest. "I don't intend to undermine your investigation. I'm here if you need me. I understand you're running the show. And that's how it should be. I'll give you my contact information. You can reach me anytime, day or night, at one of these numbers." He pulled a business card from his pocket. "The number printed on the front is for my business, Boston Blackies. The ones I wrote on the back are for my home and my cell. Don't hesitate to use any one of them." He checked his watch. "The booze bunch doesn't wait for anyone. I've got to get back to L Street." He stood and extended his hand.

14

"Nice to meet you. We'll talk soon." He turned to Marnie. "Keep Rusty in line and tell him I said 'hi'." He gave us a two-finger salute as he walked out the door.

"One of my best friends. You don't have to worry about him."

"I have no way to get ahold of Patrick O'Malley. He wanted me to talk to you first before I took the case." I shrugged. "Now that we've talked and I'm on board, I've got a few ideas on how I should approach it, but I have to organize them before I go off half-cocked. And, as Marnie reminded me, we're in Boston, which is a far cry from Cape Cod. I need to get all my ducks in a row and do preliminary investigating before I start skulking around."

"When will you be ready to meet with Patrick?"

"Today is Tuesday. I should have some stuff on the burner by next Monday. Tell him I'll meet him someplace convenient in the Boston area."

"I'll give him a call, then let you know. I'll be there too."

"Sounds like a plan."

"You girls should start back so you don't get stuck in the five o'clock gridlock."

Chapter 6

"Are you getting any closer to what this is all about?" Marnie asked.

"Yes and no. Yes, because the O'Malleys think their granddaughter is still alive and no, because why didn't she die in the fire?"

"So, are you thinking the fire wasn't an accident?"

"I am." I gave Marnie a quick glance then focused back on the road. "Something doesn't set well with me regarding Charlie Davis, and not just because Big M and Jim didn't like him. Tomorrow morning I'll stop over at Sandwich PD. The reports may have been sent to archives. In that case, I'll order a copies of them. That could take a week. Same with the fire department. I've never worked with the FD, so I'm not sure of their procedures. Once I get that stuff in the works, I'll talk to Chuck about using the Tribune computer. I want to do in-depth background checks on both Megan and Charlie Davis."

"Not to change the subject, but did you have Mr. O'Malley sign a contract saying he hired you to investigate something concerning his granddaughter?"

"I didn't. Now that I've talked to Big M, I'll draw something up and bring it with me next Monday."

"Don't forget the confidentiality clause? Legally, you're supposed to get permission to discuss the case with persons other than him and/or his wife. And, that brings us to another question: Is his wife a part of this? Does she know what he's doing?" Marnie hesitated. "If she doesn't, then you'll have to get his permission to talk to her, too."

"Okay, legal beagle, I'll take care of the paperwork before I get too involved." I smiled. "Hey, we're going to be near Manomet, just past Plymouth. Do you remember going to 42 Degrees with Sam and Maloney on our way back from Boston last year?"

"That was the one with the great lobster roll."

"How 'bout we stop and have one?"

"You're driving. I'm just a passenger, but if you don't stop, I'll pout."

"We can't have that now, can we?" I smiled. "I'm glad Sam took Watson to his house this morning. Poor little guy, I hate leaving him alone all day."

"Is Sam coming to Hyannisport tonight?"

"No. He's working on a grant. Something to do with that terrorism conference he attended at Quantico last year. He said it's for some serious money to get specialized equipment for training."

Chapter 7

There were people at the bar and several tables close to the windows were taken. We headed for one towards the back of the restaurant where we could talk without an audience.

"I'm going to have a White Zin. How 'bout you?"

"Twist my arm." Marnie reached across the table. "Make mine Pinot Noir. We're not in any hurry. We don't have to order food yet. Let's unwind and hash over the conversations of the day."

The server came and took our drink order.

"Tomorrow I'm going to head to the office and draft a plan of action. Per my lawyer's advice, I'll prepare a contract for the O'Malleys to sign. I know I'm putting the cart before the horse, but I'm going to start my investigation before I have the signed copy. I don't anticipate any problems."

"I have to work on a briefing for a case Michael is working on, so I'll be in the office all day. If you need me to look up something, give me a call."

"Why don't I meet you and Annie for lunch at Finn's?"

"Yes for me, but let me check with her."

"Okay. Now, back to the case at hand." I stopped when I saw the server coming closer with our drinks.

"Would you like to order food now?"

"No, we're going to do a little talking first. I'll move the menus to the edge of the table when we're ready."

"The first thing after the contract is to head over to Sandwich PD and Fire Departments. While I'm in Sandwich, I'll take a ride by the area where the fire took place. I forgot to ask Big M if the

18

property was sold and, if so, did the new owners rebuild. That was twenty-five years ago. The house sat on four acres. There could be a whole bunch of houses there now."

"Earlier, you mentioned asking Chuck if you could use the computer at the Tribune to research some articles. It might be helpful if you did that before you talked to the police and fire departments? You might get some insight from what was written."

"Good point. I'll also get a copy of the obituaries. Since Megan and Charlie were relatively new to the Cape and their families were from the Boston area, their funerals might have happened off Cape. That's easy enough to find out."

"We took a few minutes to scan our menus, and then got back to the case. What are your thoughts about baby Carleen being alive? She'd be twenty-five years old now."

"That all seems strange, doesn't it? I'm going to do a lot of thinking and write down anything that comes to mind, whether it's nutty or not." I shook my head, then took a sip of wine. "If only Raggedy Ann could talk."

Chapter 8

Wednesday

My alarm was set to go off at seven, but I was wide awake at six. I wasn't used to no Sam to snuggle with or no Watson curled up at the foot of my bed. There was no smell of coffee brewing in the Keurig or English muffins crisping in the toaster. I didn't like it.

I couldn't call the Tribune before eight. Sam was in Bourne, and I didn't want to bother him in case he was working on the grant. I took my shower, got dressed, and made a pit stop at Dunkin's to grab a couple jelly donuts and a large French Vanilla before I went to my office.

I pulled into my parking space behind my building. There were two cars parked next to mine in spaces clearly marked for clients. Since I wasn't expecting anyone, they were obviously poachers. "Apparently, these people can't read English. I'll stick a note on their windshield." I grabbed my briefcase, coffee and donuts and proceeded to unlock the back door.

It was only seven-thirty—too early to call Chuck. I plated my breakfast, poured my coffee and headed to my desk.

I'd just gotten my computer booted up and taken my notes from my briefcase, when I looked up and saw a silhouette of a person outside my front window. Last week I put a small bistro table with a weighted down petunia, daisy, and vinca vine arrangement and two small chairs in the narrow grassy area. Apparently, it invited someone to sit down and make themselves comfortable. I had too much work to do, so I ignored my human lawn ornament and started to write the contract for Patrick and Mary O'Malley. I'd just

20

swallowed a mouthful of coffee, when there was a knock on the door.

The silhouette I'd observed earlier had acquired a partner.

So much for getting an early start.

My face emoted pure shock when I opened the door and saw Patrick O'Malley and a woman, I assumed to be Mary, standing perfectly still, holding hands, waiting for me to ask them in.

I stepped aside and invitingly swept my arms across my body giving them permission to enter.

Patrick spoke first. "Casey, I'd like you to meet my wife, Mary."

Instead of shaking my hand, she leaned forward and hugged me.

I was totally unprepared for their unannounced visit. "I thought Big M said he would set up a meeting for next Monday? That was the plan when we talked yesterday afternoon."

"He called and told me about Monday, but I wanted Mary to meet you. Besides, I know we have to sign a contract. You're not doing this for nothing. We brought a check. Tell us what you need to get started and we'll take care of that right now."

"I was just about to write it up." I walked behind my desk. "I have a suggestion. Nancy's Donut Shop is a few doors up the street. She has great coffee and makes the best sticky buns around. Take a half-hour, let me get the paperwork ready, then we'll go over it. Once that's done, we'll talk more about the case."

Mary smiled.

"We can do that." Patrick turned toward Mary. "I told you you'd like her. We'll be back in a half-hour." They headed out the front door.

The digital display in the bottom right corner of my computer read eight-sixteen. I didn't have time to call Chuck, but I needed to give Marnie a heads-up about lunch. I speed dialed her. She answered on the first ring. I put my phone on speaker.

"You're too early. I haven't had time to ask Annie about lunch yet."

21

"Hold off. I've already had company this morning. I got here at seven-thirty and the O'Malleys were waiting for me."

"Where are they now?"

"I sent them to Nancy's for coffee. I'm supposed to be working on their contract, so I can't talk. I'll call you later." I didn't wait for a reply.

Fortunately, my basic contract was a fill-in-the-blank I'd developed before my first case, then tweaked it so I could use it for future jobs. My standard up-front retainer was two thousand dollars, then fifty dollars an hour, plus expenses to include mileage, any documentation I'd have to pay for and lodging, if I had to travel. That was standard. I couldn't fill in what the actual investigation was because I wasn't one-hundred percent sure. After talking to the O'Malleys, I'd be able to incorporate that part.

I expected the O'Malleys to come through the door at any minute when my cell rang. It was Sam. "Good morning." It was good to hear his voice.

I looked up. "I can't talk right now. The principals in the Big M case are about to walk through my door. I'll call you later." I ended the call, shut off the ringer and set my cell on the corner of the desk.

This time the O'Malleys didn't knock.

"You were right. The sticky buns were wonderful," said Mrs. O'Malley. "Almost as good as mine." She took a seat in front of my desk. Patrick sat beside her.

"Let's go over the contract basics, then we'll talk specifics." I printed a copy and handed it to them to read.

After they read it, Patrick passed it back to me. "That's fine. We agree to your terms. We'll write you a check before we leave." He took a deep breath. "Can we talk about the particulars now?"

"We can, but before we do, I'd like to ask you both a question. As a licensed private investigator, I'm not supposed to discuss your case with anyone without your permission. We know that Big M, legally Tom Maloney, is involved. There are a couple other people I'd like to include in my circle who can help me get information useful in solving the case."

"Do I know them?" Patrick leaned on the desk and rubbed his chin.

"I have a friend, Marnie Levine, who's an Assistant District Attorney in Barnstable County. Her office is across the street. She's helped me on several cases I've worked. Next is Detective Sam Summers. He's the head detective in Bourne. Again, his background and knowledge have been invaluable to my success. Those are the two you don't know, but probably will meet at some point. The next person you do know. Big M introduced me to him yesterday—Jim Kelly."

Mary and Patrick shared a glance before Pat spoke, "There's no problem with any of them. If there's somebody else to add to the list, we give you our permission to do so without having to ask. Can we do that?"

"We'll put it into the contract." I found the clause about permission to consult with other professionals, then added a passage giving the O'Malley's consent to use my discretion regarding who I might share information with.

"Can we sign the paperwork now?" asked Patrick.

"After we talk about the case."

Patrick took a deep breath. "This isn't going to be easy."

"Reminiscing about a tragic experience is never easy." I took a second to compose my thoughts. "I planned on gathering information from various sources so I could intelligently relate to the incident and surrounding circumstances before I sat down with you." I leaned forward on my desk. "Does Big M know you're here?"

"No. I wanted my wife to meet you. Besides, it isn't Big M who's retaining you."

Chapter 9

"It was twenty-five years and four days ago that we received a telephone call from our son-in-law's parents telling us that their son, Charlie, our daughter, Megan, and our granddaughter, Carleen, were victims of a horrific fire. The kids lived in Sandwich. It took two days before any family members were notified."

I made notes as Patrick spoke.

"They lived way off the main road on four acres of land—their house was situated towards the back of the property. They also bordered defunct cranberry bogs on two sides, making them very isolated. By the time the fire department was notified, it was too late. The structure was in rubble. Charlie's car was parked far enough away from the house that it didn't catch on fire, but the car was an indication there was at least one person inside."

"Why did the authorities wait two days before notifying next of kin?"

"First of all, they weren't familiar with my daughter's family. They'd only been in Sandwich for four years and kept to themselves. The police department got the owner's name from the Sandwich clerk's office, but of course those records don't give any other information. They did find where a building permit was taken out four-and-a-half years previous. They pulled a copy which listed a Dorchester address for Charlie. Between the Dorchester and Sandwich departments working together, they located Charlie's parents."

"Okay, that's the background on how you were notified. For my records, I'll get copies of reports filed by both the fire and police departments."

Patrick's eyes welled up. "Whatever you need to do. The state fire marshal's office conducted an investigation. That's when they found Charlie and Megan's remains."

Mary stared at the floor.

"I know this is hard. Let's take a break. I'm going to make a cup of coffee. Will you join me?"

Mary nodded. Patrick didn't say a word.

She opened her purse and pulled out a tissue.

I walked back from my kitchen. "It'll take a minute for the water to heat." I took a deep breath. "You said they found Charlie and Megan's remains. They didn't find Carleen's?" I knew the answer. Big M had already filled me in, but I needed to hear it from both the O'Malleys.

"No. She was only one month old. They said her room was closest to the garage where the fire was the most intense. The fire was fueled by gasoline stored in the garage. Carleen's room was reduced to cinders. They couldn't link any ashes to her, so it was determined her remains were cremated beyond recognition."

"It does appear to be a tragic accident."

"We never felt that way."

I needed another breather. I stood up from my desk. "How do you take your coffee?"

Mary raised her eyes from the floor. "We both use cream."

I brought them their coffee, then went back for mine.

"Thank you," they said in unison.

"This is what keeps me going." I smiled. "How did Charlie's parents feel about the fire?"

"His parents were divorced, but came together in light of the fire. They accepted it as an accident. We were never close with them. Right after it happened, we leaned on each other for support. But in the last twenty-five years, we've probably talked to them only four times."

25

"Do they know about the bag with the Raggedy Ann doll?"

"No. And, at this point, I don't want them to know. If you think it becomes necessary to inform them, we'll discuss it."

"Let's talk about the doll." I waited for a response, but got none, so I continued. "Why did you give her a Raggedy Ann? And, are you sure this is Carleen's doll?"

Mary spoke up. "My daughter, Megan, was true to her heritage. She had beautiful red hair that any proud Irish girl would love. When Megan was born, my parents, her grandparents, gave her a Raggedy Ann doll because of the red hair. We always made a joke of it. So, when Carleen was born and we saw the same red hair her mother was blessed with, we carried on the tradition and gave our granddaughter a Raggedy Ann doll too." Mary sipped her coffee. "I know the doll that somebody left on our stoop last week was Carleen's because I embroidered her initials on the doll's foot."

This new information made me sit up and take notice. So much for a boring missing person case. "Now, that's something to sink my teeth into. I'll get you answers, but it's not going to happen overnight."

"We understand that. Given the years and all," said Patrick.

"I understand the twenty-five years, but you've just been handed a tangible memory. I need your word you won't go off on your own trying to get answers. If you do, you'll cloud the investigation and we may never uncover the truth. I'll keep you informed as to what you need to know." I bit the inside of my lip. I was about to say something I probably shouldn't. "If Carleen is alive, I will find her."

Mary started to cry. Patrick's arm around her shoulder didn't provide much comfort. "Casey, we'll do whatever you say. We'll help you anyway we can and we won't hinder your investigation. Our contact and conversation will be strictly with you. Please find our Carleen."

Chapter 10

Marnie answered on the first ring.

"You still up for lunch?" I asked.

"Been waiting for your call."

"Is Annie coming?"

"No, she has an appointment for her car. She took a half day."

"Why don't you meet me at Finn's in fifteen."

"I'll be there." And in the usual Marnie fashion, her phone went dead.

I closed my eyes, wrapped my hands behind my neck, leaned back in my chair and rocked gently back and forth trying to compartmentalize my thoughts. I wasn't a quarter way through when my cell rang. The screen displayed the hated "unknown caller".

"Hello."

It was Sam. "Is that all I get?"

"That's all you're going to get right now." I laughed. "I had visitors this morning."

"Anyone, I know?"

"Mr. and Mrs. O'Malley."

"I thought you were going to meet them next week in Boston."

"That was the plan, but Patrick wanted his wife to meet me. I guess when you're on a mission and have all the time in the world, scheduled dates and times aren't always going to be adhered to."

"You can work around that, unless they start probing on their own. If that happens, it can screw up your investigation."

"I basically told them that." I checked my watch. "I'm meeting Marnie in five minutes for lunch. I'll call you back later."

"Actually, I'm calling to tell you I've finished my part of the grant, so Watson and I are ready to head back to Hyannisport tonight. The little guy misses you—almost as much as I do. I figure we'll take the boy for a walk on the beach, then head over to DiParma's for dinner."

"Welcome home. See you around fiveish." I held my cell against my chest. I wasn't sure if I was ready to make a permanent commitment, but life was lonely without my man and my dog. Sam didn't spend much time anymore at his condo in Bourne, but it was still his. My little place in Hyannisport wasn't technically mine, since I rented. *Someday.*

Marnie had just walked out the front door of the DA's office across the street. I waved and waited for her to join me in front of Finn's. The people sitting at the corner table by the window were leaving. Perfect timing. We stood aside for them to pass, then sat down.

"We have the best conversations at *our* table." Marnie smiled.

"That we do."

Karen knew we were on lunch and had to get back to work, so she came right over to clear the table and take our order.

"The special today is Kale soup and a BLT."

"I'll pass. Crab salad on toasted sour dough with fries and a Diet Coke is calling my name."

Marnie was still studying the menu.

"You can recite that in your sleep, what's the problem?"

"I was thinking about the special until you ordered." She looked up from the menu. "I'll have the same."

"Be right back with your drinks."

"So, what was the reason for the surprise visit, other than the fact Mr. O'Malley wanted to introduce you to Mrs. O'Malley?"

"I don't think there was much more of a reason. They truly believe their granddaughter is alive. My problem with the O'Malleys will be to keep them from interfering. I tried to impress

28

them with the importance of letting me do my job and if they didn't, we might never know the answer—that if they stay quiet and Carleen is alive, I will find her."

"Whoa. That's a pretty strong statement to make."

"I know."

"Have you talked to Sam yet?"

"He called a half-hour ago. He'll be back in the big bed tonight. He finished what he had to do for his chief. The grant's being reviewed, then it'll be ready to submit. Detective Summers used the excuse that Watson wants his mommy. We're going to do a beach walk with the boy, then out to dinner."

Marnie grinned. "Maloney's coming up late Friday and staying until Monday morning, so we've got the whole weekend if you guys want to do something."

"Let me check and I'll get back to you tomorrow."

Karen appeared with our drinks. "Food's almost ready."

"Thanks," we said in unison.

"This afternoon, I'll get back on track. I plan to do the Sandwich location ride-by first and take pictures of the area where the house was, then head to the Tribune. I didn't get a chance to call Chuck, but I know there won't be a problem using the computers."

"I'm working a case for Mike, but if there's anything you need me to research, I can take a break once in a while."

"Thanks for the offer, but there's a lot of leg work I have to do to get this case going. Until I find and organize relevant information, I've got to fly solo."

"Do you have the Sandwich address?"

"No, I'll get it from the Sandwich PD."

"That'll alert them you've got an interest in a case they investigated and closed years ago. I know it was twenty-five years ago, but since the PD had interaction with Patrick, maybe you should find the address another way. Once you have something concrete to talk about to your friends in Sandwich, then that would be the time to tell them what you're doing."

"We'd make a good team. Wanna quit the DA's office? There's room for another desk beside mine."

Marnie cradled her right elbow in the palm of her left hand, then rubbed her chin. "Hmmm …let me think on it."

We laughed.

"Seriously, before I go back to my office, let's go over to the Registry of Deeds and see what's on the books," she said.

Chapter 11

It took less than five minutes to locate the 18 Buzzy Lane address at the Registry. I input it into my GPS. Twenty miles later, the obnoxious GPS lady piped in. "In one mile turn left onto Winter Hill Street."

My next directive was to turn right in a quarter mile onto Buzzy Lane. My final destination was two miles on the left.

The ending point didn't reveal a structure, just an opening to a thickly overgrown, car-and-a half wide unkempt path. I hesitated, then slowly moved down the dirt drive. What was probably three hundred yards seemed like three miles before I reached somewhat of a clearing.

This must be where the house was.

Scrub brush had rejuvenated and reclaimed the area. Ruminants of wooden slats lay haphazardly between picker bushes. Clusters of Seven Sister's pink roses still clung to a weather-beaten, broken white picket fence. I took my camera and walked to where I pictured the house once stood. I kicked back some brush to discover I was standing on a brick walkway. I took a few more steps, then stopped. Out of the corner of my eye I saw something that didn't fit into the landscape. A rusted metal sign with the message still bold enough to exert authority was wedged into the ground. PRIVATE PROPERTY – KEEP OUT was clearly visible. I snapped pictures of where I assumed the house stood and a handful of the proximate area. Twenty-five years ago a tragic fire ended a dream. But, today something was still very much alive. A gentle breeze brushed across my shoulders. My cue to leave. I didn't believe in the paranormal, but as I drove back to my office, I couldn't help thinking someone had watched me.

Nothing had been done to the Sandwich property since the fire. The Probate Court records listed the Estate of Megan and Charlie Davis as the owners. I needed to find out who is or who are the principals in the estate. Obviously, it wasn't the O'Malleys, otherwise they would have mentioned it to me. But, in this business, I'm finding that people like to keep little secrets—sometimes dangerous ones.

I pulled into my parking lot and headed inside my office. There weren't any notes taped to my front door and no message light flashing on my phone. It was three-thirty and I wasn't meeting Sam until fiveish, so I had plenty of time to stop by the Tribune. I put my phone on speaker and punched in their number.

"Good Afternoon, Cape Cod Tribune. How may I direct your call?"

"Hi Jamie."

"Casey, I'd know your voice anywhere. How are you? What's up? When are we going to lunch?"

"Twenty questions."

"I know, but you were supposed to call me and—"

I laughed, "I'm back on the job, so I'm fine. Second answer—I'm working a new case. And, third—we'll do lunch next week. But, right now, I need to talk to Chuck. Is he in?"

"He is." She put me on hold for a few seconds, then put me through.

"Well, if it isn't our favorite private eye. We were just talking about you this morning."

"Hope it was all good."

"I'll never tell. Some conversations between reporters are confidential, so I'll plead that for Jamie and me," said Chuck.

"Miss you guys."

"Is this a social call or do you need something?"

32

"You know me too well. I need to access the computer again. Have you filled my old office yet?"

"Door's locked, but I have the key and your password still works."

Chapter 12

Jamie was in the middle of some busy work when I walked into the reception area. She pointed at me. "Where's the donuts?"

"It's not morning."

"No excuse." She gave me a hug. "Chuck's waiting for you. I'm out of here at four today. I'll swing by your office—oops, I mean old office—before I leave."

I gave her a two finger salute, then headed down the corridor to see Chuck.

I explained I was working a new case. He knew I couldn't discuss the particulars with him. He smiled and told me to get to work.

I fired up the computer and went directly to archives, then to obituaries. Three obits grouped together came up when I entered Charles Davis. Only two of them were headed by a picture—Charlie on one and Megan on the other. Carleen's was just words, and very few at that.

I knew Megan's parents, so that information was nothing new and she was an only child, so no siblings were listed. Charlie, on the other hand, came from a broken family. It listed his mother and stepfather, then his father, but no step-mother. He had two sisters, one brother living and one deceased. I sent the page to the printer.

Still in archives, I plugged in 18 Buzzy Lane, Sandwich house fire. As suspected, there were several articles. Instead of reading them on the computer, I printed them.

Although I knew I could tap into the data bases for several of the Boston Newspapers, I'd never done it. Since the Davis' were originally from Boston, it was a logical move to give it a try. I entered 'Megan Davis'. The only thing that came up was the wedding announcement. I typed in 'Megan O'Malley'. Again, nothing newsworthy, just a listing when she graduated from UMass Boston. The last one was her obituary.

I keyed in Charles Davis. There were numerous articles referenced. I pulled them up in the order they were published in the papers. The first three articles weren't my Charles Davis. The fourth article was. He'd been arrested in Revere on a DUI. They'd found marijuana in his car, but determined it wasn't enough to get him on possession to distribute. Since I figured I was going to be introduced to many men with his name, I printed any article I thought involved my Charlie. There were more than just a few. Seems as though my Charlie Davis was no Boy Scout. They ranged from breaking and entering, speeding, assault on a police officer to lewd and lascivious behavior. I sent them all to the printer. They would give me insight into Charlie Davis' background and perhaps, personality, but it was the next group of articles I was most interested in. He had court appearances listed for drug charges. There weren't articles matching up to all the dates, but that could be because of continuances or the charges weren't newsworthy. I printed the drug-related stories, along with all the other articles pertaining to Charlie. Like Megan, the last was his obituary.

The printer tray was full. I slipped all the stuff into my briefcase and closed up the office. Chuck's door was cracked open. He was still at his desk. "Thanks, boss. Again, you've been a great help." I smiled. "If I keep this up, I'm going to have to put you on my payroll."

"Donuts will do. One of these days, I'll meet you in the Village for lunch."

"I'd like that." I waved and headed for the employee door to the parking lot. The reception area was empty. Jamie said she'd stop by before she left, but she didn't.

Chapter 13

Sam's car was already at my house when I pulled into the driveway. He and Watson were sitting on the front steps.

"What's the matter—lost your key?" I laughed and ran across the front yard to greet my boy and my man. Watson was so excited, he almost knocked me down when he jumped up to lick my face.

"Those kisses are going to be hard to follow." Sam wrapped me in his arms.

"I wouldn't mind if you gave it a try."

He did and I liked it.

"Watson's ready to head for the beach and I'm hungry, so let's get this show on the road."

"Let me change into my sneakers and we'll get going." They stayed outside. I returned in five minutes.

Sam hooked Watson to his leash and we headed down the driveway. "How did your day go?"

"It's going to take more time than a walk to the beach to fill you in." I waited for a reaction—nothing. "I want to remind you that it was you who suggested I take this case. I don't know what Big M told you, but I'm sure you only got half the story."

Sam took a deep breath. "Why am I not surprised?"

Most of the people on the beach were walking dogs. Come season, we have to go either very early in the morning or after the beach closes, usually around seven o'clock. According to beach rules, Watson isn't allowed to walk, run or play in the sand during the day.

Sam unhooked Watson's leash. "Your friends are waiting." The boy took off like a bat out of hell trying to catch one of his seagull buddies.

"Just a half-day in Boston makes me realize how good I have it. I don't think, actually I know, I could never live there—visit, yes, but live, no."

"Somedays, I feel that way about living in Bourne."

"Are you comparing Bourne to Boston?" I stopped and turned to face Sam.

"Yeah, I guess I am."

I wasn't sure what, if anything, he was getting at, but opted to change the subject. "Do you think you've got a shot at the grant money?"

"We're considered a strategic location. We're easily accessible by water. That makes the Cape appealing to terrorists. That's the same reason the Cape's inviting to drug dealers. Especially during season, boats come in and out of marinas without suspect. As far as terrorism, it hasn't been a problem, but prevention is the best defense." Sam sighed. "To answer your question, yes, I believe Homeland Security will award us a sizeable amount for equipment and training."

I closed my eyes, tilted my head down and rubbed my temples. "I see two seats in the bar at DiParma's calling our names."

"Now you're a psycho—I mean psychic."

I arm-punched him and called out to Watson. As usual, he was too busy with his gull buddies and chose to ignore me.

But when Sam gave him the whistle, he came running.

"I'll have to learn how to do that—not that the boy would respond."

Chapter 14

Ben, the manager, greeted us as we walked into the restaurant. "For some reason, I had a feeling I'd be seeing you guys tonight. There are two seats on the other side of the bar."

We walked around and sat down.

Sam looked at me out of the corner of his eyes. "Don't say a word, Miss Psychic." He caught the attention of Gabby, our favorite bartender.

"The usual?"

"Yes to her White Zin with a side of ice, but instead of beer, I'll have a glass of Merlot for a change."

We toasted and opted to relax a while before we ordered dinner.

I ran through Patrick O'Malley's Monday visit to my office in Barnstable, then the Tuesday morning alley walk in the North End, that ended with a meeting at the Black Rose Pub next to the Marriott Custom House. "I know you talked to Big M, but like I said before, I don't think he told you the entire story."

"From what you just told me, I only got highlights. I respect the fact that he talked to me first, knowing I was concerned about your involvement in another high-risk investigation immediately following the one in Falmouth." Sam took a drink, then continued. "I didn't ask him any questions. It's your business and I have no right to screen what cases you take or don't take."

This was a new twist.

"All I ask is that you be careful, cover your ass and let somebody know if you're entering a danger zone." He propped his elbows on the bar and supported his chin on his fists. "And, know I'm here to be a sounding board and help in any way I can."

I leaned over and gave him a kiss. "I love you, Sam Summers."

"And, I love you too, Sherlock."

We clinked glasses again.

Sam got Gabby's attention. "We'd like an order of calamari and two more wines, please."

"I'll put in the order and get your drinks."

I caught Sam up on my comings and goings. "This morning, I got a surprise. The O'Malleys showed up in Barnstable."

"Weren't you planning on meeting with them next Monday in Boston?"

"That was the plan, but Patrick O'Malley said he wanted his wife to meet me. He also wanted to get a contract signed. I already knew I was going to take the case, but wanted to do a little research before I met with him again." I turned towards Sam. "We did do a lot of talking and it gave me more insight into the case."

"A client in a hurry to sign a contract. Now that's unusual. Apparently, he wants to get you started pretty darn quick."

I smiled. "After I had lunch with Marnie, we went over to the Registry of Deeds and looked up the address for Charlie and Megan Davis in Sandwich."

"I'm assuming that's the daughter and son-in-law."

"It is. According to records, the property never really changed hands. Ownership is listed as the Estate of Charles and Megan Davis. Now I have to find out who controls the estate."

Our drinks came. I dumped half the glass of ice into my White Zin, swirled it around and took a sip. "Marnie went back to work and I headed towards Sandwich. Fortunately, the obnoxious GPS lady was cooperative today. But, here's the thing. The Davis house was on approximately four acres of what looked like prime land. It's surrounded by two defunct cranberry bogs. I can't imagine why someone didn't buy it up, either to build a showplace or for development. If you go about five miles away, there's an area of

39

beautiful designer houses that could be the centerfold for the *HGTV* magazine."

"Did you find anything interesting at the Davis property?"

"Not really." There was noticeable doubt in my voice.

Gabby set the plate down. "Enjoy your calamari. Give me the high sign when you want to order dinner." She walked back to some customers sitting across the bar from us.

Sam dipped a tentacle into the spicy marinara sauce, stuffed it into his mouth, then washed it down with a drink of wine. "Don't get any better than this." He smacked his lips and repeated the process. "I'm all ears. What are the *not really* interesting things you found at the Davis property?"

"Seriously, there wasn't much. I drove down the overgrown dirt driveway that ended at a clearing, which I presume was where the Davis house once stood. There were remnants of a white picket fence, charred pieces of wood, a brick walkway and a 'No Trespassing' sign. I took pictures. My camera's at the office. I'll print them out tomorrow."

"Were there any signs of human life anywhere around?"

"No. Even the vegetation that flanked the area was dead, except for the scrub pines and Seven Sister's roses. It was a little unsettling." I neglected to tell him about the breeze that came from nowhere and brushed against the back of my neck.

"You haven't touched the calamari. Better have some before I eat it all." He held out a sauce soaked ring for me to taste. "Ready to order dinner?"

"Yeah. I'll have the Mussels Bianco appetizer and an order of garlic bread."

"I've got a suggestion. Why don't we get the mussels, bread and an antipasto and split?"

"That works."

Sam gave Gabby the order.

"Interested in hearing about the rest of my day?"

"There's more?"

"Wise guy. I went to the Tribune to use their computer."

"One of these days, Chuck is going to replace you and the source for some of your information is going to dry up."

"I know. Someday, but not today. I got copies of obituaries and checked several of the Boston papers. I found lots of articles and a couple arrests. I printed them. Tomorrow I'll comb through what I got, put it in order and pull out anything that might give me a hint as to what my next step will be."

"Do you think with all this research and homework you'll have a little time for a houseguest?" Sam gave me a kiss on the cheek. "I'll make your French Vanilla in the morning."

I whispered in his ear, "We can work something out, especially if you'll keep the other half of my bed warm."

Chapter 15

Thursday

I could have slept at least another hour, but the smell of coffee brewing and a Mr. Thomas crisping up in the toaster got the better of me. "Good morning," I called out. When I didn't get an answer, I figured no one was going to come join me, so I got up.

Sam and Watson were coming in the front door just as I walked into the kitchen.

"Mornin' sunshine." He let go of Watson's leash and gave me a hug and kiss. Watson followed, jumping up, trying to lick my face.

"Not quite tall enough." I bent down and tussled with him for a few seconds, then reached up and took a treat from the bowl on the counter.

Sam poured our coffee and I buttered the muffins, then brought them to the table.

"Marnie said Maloney is going to be in town for the weekend and wants to know if we'd like to do something."

"It's supposed to be great weather. If we take the high speed ferry from Hyannis, we can be in Nantucket in an hour, hit the beach for a couple, then get a late lunch. There's an Irish pub, Kittie Murtagh's, not too far from the beach. The island bus stops near it or we can take a taxi. And, if you and Marnie are good girls, we might let you do a little store poking." He smiled and went back to his muffin.

"I don't think she's been to Nantucket. I'll call her this morning." I got Sam and me another coffee. "I'm going to be in the office all morning, but after lunch, I might see if Ernie's around."

"Are you planning on going to the Sandwich Fire Department today?"

"Probably not. I want to be comfortable with information I've already got so I'll sound halfway intelligent when I talk to Chief Monroe."

"He's a friend. Do you want an introduction call?"

I didn't say a word. I didn't need to.

"Okay, I know. If you need my help, you'll ask."

I smiled.

Sam brought his dishes to the sink. "I've got to get going. Pizza and frosties tonight?"

I nodded. "Talk to you later." Watson and I stood in the open doorway and watched him drive away. I gave my boy a pat. "He's a good daddy. Let's keep him around."

Chapter 16

I waved at the Dunkin Donuts as I rode by on my way to the Village. "Not today. My man made me breakfast."

The traffic on Phinneys Lane was light, but then it wasn't season yet. I pulled into my parking space behind my building, went inside to start my morning ritual. I made a coffee, opened the shades on the front picture window, unlocked the front door, fired up the computer and got myself settled in. Sam had put me in a good state of mind, and body, last night. It carried over to morning.

I emptied my briefcase on the desk. I'd printed an impressive pile yesterday. Now I had to rank each one in order of relevance before I started to analyze. Organizing information in a case is much like writing an outline for a book. *Maybe someday I'll try that too.*

The obituaries were routine. They provided dates and some family background information. They warranted a separate pile. The next batch consisted of articles on Charlie Davis. I had to be careful to make sure they were my Charlie Davis. I'd tried to do this when I looked them up yesterday, but I could have easily made a mistake. Now it was time to scrutinize them.

"Shit." I hastily thumbed through the stack of papers in front of me. I didn't run Charlie through the DMV data base. I know Marnie is able to access it at the DA's office, but I don't want her to get in trouble. I pushed the number one on my cell. It went to voice mail. "Sam, it's me. Please give me a call when you get a chance. Thanks." I checked my watch. It was eight forty-five. He must be in a meeting.

I took the memory stick from my camera, put it in the computer and printed off the pictures I'd taken of 18 Buzzy Lane.

Nothing unusual stood out in obits for Megan and Charlie. Besides, any information I pulled was twenty-five years old. But then, this whole case was twenty-five years old. I took a couple blank sheets of paper from the tray beside my printer and started to construct a family tree for both the Davis'. Since Megan's obit only listed her parents, hers wasn't much help. I should have run obits for Charlie's parents and stepfather to see if they're still living. I made myself a to-do-list—the DMV and Boston obits. One of his sisters still had the Davis name, but the other one's last name was Gerber. The living brother's name was Richard. The deceased brother's name was Stanley. Their last names were both Davis. I added a note to my list—look up Stanley Davis's obit. I clipped the pages together and set them aside.

Now to the meat of my 'to date' research. I sifted through the Charlie Davis articles. Two of them weren't the right Charlie, so I tossed them into the round file. I'd written the names of the newspapers and dates on the top of my copies where my Charlie's stories appeared. He was an active individual. Judging from the number of pages, it appeared his bad boy escapades didn't start at eighteen—the legal age he could be identified in print. Sam could be my ace-in-the-hole if I needed actual copies of the arrest sheets. I could ask Big M, but I got the feeling he'd help me only if it was off the record. Hence, the meeting in the North End, rather than in his office at the South Boston precinct.

I was in the process of separating the clippings into like categories when my cell rang. It was Marnie. I pressed speaker. "Casey Quinby, Private Investigator."

"Didn't you know it was me?"

"I did, but I want to feel important."

"What are you doing for lunch?"

"Going up to the deli for a sandwich, then eating at my desk. Want to join me?"

"It's eleven-twenty-five, I'll meet you there in fifteen minutes. That way we can get there before the lunch bunch."

"Is Annie coming?"

"If I can find her, I'll ask."

"See you in a few." The end of my sentence is Marnie's good-bye.

I browsed the articles. The first one was something to do with a DUI. The second one involved a fight at a bar on Revere Beach. Charlie and three others were arrested. Again, I'll note the charges after Marnie leaves. I had a few minutes left, so I started to read the third one in the pile. This one I didn't put down. It involved a drug bust that ended with one person dead and two taken to the hospital with non-life-threatening injuries. Charlie was one of the lucky ones. I put this article aside.

I was already three minutes late. Marnie would be waiting—she was always early. I grabbed my purse and ran out the door, making sure it was locked.

She was sitting on the bench in front of the deli. "Must need a new battery in your clock."

"Smartass. I'm here and it's not crowded. Let's order."

We said our hellos and goodbyes to a couple of the neighboring merchants, then headed back to my office. Instead of eating in the kitchen, I suggested we sit outside the front window at the bistro table. "I'll be right back. I've got chips and Diet Coke in the back."

Marnie had her eyes closed and was facing the sun when I came back outside.

"Did you use sun screen?"

She ignored me. "I could get used to sitting here."

"I should put up a sign—Reserved for Employees and Clients only."

"I distinctly recall you asking me Wednesday if I wanted to quit the DA's office and come to work with you?" She smiled.

"I did?"

"Change of subject. Did you ask Sam about this weekend?"

"We talked about it last night. He suggested we go to Nantucket for the day. We can take the fast ferry from Hyannis. It only takes an hour, spend some time on the beach, have lunch, do a little shop poking and then head home."

"I've never been there, so I'd love it. I'm sure Maloney will agree."

"You kidding, Maloney does whatever you want."

Marnie shrugged. "He loves me."

"You're such a brat."

"I know. I'd love to sit here all day," she checked her watch, "but I've got to get back to work. You know—Friday afternoon— all the loose ends to sew up before I go home."

"I'll call you tonight with the time."

She put her sandwich wrapper and empty soda bottle in the bag and handed it to me. "Present for you."

"Talk to you later."

She walked away and I went inside.

I reread the Charlie article relating to the Dorchester drug bust. It was dated May 5, 1977. That would make him seventeen. I added a note to my to-do-list—check the Dorchester area for drug problems around the time Charlie was busted. There were three others involved, but no names mentioned in the case.

With all the incidents relating to the DMV, I couldn't imagine Charlie held a valid Massachusetts license. Was Megan his chauffeur?"

The story reporting an assault on a police officer caught my interest. Charlie was mentioned along with four other guys. I recognized one of the names—Martin Gerber. In Charlie's obit one of his sister's last name was Gerber. *Interesting.* Again, there was no indication he was arrested for the offense. My to-do-list was growing.

The lewd and lascivious behavior charge disappeared too. *Strange.*

I knew Sam was going to ask why I wanted this background check. After all, my contract was to find a missing person. The way

I saw it, everything that lead up to Carleen's death or disappearance was relevant to my doing that.

I took a break and made a cup of French Vanilla. The aroma filled the air. "Ah, my drug of choice is working." When I sat back down, my cell rang. I didn't bother to check the caller ID, I just answered it. "Casey Quinby, Private Investigator."

"So formal." It was Sam. "Sorry I didn't get back to you sooner, but I was in meetings all morning. In fact, we're on our way to lunch now."

I glanced at the clock. It was two-ten.

"How's things going?"

"Just fine. I'm in no danger—at least not yet."

"That's not funny," he said after I punctuated my comment with a chuckle.

"It wasn't meant to be. I'm working on a missing person case. That's a biggie in the world of private investigators. If I start compiling a murder book, you can worry. I should be home by four-thirty. Do you want me to pick up the pizza at Jack's?"

"That's a little early. I won't be leaving the station until five. I'll call you, then you can order and I'll pick it up."

"See you then." I made a silent kissing gesture into the phone.

I called Ernie Mullins at the ME's office.

He picked up on the fourth ring. "Medical Examiner's Office."

"Hi, Ernie. It's Casey Quinby."

"Casey, how are you? Or should I ask?"

"I'm fine, but I need your help again." This time I didn't wait for him to answer. "I'm back on the job and working a missing person case. There are a couple deaths involved and I'm sure you can fill in some of the blanks."

"No need to talk on the phone. I'm here for the next couple hours. Why don't you stop over?"

"Thanks, I will. Do you want names so you can get a head start?"

"I'm listening."

"Charles Davis, Megan Davis and Carleen Davis—all from Sandwich."

"They do and they don't sound familiar."

"Probably because you met them twenty-five years ago."

Chapter 17

There were only two cars in the ME's lot. I parked beside the spot reserved for Ernie. I didn't bother to take anything but a notepad in with me. When I pushed the button on the side of the door and announced my arrival, Ernie buzzed me in and instructed me to come to his office.

He looked up from his computer as the sound of my footsteps reached out to him.

I walked over to his desk. "Good afternoon."

"I've found information on the Davis'." He kept his eyes glued to the screen, but lifted his hand to wave me forward. "It appears to be routine. According to the Sandwich Fire Department, there were three occupants inside a structure at 18 Buzzy Lane. By the time the fire was reported, there was no way anyone could have survived. I was called to the scene to gather evidence to substantiate the fact there were three victims. It was an eerie site and the smell of death by fire—I don't know which is worse."

I stepped closer and leaned in, my hands flat on the top of his desk. "Were you able to retrieve any remains that would provide viable DNA?"

Ernie printed off copies of his reports and handed me a set. "You'll see in the reports for Charles and Megan, I found bone fragments. A neighbor told the fire department they thought the couple had a newborn. The chief, along with his arson squad, determined the baby's bedroom was located behind the garage. Since the garage was where the fire was the most intense, the baby's bedroom was completely obliterated. There were a couple places where a crib could have been, so we took samples from those locations. I didn't hold out any hope the sample ash, or should I say dust, would offer any proof of identity. I labeled everything and sent the entire package to the Boston Crime Lab."

"How were you able to determine the two adults were Charlie and Megan Davis?"

"The Sandwich PD did their homework and contacted both sets of parents, who submitted blood samples to use for DNA testing. These samples, along with ashes gathered from the scene, were also sent to Boston. After a couple days, we received a report. It was confirmed Charlie and Megan Davis, the owners of the property at 18 Buzzy Lane, were the ones who died in the fire. DNA testing back then wasn't as sophisticated as it is today, but we were fortunate enough to get a match."

"Were they able to do anything with the samples you sent from the baby's room?"

"Nothing. As I said, that room was reduced to ashes and anything and/or anybody in it was just a memory. After a complete investigation by the arson squad and a Sandwich PD homicide detective, the state fire marshal ruled the fire an accident. They didn't find any reason to suspect the fire was started by a third party. I listed the cause of death on the certificates as asphyxiation by smoke."

The report went on to say what remains there were got picked up by Wilmot Funeral Home in Dorchester. Patrick hadn't said anything about where his daughter was buried. I made a mental note to check.

Ernie tilted back in his chair. "What's your interest in this closed case?"

"It's a missing person case."

Ernie gave me a puzzled look. "Who's missing?"

"The granddaughter, Carleen."

He shook his head. "Isn't Carleen the child in the fire?"

"She is."

"Then I don't understand. She's dead."

"Megan Davis' parents don't think so. It's bizarre, but they appear to have proof she may be alive."

"I don't know how you find these screwy cases, but you certainly do."

"This one found me." I smiled. "A friend in Boston recommended my services." I checked my watch. "As always, thanks for your help. I'm sure your reports have all the information."

"If you need me, you know where I am." Ernie stood up as I started to leave.

"Thanks." I headed down the corridor to the parking lot.

Chapter 18

It was four-fifteen when I pulled into my driveway. I knew Watson would be impatiently waiting for me to unlock the door and let him out to run around the yard. I opened the door and quickly stepped aside.

I put my briefcase and purse on the top step and sat down on the bottom one, knowing, in a few seconds, he'd want to give me dog kisses and tussle with me on the grass.

"Hey, boy, want a treat?" Whenever I say that to him his tail wags non-stop. I laughed while scuffing up the hair on the back of his head. "Let's go inside and I'll get you some."

No sooner did I get the box down from the cabinet, my cell rang. I poured a few treats on the counter and managed to answer the call at the same time. "Hi, are you on your way home?"

"I got out a little early. I'm in Mashpee. Call Jack's and I'll get the pizza. I should be there in twenty minutes to a half hour."

"Will do."

I freshened Watson's water and filled his food bowl, checked the fridge for Sam's beers and my White Zin, then the freezer for his mugs. We were set to go.

I got through to Jack's on the first ring. "I'd like to order a medium pepperoni, sausage and feta pizza—extra crispy please. The last name is Summers." Watson listened while I placed the order. If I didn't know better, I'd swear he understood every word.

"Be ready in twenty minutes."

"Thank you," I said, and hung up.

I was anxious to talk to Sam about my new case. Since we were staying in, and there was nothing but reruns on TV, tonight would be an ideal time to start sorting out events in the order they occurred. I sat down and stared at the empty table.

When I did cold or closed cases, some of the investigative work was already done. My last case, actually my first case as a PI, was ruled an accident, but Rocco DeLuca's niece, Bella, was sure he was murdered. He was, and his killer was finally unmasked. That was a hard one. Now, I had a missing person who was reported dead in a fire twenty-five years ago.

I didn't hear Sam pull into the driveway or notice Watson scurry for the door. I jumped when my man came in unannounced.

Sam set the pizza box on the counter. "A little edgy are we?" He took a couple plates from the cabinet and handed them to me. Before I could empty my hands, he walked behind and gave me a hug and kissed the back of my neck.

"You've got all the bases covered."

"Yep. You gonna sit there, or are you going to stand up and get the drinks?"

"Wine for me and a frostie for you. Grab me a wine glass," I said as I got up from the table.

"Your command is my wish." He gave me a pat on the ass.

I shook my head, then got our drinks ready.

Sam put a slice on our plates. "My day was boring. Tell me about yours."

"I went to see Ernie Mullins at the ME's office. He saves everything. The records for the Davis' were already on the computer screen when I got there. For him, twenty-five years is the same as yesterday. He'd already read through them and actually remembered the fire, mainly because of the baby."

"Do you have copies?"

"He gave me a full set." I gave Sam another slice and took one for myself. "After supper I'll show you what I've got."

Chapter 19

I handed Sam the pictures I'd taken of Buzzy Lane. He studied them as I got Ernie's reports out of my briefcase.

"Ask the O'Malleys if they have a picture of the house before the fire."

I took a mini legal pad and noted Sam's suggestion, then slid the copies of the ME's certificates across the table. "I'm going to have a coffee. Want one?"

"Sure," he said without looking up.

They were cut and dried ME certificates. What did he see that I didn't?

"You said you also found news stories in several of the Boston papers spotlighting Charlie."

I handed Sam his coffee, took mine from the Keurig and sat back down. I removed the last group of clipped paperwork from my briefcase. "I've skimmed over these several times. I need to delve into them and pick them apart. In my opinion, there's stuff written between the lines that's going to answer lots of questions."

"For tonight, I'm going to do what you did and just scan them. Tomorrow I'll take a closer look." He clasped his hands behind his neck and squeezed his forearms against his head. "I don't feel like watching TV. Let me play with these for a little bit, then we'll go to bed."

"By the way, we're on for Nantucket on Saturday."

Chapter 20

Friday

Nobody stirred until the alarm went off. I wanted to hit the snooze button, but knew we had to get up, so instead I gently hit Sam's shoulder several times. "Hey big guy, time to rise and shine."

In a split second, sleeping beauty's prince rolled over and wrapped me in his arms. "Just another ten minutes?" he whispered.

I peeked over Sam's shoulder. "Our boy has other plans that can't wait." Watson was standing beside Sam's side of the bed tugging on the sheet.

"Yeah, yeah, yeah."

When I heard the outside door shut, I got up and popped a K-cup into the Keurig. The least I could do was have a cup of coffee waiting. Sam was a regular kind of guy. I was a French Vanilla girl. Two minutes later, Sam and Watson returned. "Want some breakfast?" I asked.

"Your DD jelly donuts have rubbed off. I'm going to pick some up on the way to work. Actually, I'm going to treat the office and pick up a couple dozen."

I played with the short hair at the back of his neck. "Jelly donuts—can I come in with you today?" I teased. I didn't get an answer, just a smile. "Did you hear me last night when I said we're on for Nantucket tomorrow? You only nodded and sometimes that means my words fell on deaf ears."

"I did, but I wanted to finish reading the Charlie articles."

"So, it's yes to Nantucket. Now what's your take on the articles?"

"Charlie was a bad boy from a young age. Before I can determine much more I need to dissect what the reporter was trying to say. These are not technically related charges, but one could lead to another." He took a deep breath and let it out slowly. "Do you understand what I'm trying to say?"

"I do, because that's basically what I thought when I read them."

"You've been hired to find a missing person—if this person is actually missing. What I'm seeing is a strong possibility the O'Malley's claims are true. The other thing I'm considering is that the Sandwich fire wasn't an accident, but rather a homicide."

I picked up my cup with two hands and slowly took a drink. When I glanced over the rim, I was paralyzed by Sam's intense stare. I knew if I spoke first, I'd lose the upper hand. For once, I kept quiet.

"You can recite my 'be careful lecture' in your sleep. All I'm going to say is, if you go snooping under moss-covered rocks, let someone know."

"Will do." I got up and kissed his forehead. "I have a favor to ask. I forgot to tap the DMV site to run both Charlie and Megan's motor vehicle histories. Instead of going back to the Tribune or asking Marnie, could you do it for me?"

"I've got a slow day. I'll have it for you tonight. Is there anything else?"

"Not at the moment."

"So Miss PI, what are your plans for today?"

"Since my trip to the Sandwich PD kept moving to the back burner, I intend to get up there today. I'll decide later if I'm going to stop at the fire department. Do you know Billy Bumpus at the PD?"

"He's a lieutenant, isn't he?"

"He is. I met him when I first came to the Cape. We were both doing rehab at Spaulding. He had been in a work related car accident and I was rehabbing from my fall at the Shrewsbury Police Academy. I never worked a case with him, but we remained friends even though I haven't seen him for a few years. He used to stop over to the Barnstable Tavern every once in a while. Since his wife died he's kept pretty much to himself." I put my cup down and rested my arms on the table. "I'll give him a call before I go."

"If you run into a problem, don't forget I said I'd furnish an introduction for you."

"I won't."

Sam looked down at Watson. "It's supposed to be nice today and I know I won't be late getting home, so we'll leave the boy outside on his run."

"It would be better than staying inside."

Within forty-five minutes we were ready to face the world. Watson had food and water and appeared content to guard the backyard while we were gone. I followed Sam until I came to Old Craigville Road, then turned right towards the Village. I parked behind my office, dropped my briefcase off inside and headed to Nancy's Donuts.

She came out from behind the counter and gave me a hug. "Where have you been?" I saw you more when you worked at the Tribune. Now you're next door and I hardly see you."

"No excuse," I mumbled. "But, I'm here now and I want one of your famous sticky buns and a cup of coffee."

"For here or to go?"

I didn't have the heart to say to go. What was another half hour anyway? "Here."

She smiled.

I got a Tribune from the stack beside the counter and went to an empty table by the window. I hadn't finished reading the front page when Nancy set two cups of coffee and a sticky bun on the table.

"Since you're early and nobody's at the counter, I'm going to join you."

"Like old times." I folded the newspaper and set it aside.

Chapter 21

It was eight o'clock when I left Nancy's. It was nice to sit and talk, but she was beginning to get busy, and I had to get started.

I called the Sandwich PD and crossed my fingers that Lieutenant Bumpus was working. He was. They put me through to him. "Billy, it's Casey Quinby."

"A welcome voice from the past. How are you?" He sounded upbeat. "Rumor has it you hung a shingle in Barnstable Village. I'm impressed. Makes me remember our conversations in the conservatory at Spalding."

"Lots has happened since then."

"It has," he said ruefully.

I screwed up. I forgot about him losing his wife. I changed the subject. "Billy, I need your help with something that happened in Sandwich."

"Sure, what is it?"

"It happened twenty-five years ago."

"Whew. That's ancient history. I was only on the job a couple years."

"That's why I didn't just stop in. I figured you'd need time to find where the reports are filed."

"Depending on what the incident was will determine how easily I can put my hands on them."

"It was a fire on Buzzy Lane. Three people died. A young couple, Charlie and Megan Davis, and their one-month-old baby, Carleen, were the victims. Do you remember it?"

"I'll never forget it. It was horrible. The Davis' were only a couple years younger than me—and the baby ... whew. One of the cases that hang in your mind. Me and my partner, Munge Marston, were the first on the scene. Munge wasn't a new kid on the block, but I was. After that one, I had to do a lot of soul searching to decide if I wanted to stay on the job. If it wasn't for Munge I'd be gone."

"I'm sorry to bring up such a bad memory."

"I know exactly where the paperwork is. It'll take me a bit to get to it. When will you be here?"

"How 'bout I get there around noon, pick up the reports, then we do lunch?"

"Better still. I'll meet you at the Marshland Restaurant just up from the station at twelve-thirty."

"I'll be there. And, Billy, thanks."

That gave me a good three hours to examine the Charlie articles before I had to leave to meet Billy. I pulled my to-do list from yesterday. I already asked Sam about checking the DMV site, so I didn't need to concern myself with that chore. I wanted to run family names through obit archives of Boston newspapers to check if any of Charlie's parents or siblings had passed. I knew if I pulled up either the Herald or the Globe on my computer, I wouldn't be able to go that far back. The same for the Dorchester area check indicating drug problems around the time Charlie was busted. I reread the article about the assault on a police officer—the one that mentioned Martin Gerber. Something didn't sit right with me. All these offenses should have had some kind of consequences, and, from what I read, they didn't. Just as I picked up the phone to call Sam, my cell rang. "Casey Quinby, Private Investigator."

"Sounds better every day."

"Why thank you kind sir. How did you know. In fact, you're just the person I want to talk to."

"I knew I shouldn't have called."

"Since you did, I have an assignment for you." I smiled to myself. "Is it possible to get copies of old arrest records? I don't believe there were never charges attached to them. It's like they disappeared."

"I can check. Do you have the names and dates?"

"Give me fifteen minutes and I'll call you back with the info. Also, do you have any friends on the Dorchester PD or at headquarters that could check a couple names to see if they were ever associated with one of the Boston Police Departments? I'm talking at least thirty to thirty-five years ago."

"I can handle that. Get me the information and I'll get you answers, if there are any."

"I talked to Lieutenant Bumpus this morning. He remembers the fire well. I'm meeting him for lunch at Marshland and he's going to bring me what he can find. I'm contemplating what and how much I should tell him about what I'm doing."

"He might not even ask you. As long as the reports are closed and not part of an ongoing investigation, he'll probably be curious, but not press the issue. If you have to, you can remind him of your confidential responsibility attached to your license."

"Yeah, I know. Let me get that information and call you back."

"Later," he said and hung up.

I needed Sam to check old arrest records for Charlie Davis and Martin Gerber and any other names mentioned in the various newspaper clippings. I dated them as best I could from when they appeared in print. There was a second set of names I wanted checked for any type of police affiliation—Robert Cushing, Charlie's stepfather; Harold Davis, Charlie's father; and Elaine Gerber, Charlie's sister. I had to do more research before exploring old drug busts in Boston. I had stepped out of my comfort zone the minute I started to probe life in the Big City.

I called Sam back, gave him the information he needed, then packed up and got ready to head to Sandwich.

Chapter 22

I got to the Marshland a few minutes early. Billy was even earlier. He was sitting at a table reading the menu as though it was a New York Times best seller.

"Hey, Mr. B, how the hell are you?" I bent down to give him a hug.

He got up and almost smothered me against his chest. "It's been too long. Still seeing that Bourne detective?"

"Yeah. He's a good guy. I'm gonna keep him around."

"Shit. That means I haven't got a chance. Say 'hi' to him for me."

We laughed and sat opposite each other.

"I felt terrible when I heard about your wife."

"It's been hard, but I'm doing better now. It was cancer. I can't believe it's been three years since she passed. Time doesn't stand still."

I reached across the table and took his hands in mine.

Out of the corner of my eye, I saw the server heading toward us. "Lieutenant, it's good to see you. Been a while."

"I've been working on my girlish figure, so I'm trying to eat healthy."

"Likely story." She put her hands on her hips and chuckled. "We do serve salads. Can I get you guys something to drink?"

"A Diet Coke with a lime, please."

Billy patted his chest. "I'll take the same, except for the lime."

"Let me get those, then I'll return to take your order."

"So Casey, what in the world are you up to? You had a great job at the Tribune. And, didn't you dabble in cold cases for some of the Cape PDs?"

"Like you said when we talked earlier, you remember my dream of becoming a detective. That ain't never gonna happen. I did have it good with the newspaper and my association with the PDs was great, but that devil on my shoulder kept prodding me with his pitchfork. I figured a private investigator was the closest thing I could do to realize my dream."

He shook his head, then laughed. "I have no doubt, you'll do just fine. Now I know someone I can refer the crazies to. You know, the ones that come into the station looking for the person who pushed Humpty Dumpty off the wall."

"Don't you dare or I'll send you a bill for wasting my time."

"It might be worth paying, just to see your face."

"I'm changing the subject. What's good here?"

"It's Friday. They usually have fish tacos on special. Their chowder is really good, too—homemade. Not that stuff that comes in a plastic bag."

No sooner did Billy finish his sentence, the server appeared with our drinks and looked straight at me. "You ready to order?"

"What's the special today?" I asked.

"Fish tacos."

Billy was right. I handed my menu to the waitress. "I'll have a cup of chowder and the tacos."

Billy closed his. "Sounds good to me. The same."

The conversation stopped for a few seconds. Billy reached down to the seat next to him and picked up an overstuffed nine by twelve envelope. "This is a complete copy of the reports regarding the fire twenty-five years ago at 18 Buzzy Lane." He handed it to me. "I've been on the job for twenty-eight years. In that time, I've never seen anything so intense, so devastating or so heart-breaking. It seared an image in my mind that will stay with me forever."

"Billy, I'm sorry."

"I want to ask you why you need these, but know I can't."

"Thank you."

"I have an idea what you're up to. If after you read these and have questions, don't hesitate to call. Our conversations will be kept strictly confidential." He managed to give me a slight smile. "Now, let's change the subject."

Chapter 23

I thought about stopping at the fire department before I headed back to the Village. But I chickened out. I didn't want to face a barrage of questions I wasn't ready to answer. I didn't know anyone at the Sandwich FD, so I had to tread carefully. Besides, I wanted to go over the paperwork Billy gave me, and run some things by Sam.

The incoming call light on my desk phone was flashing. Big M left a message. "Casey, I misplaced your cell number. Give me a call so we can firm up the meeting on Monday with the O'Malleys."

I sat back in my chair and contemplated the impending conversation I was about to have with Big M. I tapped my fingernails in a rhythmic pattern, first one hand, then the other. I didn't see the need for a Monday meeting. I'd already told the O'Malleys I'd let them know when I had something concrete to report. I didn't plan on Big M sitting in every time I spoke to Patrick and Mary.

It was time to make the call. It only rang twice. He must've checked the caller ID before he answered.

"Casey, you got my message."

"I just got back to the office. I've been putting some things together so I can structure some kinda game plan. Until I get that done, I'm not going to schedule a meeting." There was a dead silence. "Hello…you still there?"

"Yeah, I'm here. I understand you talked to the O'Malleys Wednesday."

Obviously Patrick told Big M they made the trip to the Cape. "They wanted me to get started. They're eager. Monday seemed too far away. It all happened so quickly, I didn't have a chance to give

65

you a call. Saturdays and Sundays are tough days to get reports from police or fire departments. I had to move quickly." I danced around the fact that I didn't want to tell him exactly what information I'd gotten my hands on.

He hesitated. "We should still have a meeting. Maybe not Monday, but early next week."

I was between a rock and a hard place. "Big M, I'm very appreciative that you referred a friend of yours to me. I know what this case means to you, but you have to understand that I'm the one who's calling the shots. Once I get my ducks in a row, I'll need your help to fill in the blanks. Until then, you need to step back and let me do my job."

He took a deep, unquiet breath. "I didn't mean to come on so strong. You're right. I'm too close to the case and, at this time, I could hurt more than help. You would have made a great police detective. And, let me be the first to say, your choice to become a PI will be very rewarding not only to yourself, but to those who use your services." He hesitated. "By the way, the O'Malleys were very impressed."

I smiled. "Thank you. I'll call in a couple days." The monotonous hums of a dial tone warbled in my ear.

The Sandwich PD envelope on the corner of the desk was calling me. Judging from Billy's interest, I surmised he had an opinion regarding the fire, but didn't want to voice it until after I'd finished the reading material he'd furnished me.

I pulled the paperwork from the envelope and laid it on my desk. It had already been divided into groups with a sticky note attached to the first page of each set. One was labeled PD reports, the second was pictures, another was marked test results and the last one FD reports. The last group puzzled me. I made a mental note to ask Sam if the police and fire are jointly involved in a case, do they each get copies of the entire investigation process from start to finish. If they didn't, Billy must have gotten the fire reports I would need to combine with the police reports in order to get a complete picture of what happened.

I set the pictures I took, and the ones from Billy, in front of me, and put the other piles off to one side. Sometimes pictures speak louder than words. I hoped these would scream. The FD's were graphic—not gory, just graphic. By the time they arrived, there was basically nothing left except for a few half-burned king studs on the outside wall of the room furthest away from the garage. I closed my eyes and tried to visualize the scene—the flames, the black smoke, the collapse of the timbers. The roar of the fire daring anyone to challenge it, and the nauseating stench of the smoke and dead bodies. Reality bites hard.

I matched my pictures with the FD pictures taken from similar angles. After twenty-five years, my pictures should depict a more peaceful, serene image, but they didn't. I stared at the ones I took two days ago.

There's a secret buried at 18 Buzzy Lane and I intend to dig it up.

I looked at the rest of the photos, then clipped them together and slipped them back into the envelope.

As I started to get up, my cell rang.

"How's my Sherlock doing?"

"Lots of stuff happening. I'll run it all by you tonight." I smiled through the phone. "I don't feel like going out for supper. How about I stop at the market and pick up a couple steaks and all the fixin's?"

"I'd like that. Beside, we're heading out early tomorrow, so an easy night at home would be nice."

I was so glad Sam was back in the big bed. "I'm going to pack things up and head out in about a half hour. Watson won't be crazy since he's been outside all day, but I could still do a beach walk and a glass of wine before we eat."

"In that order?" He laughed.

"I might even paper cup one, so I can walk and drink at the same time."

"You're smarter that I thought."

"Quit while you're ahead. See you in an hour."

Chapter 24

Sam and Watson were playing Frisbee in the back yard when I pulled into the driveway. I left my paperwork and the groceries in the car, ran around the house and tried to intercept the flying red disc. I missed.

"You'll never make the team playing like that."

Watson barked as if to mimic Sam's taunting.

"Not fair," I called. "It's two against one."

As I ran past the deck, I caught a glimpse of what appeared to be a glass of White Zin with an ice cube chaser. I stopped abruptly, walked up the steps and hoisted the plastic flute. "I'm assuming this is for me?"

"If it's not, then you got home early and I got caught." Sam grabbed a Coors and joined me.

"Before we get settled in, the groceries and my briefcase are still in the car."

"Allow me, my princess." Sam cut through the house to retrieve the food and paperwork.

The sun was warm for early April. I leaned back in my chair, rested my legs on the ottoman and wrapped my hands around my glass of wine. It doesn't get much better than this.

We skipped the walk and just kicked back and relaxed. It wasn't long before the sizzle of the Kelli potatoes let us know it was time to put the steaks on the grill. Even Watson took notice, knowing he might get a bite or two.

"I'm going inside to set the table. Want some sliced tomatoes?"

"No, I'm good." Sam came up behind me, leaned over and gave me a couple quick kisses on my neck. "I could get used to eating at home."

"You saying you like my cooking?"

He made sure my hands were preoccupied. "You do have your moments."

"You get the food and I'll get drinks. I'm having another wine. You want another frostie?"

"Does a bear shit in the woods? Of course I want one." Sam handed me his mug. "You said you had lots happen today. Feel like talking about it?"

"I told you I was meeting Billy Bumpus at the Marshland for lunch. He gave me an overstuffed nine by twelve envelope. It's in my briefcase. We'll look at it later. There were also pictures taken at the scene and reports from the fire department. I've glanced at the stuff, but now need to scrutinize it. He asked me if you were still in the picture. When I told him you were, he said 'shit, I don't have a chance'." I let out a little chuckle.

"Dirty old man—he's got to be at least fifty-five." Sam smirked.

"Be careful, he's only got fifteen years on you. By the way, he told me to say 'hi'. Back to business. Did you find anything on those names I gave you?"

"Charlie's stepfather, Robert Cushing, was a Boston police lieutenant in Dorchester. He was ten years older than the mother. He died of a heart attack fifteen years ago. My contact at Boston headquarters said Robert was a good guy, kind of reserved, but mostly a happy-go-lucky person. He received several commendations from the department."

"What about Charlie's biological father?"

"Charlie's father, Harold Davis, had his problems—probably why the mother divorced him. He'd been in and out of jail, mostly for petty theft, driving under, leaving the scene and fighting. I figure that's where Charlie got his 'bad-boy' habits. My contact knew him well."

69

"Did your contact say anything about Charlie?"

Sam nodded and thumbed through his papers before he answered. "Here it is." He handed it to me. "Charlie's rap sheet mimicked his father's with the exception of the drug charges."

I read down to where they started. "This lists a couple possessions with the intent to distribute and a separate charge for growing marijuana." I read the report again. "Did he do time?"

"Only a couple overnights."

"What?" I looked at Sam. "Don't tell me his stepfather got him off."

"Yep."

I was disgusted at the system. "I'm going to make a coffee. Want one?"

"I do and while you're doing that, there's something else you're going to find interesting. The guy his sister married, Martin Gerber, was also named in conjunction with the drugs. Martin's rap sheet could wallpaper more space than Charlie's, but I'm guessing it's only because Charlie's charges went away before he got to the station."

"I know you're a cop, doesn't this piss you off?"

"It does—gives us a bad name. It gets worse. I checked deeper into Martin Gerber. Seems as though he saw the light around the age of twenty-one, twenty-two and all I could find was a couple continuations of DUI charges that were eventually dismissed by the courts."

"Am I to assume Martin married Elaine Davis around that time?"

"Exactly. When I checked the DMV, the date Elaine changed her name to Gerber coincided with the move to sainthood for Martin. Believe me, the Vatican doesn't move that fast."

"Did you find any obituary for Martin or Elaine Gerber?"

"As far as I can determine, they're alive and well, still living in Dorchester. The telephone directory listed two Gerbers."

"Did you get the first names or initials?" I asked.

"I didn't."

70

I made a note to recheck the directory. I knew, at some point, I'd have to talk to Martin and Elaine, but there was a lot more research to be done before that was going to happen.

Sam took my hands in his. "You took on a missing person investigation. That's what your contract says. I know you have to do intensive research and, because the case dates back to 1990, it's not going to be easy. When you step out of your comfort zone, where you feel your most control, you'll experience raised anxiety and generate stress response. Trust me I've been there. Keep your focus and concentration in line. Don't make impulsive decisions. "

"I'll be fine, Doctor Summers. I don't need the textbook lecture." My eyes expressed anything more that needed to be said.

Chapter 25

We met Marnie and Maloney at the docks in Hyannis. As agreed, we picked up coffee and a twenty-four count box of Munchkins. It was early in the season, so there wasn't a waiting line for the high-speed ferry. Sam and Maloney got the tickets, while Marnie and I found a place to sit until we could board.

"We couldn't have asked for a better day." Several of the pleasure boats housed at Hyannis Marina slowly made their way to the channel. Memories of the Mary Kaye Griffin case clouded the horizon.

"You okay?" Marnie asked. "You're awfully quiet."

I shrugged my shoulders. "Just thinking about last year when I was a below deck guest, not knowing if I'd ever see the light of day again."

"Well, here we are and that sun's about as bright as it can get. That's over. It's time to live for the future and our jaunt to Nantucket." She put her arm around my back and laid her head on my shoulder.

I smiled. "Wait till you see the beaches, better still, the stores."

Sam called to us from the shore end of the gangplank, "They're starting to board."

"We're coming," I called back, then turned to Marnie. "I've taken the high-speed ferry four times since I lived on Cape. It's fun."

On board, we found a table in the lounge and made ourselves comfortable. "Did you know there was a bar? The group that came on after us are belly-up, ordering bloody marys."

Sam watched as they took up residency on the opposite side of the ferry. "I suggest having a cocktail on the way back—not on the way over."

While Marnie doled out the coffees, Maloney opened the box of Munchkins.

Sam took a sip, then closed the tab on the cover. "We got three regulars and one French Vanilla."

"Judging from the expression on your face you got mine." I laughed and took it from him, then popped a chocolate glazed hole into my mouth.

"Marnie told me about your new case," said Maloney.

I looked at him, but didn't respond.

"Was she not supposed to?"

"Legally no, but the principals have authorized Sam, Marnie, Jim Kelly and your father to work with me. If we happen to discuss the case, don't let it leave our circle." I turned to Marnie. "Counselor, did I cover that base?"

She shrugged. "I believe you did."

I checked our immediate surroundings before I continued. "How much did she tell you?"

"About the fire, the O'Malleys and the Raggedy Ann doll." Maloney took a couple holes and washed them down with coffee. "I'm sure Big M gave you the background between our family and theirs. Patrick O'Malley is like an uncle to my father."

"He did mention the families were close. I'm also sure Big M filled the gaps in Marnie's version."

"Yeah, he might have done that."

I shook my head. "I suppose I can't complain. I've got an Assistant District Attorney, a lead detective, a father/son cop team and a South Boston bar owner on my workforce, and I don't have to pay them."

The bloody mary group had finished their second round when the captain announced we'd be docking in ten minutes.

"It's less than a mile to Children's Beach from the Hy-Line docks." I gathered up my canvas bag and checked my surroundings to make sure I didn't leave anything. "There's a couple different beaches, but since we're not sun-bathing all day, we're better off to stay in town."

Marnie finished her coffee and stuffed her crumpled napkins inside the empty cup. "When's your next trip to Boston?"

"It was supposed to be Monday, but that changed when the O'Malleys showed up in the Village. Tomorrow I'll sort out the information I've already got. If Big M's available, I'll drive up on Wednesday." I sensed both Marnie and Maloney wanted more, but until I had something concrete to share, I didn't want to get further into the discussion.

Sam changed the subject. "Hyannis has an opening for a detective."

Maloney nodded. "My chief told me about it yesterday morning." He rolled his eyes sideways in Marnie's direction.

"Did I put my foot in my mouth?" Sam didn't wait for an answer. "The boat's pulling into the dock. Let's get up by the gangplank."

Marnie nudged Maloney as she got up from her chair. "Something you forgot to tell me?"

"Not forgot, just trying to figure out what to do about it." He stepped aside to let her go ahead of him. "We'll talk."

Marnie didn't say a word as she walked up beside me.

"He got here late last night and you met us early this morning, it's not something he wanted to matter-of-factly throw out to you. Trust me; he must have good reason not to have said anything yet."

"You're probably right. I just didn't expect it." Marnie turned to Maloney and gave him a kiss. "Love you."

"Love you, too."

"Hey, you two—get a room," Sam laughed. "Young love."

"What does that make us?" I danced around him like a little kid. "I still got spunk."

"Move it, move it, move it." He tickled my side and motioned for me to walk the plank.

There weren't many on the beach for a Saturday. Better for us. Come here in the summer and there are wall-to-wall people. We laid our blankets down, took out the necessary lotions and balled up our towels for pillows. It was only eleven o'clock, but the sun was smiling at us.

Marnie and I walked down to the water. She put her feet in, then jumped back. "Yikes. It's freezing."

"After a while they become numb, but I'm not going anywhere past my ankles anyway."

We did a mini-run along the water's edge, then headed back to the blankets.

"What's the matter?—cluck, cluck, cluck—chicken?" I asked the guys.

"You know Maloney, they only went up to their ankles. Do you think that means the water was a little too cold for the girls to take a full body dip?"

"Sam Summers, I see that look on your face. Don't you even think about it." I quickly sat down before he got any ideas.

Marnie was already back on the blanket trying to catch some rays.

As I turned on my stomach, I caught sight of a young family with a baby in a carrier setting up their blanket and umbrella. The image danced across the back of my eyelids. I couldn't help but think of Carleen and who put her Raggedy Ann on the O'Malley's stoop? Obviously, someone who wanted to remain anonymous. Was it someone who was at 18 Buzzy Lane the day of the fire? Or, was it possible that Charlie and Megan were murdered a day, or even more, before the fire? Was Carleen taken then? Did her kidnappers know the family? Is that why Carleen wasn't left to burn? After all, she was only one month old. Somebody cared, and I've been hired to find out who. When I do that, I'll find Carleen. I took a deep breath and rolled over on my back.

"Anybody hungry?" It was Sam back from his beach walk. "I'm ready to eat."

I must have fallen asleep, at least for a little while. I didn't realize he had left.

Maloney and Marnie sat up. He pulled his watch from her bag. "I can't believe it's two o'clock. I could do food."

"If we're going to Kittie Murtagh's, we have to take a taxi." Sam was on his feet and ready to go.

"Fine with us. Taxi up and back—that way we'll have time to hit the shops." I nudged Marnie with my elbow.

Sam arranged for the taxi that brought us to the restaurant to pick us up at four o'clock and bring us back into town.

*****

"Go figure. We went to an Irish Pub and all ended up with burgers," I said.

Marnie grabbed Maloney's hand. "It's okay with me. I've got all the Irish I can handle right here." She leaned over and gave him a hug.

Marnie and I walked around admiring the wares of local artists and craftspeople. "I never get tired of this place. Nantucket has its effect on people. It's mega-bucks to live here, but as long as they let us common folks walk their streets, it will always be a dynamite place to visit. A couple years ago, Sam and I came over for a weekend. We stayed at a bed and breakfast within walking distance of the town center. It was wonderful. Maybe this summer we can do it again and you two will join us."

Maloney put his arm around Marnie. "That could be a strong possibility."

The clock in the harbor bell tower rang six times. "That's our cue to head back to the docks. The next ferry leaves at six forty-five," said Sam.

It was a beautiful ride back to Hyannis. "I'm glad the ocean is our friend tonight. The fast ferry is just that—fast. The only problem is, when the seas are unsettled, so is the ride back to the mainland. And the fast pace makes it even worse." I looked around for the bloody mary group, but they weren't on board. *Just as well.*

"The Raw Bar is still on off-season hours. That means they won't be open when we dock. If you want, we can walk up to the Black Cat and grab an early nightcap before we head home." Sam looked at the three of us. "Any takers?"

"Since I'm riding with you, I guess there's a White Zin calling my name."

Maloney turned towards Marnie. "It's up to you."

"We're in," she said.

Chapter 26

Sunday

Sam was already up when I dragged myself out of bed and slowly made my way to the kitchen. The normal person reads the paper in the morning, especially on Sunday. Not Sam. He had my case files piled all over the table.

I popped a K-cup into the Keurig. "Find anything interesting?"

"Not really. When I think I've found something, it leads back to what we've already talked about. There's a couple key puzzle pieces missing."

I looked around the kitchen. "Doesn't look like you've had anything to eat. How 'bout we go to Stella's for breakfast, then take a ride to Sandwich and I'll show you where 18 Buzzy Lane is."

"You're on."

"First in the bathroom," I said.

"Make it quick if we're going for breakfast."

I was in and out in twenty minutes.

Sam leaned against the wall outside the bathroom door. He glanced at his watch. "You're getting better."

He grabbed the corner of my towel as I walked by, leaving me standing stark naked in the middle of the hallway. "Sherlock in the buff." He gave me a thumbs up.

"You're sick. Payback is a bitch." The lock on the bathroom door echoed down the hallway. He knew about payback.

When he's here, he drives me crazy. When he's in Bourne, I can't wait for him to come home. *Home, the place where one lives permanently, especially as a member of a family.* I snapped back to reality when Sam walked into the bedroom. "Whoa, big fella." I looked him up and down. "Like those tighty whities!"

Breakfast had to wait.

78

Chapter 27

The parking lot at Stella's wasn't even half full. The church crowd wouldn't arrive for another hour and a half.

Stella saw us the minute we walked through the door. She hustled from behind the counter to give us hugs. "Where've you guys been?" She held tight to the top of my arms, but spoke to Sam. "You never know what this one is going to get herself into."

"You've got that right. And, I live with her. How do you think I feel?" he laughed.

There he goes again. He lives with me, but if things get testy, he has his what-am-I-doing-here place to retreat to.

"Your favorite table is available. Want coffee?"

"Yes, please." I picked up a newspaper on the way.

Sam faced me. "I'm in the mood for blueberry pancakes. You?"

"I'll have pancakes, but plain, and a glass of apple juice."

When Stella brought our coffees, Sam placed our order. "If you're in no hurry, neither are we."

Stella smiled. "Then I'll take care of those couples first. My daughter's in the kitchen, so hopefully, I'll be able to visit before church gets out."

Sam scanned the front page and I took the local section. There was an article about the Figawi festivities. "Last summer I mentioned the Figawi Ball to Marnie. After she got by the name, she thought it sounded like fun. I know it's black tie and evening attire, and it might be sold out, but do you think you could get four tickets?"

"You really want to go?"

"I do."

Sam rolled his eyes. "I'll make a couple calls tomorrow."

"Don't sound so enthusiastic. Promise me you'll really try."

"What's the date and place?"

"May sixteenth at the Resort and Conference Center in Hyannis. You know, the one across the street from the Melody Tent."

"I know where it is." He went back to his reading.

I sarcastically shook my head and silently mouthed, *I know where it is*.

"I heard that."

Ten minutes later, Stella brought our food, a blueberry scone for herself and three fresh coffees. "Beth told me to sit and visit with you guys for a bit. She's a good girl." Stella looked towards the kitchen and waved. "I don't know what I'll do when she goes away to college."

Sam took a bite. "As always, your blueberry pancakes are the best."

"Thanks. Casey, tell me, are you working another case?"

I knew she'd ask before we left. "The first day back to work I had a visitor from Boston. He and his wife hired me to find a relative." I noted Sam's approval of my case description.

Stella looked at Sam. "I'm glad she's taking on something easier than her last two."

"Me, too. Keeps her out of trouble."

Stella tapped the back of my hand. "Actually, I think trouble is her middle name."

"You know Sherlock better than I thought you did."

A family of four came in and headed towards the big table in the corner. "My rest period is over. Time to make the donuts." She walked over to greet the family.

Sam tucked the Tribune under his arm and went to the counter to pay. Beth was at the register. Stella was just coming out of the kitchen. I walked over and gave her a hug.

"Don't make it so long next time."

"We won't." I waved to Beth as we headed out.

80

Chapter 28

We took backroads to get to Sandwich. It was definitely the long way, but we had nothing else to do.

Sam touched my forearm. "When we get to Route 6A, which way do we turn?"

"I'm not sure where you're getting onto 6A, so I'm giving the address to our favorite GPS lady."

"In three miles, take a right."

"There's your answer," I said.

Seven miles later, our friend let us know she was still in command. "In one mile, turn right onto Winter Hill Street." Silence. "In three hundred feet turn right."

"You can shut that off now. We have to turn left—right?" Sam laughed and made the right turn.

"Buzzy Lane isn't far up on the right. Then, number18 is two miles on the left."

Sam slowed when we came to the driveway I'd turned down just days before.

"Here it is." I took my camera from my purse. "I want to take a couple pictures of this end of the driveway. I didn't take any Friday." Somehow I missed the pole with the half-hung address sign displaying a worn-out number 18.

Sam stopped. We got out of the car and looked around.

"This is really out in the boondocks. I can understand why nobody discovered the fire before it was too late," said Sam.

I snapped a couple pictures of the sign and a few more of the surrounding area. "If you think this is way out, wait until you see

81

where the house was. I didn't check the distance, but I figured it to be about three hundred yards in."

"Get back in the car and we'll check it out."

"I got an eerie feeling when I was here by myself."

"I'll reserve comment until we walk the area." Sam glanced from side to side as he drove slowly down the driveway. He stopped when he saw the weatherworn, broken pieces of the white picket fence. "I presume the house was at the end of this brick walkway. If it wasn't enveloped by sand, you'd never find it without removing some of the overgrown brush. Did you walk the red brick road?"

"I did, until I came to a private property sign. It was old and rusty, but I don't think it's been here for twenty-five years." I got out of the car and started down the walkway. "Follow me and I'll show you."

"You're right. This sign hasn't been here that long. It would have been completely rusted through. Something's not right with this picture."

"I have questions for the O'Malleys regarding this property."

"I'll be interested in what they have to say." Sam walked the ground where he presumed the house once stood. "This fire had to be a raging inferno." He kicked some picker bushes aside and uncovered part of a foundation. He followed it. When it turned right, he turned right. He step-measured, what he deemed to be was the back of the house, from one corner to the other, then did the same thing down the side. "This wasn't a small house. I figure it was approximately forty-eight feet long and fifty-eight feet deep, not counting the garage. If my math is right, the house was 2,700 plus square feet, probably a ranch."

"Since they built the house, there has to be a copy of the footprint somewhere. I'll check with the Registry of Deeds tomorrow. I'll get the name of the builder too."

Sam crossed his arms over his chest. "Big house, lots of toys—what did this guy do for a living?"

"Good question. I intend to find out."

"Do you have all the pictures you want?"

"I do. At least for now." The panoramic view surrounding the spot where the Davis' house once stood was as dead as the Davis'. "There's a story here and it's begging to be told." I should've never let that sentence come out of my mouth for anyone, let alone Sam, to hear—but it was too late.

"You were hired to find a missing person, not to re-write history."

I knew not to question or even reply to Sam's comment.

Nothing was said until we were away from the Buzzy Lane property.

"Do you want company when you go to Boston this week?"

"Not this time. Save it for when I want an introduction to one of your cronies in Dorchester. I might need to ask questions about a crooked cop and they might not take well to a PI from Cape Cod messin' with the Boston 'big boys'."

"You've got that right."

"Besides, maybe the day you come with me, we can stay overnight and take in a show."

"You think you're cute, don't you?"

"Don't you?"

"Enough said. I don't know what you want to do now, but Sox are playing the Yankees at eight o'clock in New York. Our boys beat them last night and Buchholz is pitching tonight. Dino's or Red Face Jacks will have the game on the big screen."

"I opt for Dino's. Pizza, chicken wings, keno and the Red Sox—I can handle that. But, now we better get home and make sure Watson's still talking to us."

*****

Sam beeped the horn when we pulled into the driveway.

"You're cruel."

"Not at all—just letting him know we're home in case he's got company and has to let her out the back door."

I took a deep breath. "My father never gave me a warning."

83

Sam smirked.

"You up for a walk?"

"I was going to sit, finish reading the paper and enjoy a nice cold frostie."

I pulled two spill-proof Dunkin Donut travel tumblers from the cabinet beside the refrigerator. "No problem—one for you and one for me. They're perfect to camouflage your beer and my White Zin."

Sam laughed, "When did you get those?"

"They came in last week when you were in Bourne. I actually forgot about them until now. Perfect time to break 'em in."

"Then, a walk it is."

All Watson had to hear was 'walk' and he scurried to the front door, sat at attention and yipped until we acknowledged him.

"He's getting far too smart. I think he turns the TV on while we're not here and watches the Dog Channel."

"Dog Channel?"

"Yeah, somebody's making big money. They created a channel specifically designed for dogs as viewers."

Sam looked at Watson and shook his head. "You've got to be shittin' me."

"Nope and if I didn't know better, I'd say he understands every word you're saying, so please refrain from swearing in front of our boy."

Chapter 29

The parking lot at Dino's was full. After all, it was the beginning of the season, and it was a Red Sox vs Yankees' game. We found a spot around the corner in front of the Chinese take-out place.

Bob, the bartender, pointed to two stools open at his end of the bar. "Perfect timing, Dino and his buddy just got up, so his loss, your gain." He smiled. "What can I get you to drink?"

"A bottle of Bud with a frosted mug and…" Sam looked at me.

"I'll have the same."

Bob shrugged. "No White Zin with an ice cube chaser tonight?"

"Not in the pink shit mood."

Sam laughed, "See why I don't order for her."

"Smart man, my friend. Smart man." Bob left to get our drinks.

"Have you made plans for tomorrow?" Sam asked.

"I'm going to stick around the Village. I want to be prepared before I venture into Boston. If I forget something, it's not like I can take a half hour ride back to the office to get it. And, since I'm going to be around, I'll take Watson to work with me."

Bob came back with our drinks. "You ordering any food?" He looked around the restaurant. "It's going to take a while, so I suggest you put at least part of it in now."

"We'll take an order of cheese fries and an order of wings with teriyaki sauce on the side. Better give us some ranch dressing too." Sam looked at the pizza the couple beside us was eating. "We've got time before the game. We'll just get the wings and fries to start, then maybe order something else later."

"Good choice." I held up my mug to toast. The Keno holder was sitting smack in front of me. "Those Keno slips are calling my name. Who knows, I could get lucky."

"The only lucky you're going to get is when we get home." Sam leaned over and gave me a kiss on the check.

"Really," I said and proceeded to fill in my numbers—seven, nineteen, sixteen, thirty-seven and forty-eight.

"How many games you going to play?"

"Ten—a dollar per game. You playing?"

"Waste of money."

We had a half hour before the ballgame started. I looked around, but didn't see anybody I knew until Dino walked out from the kitchen.

"Aren't you glad I saved you two seats?" He smiled. "Been a while. What brings you guys to Mashpee tonight?"

I gave him a hug. "It's the wings, of course, and maybe a few innings of the game."

"A few innings? I don't think so. We'll be warming these seats for the whole game."

"I've got season tickets in the Budweiser section. How 'bout you guys come to a game with me? Check their schedule and yours and get back to me. Do it as soon as possible 'cause I've got a lot of 'friends' wanting these tickets," said Dino.

"Appreciate it. I'll get back to you in a couple days."

Dino gave us each a pat on the back. "I've got to get going. Talk to you soon."

"That guy moves faster than anyone I know. Here one minute and completely gone the next." I shook my head in amazement. "And, with all his conversations, he never forgets one of them."

"We'll check the calendar when we get home."

"Hey, I wasn't watching the board. I'm already on the seventh game and just won a dollar."

Sam held a finger up and swirled it around. "Big deal. That's not even enough for Bob's tip."

"I've still got three more games."

Our food came along with two more drinks. "The drinks are on Dino."

"Thanks. We'll catch him later." Sam dug his fork into the cheese fries.

"I'm going to cash in my ticket before I get all greased up." There were two people in front of me at the Keno desk. "Here's the lucky one." I laughed.

Janie ran it through the machine. "I guess it is lucky. Do you want to repeat the bet?"

"Nah."

I turned in Sam's direction. He split his focus between the Sox game and his wings.

"Hold out your hand." Janie started counting money as she laid it in my palm—one hundred, two hundred, three hundred in one hundred dollar bills, then continued with a mixture of twenties, tens, fives and a one. "Four hundred and fifty-one dollars."

I could hardly speak, but managed to get out a weak, 'thank-you', then handed her a twenty dollar tip. I put my winnings, all except another ten, for ten more plays, in my pocket and walked back to my seat.

"Took you long enough. How many more games did you play?" He said in between bites.

"Another ten." I debated whether or not to 'show him the money'. *Later.* "What's the score?"

"Ten to three in the fourth—Yankees ahead."

I ate a couple more wings. "Boring game."

Half the bar had already left. "Let's finish eating, head home, watch the news and go to bed."

Chapter 30

Monday

I hit all four lights on my way to the office. It was raining and, of course, my umbrella was at home. My parking spot was only ten steps from the back entrance. I patted Watson on the head. "Stay here I'm going to unlock the door."

Watson sat patiently on the passenger seat while I reached into the back to collect my briefcase and purse. I wasn't about to sit and wait out the rain, so I ran to unlock the door. My keys slipped from my hand and fell on the ground beside the steps.

Watson, who runs faster than me, jumped out of the driver's side of the car and headed for the open office door. He was relatively dry. I was a drowned rat. Good thing I wasn't driving to Boston today. My organizational skills screamed my name—telling me to stop procrastinating. I sat at my desk and looked over the same newspaper articles I'd looked at umpteen times before. The printed words didn't change. It was the hidden meanings in-between that I couldn't make out.

I flipped through the pages until I came to the one involving a drug bust with injuries and a death. It was dated August 13, 1978. That would have made Charlie eighteen. His was the only actual name mentioned. That meant the other three involved were juveniles. Note to Sam—get me names. The Revere Beach bar fight—also involved Charlie and two unnamed cronies. Were they juveniles too? But they were in a bar. It was dated almost a year after the drug bust. Charlie would be nineteen. Note to Sam—get me names.

My cell rang. I was glad Marnie's name appeared on the screen. "It makes it much easier when you use your own phone."

"I'm so excited—I can hardly speak." Marnie gasped. "I just got off the phone with Maloney." Her voice elevated. "He's been offered the detective position in Hyannis."

"Shut-up! That's great! Oh my God, when does he start?"

"I don't have the details. He said he'd call me tonight." She was hyperventilating through the phone. "You going to be home?"

"I am. Can't wait to tell Sam."

"I'm covering the switchboard and there's a call coming in." She was gone.

Maloney certainly isn't going to travel an hour and a half, twice a day, from Provincetown to Hyannis. Marnie's about to have a roommate. I couldn't be happier for her.

I put my reading material aside. It was ten o'clock and I hadn't had a second cup of coffee. I glanced out the window at the county court complex, then headed to the kitchen for a rendezvous with my Keurig.

It seemed like forever before the stream of coffee finally stopped. Watson sidled up beside me. "I suppose you're looking for a treat." I pulled two Milk Bones from my pocket. He stood, his tail wagging so fast I thought it might fly off. "One at a time, buddy." I patted him, kept the other treat in my hand and walked back to the front office.

My brain was unclear like the greyish overcast sky. Raggedy Ann kept making a ghostly appearance in the shadows. I sensed a haunting presence of what, I didn't know. Obviously if there was cause for alarm, Watson would alert me. He didn't.

I pushed the number one on my cell, hoping Sam was out of his meeting and could answer. It rang four times before it went to voice mail. "Call me when you're free." In the meantime, I fired up the Internet and typed *facebook.com* into the search box. I wasn't very familiar with the ins and outs of the social networking service, but Marnie signed me up a few weeks ago and gave me a brief lesson on how to maneuver the site. I had two friends listed—her and Annie. My only reason for the account was to find people. She told me I couldn't find out much information on someone unless we were friends. I wasn't about to friend people who might be related to one of my cases.

"Here goes." I typed Martin Gerber into the people search box. Almost instantly, several people with the same name appeared. Some had thumbnail pictures, others had animals or strange symbols or a generic gray, male or female bust. Under some of their names, in italics, was a town or city or state. I looked down the list of the eight Martin Gerber's. The fifth one was a picture with *Boston* printed below. I clicked on it. He looked to be in his late forties or early fifties. One thing did catch my eye. He listed Dorchester High School. There was no indication of college and the space beside employment was blank.

Marnie was right. If I wanted real info, I had to send him a friend request. Not going to happen. I was ninety-five percent sure this was my man. It appeared he was amongst the living. I studied his face. He didn't have friendly eyes. He needed a shave or maybe the picture was taken with a five o'clock shadow. People don't care what they put out there. I bumped into him before being introduced, I may be able to recognize him.

I jumped when my desk phone rang. "Casey Quinby." I skipped the private investigator spiel.

"It's me. I tried calling your cell and got no answer." Sam sounded nervous.

"It was working earlier." I picked it up. "Oops, I must have turned off the sound. I'll fix it after we talk."

"You called?"

"I did. The drug bust and the Revere Beach bar fight both listed Charlie, but nobody else by name. It reported there were three others involved in the bust and two in the fight. During the drug bust, one person was killed and two went to the hospital. I'm thinking the participants involved in both incidents are the same. And, except for Charlie, they're juveniles. Can you get me names?"

"Let me make a call. If they are juveniles, you're going to have to tread softly. Those records are sealed. But, let me find out first."

"Thanks. Wait, there's one more thing—assault on a police officer. Same scenario, Charlie's name is listed, but no others."

Sam was right. Juvenile records are sealed. I needed the information, but I couldn't let anyone know Sam was my source. When and if the unnamed were persons of interest, I'd figure out how to approach the situation. I could get lucky and find at least one of them committed a chargeable offense after he turned eighteen. That would make my poking around easier—maybe more dangerous, but definitely easier.

Chapter 31

Big M closed the door to his office and settled in behind his desk. He knew his attempt at solidarity wouldn't last long, so he hastily punched Little F's number into his cell phone. It rang three times before Shamus answered.

Thomas Maloney and Shamus Flannigan were inseparable since birth. Born one hour apart, they were known as the neighborhood twins—twins similar to Arnold Schwarzenegger and Danny DeVito. Thomas was six-three and Shamus was five-nine—hence the nicknames, Big M and Little F. After finishing Boston College High, Big M followed in his father's footsteps and became a cop. Little F went on to Boston College and graduated with double Master—one in English and the other in Journalism. The Boston Globe hired him as a political correspondent. After twenty-five years, Big M still works out of the Southie precinct and Little F covers stories all over the world for the same newspaper.

"To what do I owe the pleasure?"

"I need a favor." Big M hesitated. "When we talked the other day, you told me you were going to be away on assignment for a month?"

"I did. I'm not looking forward to traveling Europe right now—especially when it's not for personal enjoyment." Little F's tone became questioning. "What does my trip and your favor have in common?"

"It's a long story which I can't get into right now. The only thing I can say is that it involves an old case."

"One of yours?"

"Not really. Actually, no." Big M took a deep breath. "It's a Barnstable County case, but …"

"Mr. Thomas J. Maloney, Big M, there's no way you'd overstep your boundaries or jeopardize your police retirement unless it involved your family. Just tell me the wife and kid are okay."

"They are. It's nothing like that. All I'll say is it does involve my family—my Southie family."

"Enough said. How can I help?"

"The use of your condo for a few nights. Like I said, I'm not working the case, but somebody I know is. She travels up from and back to the Cape the same day. It would be much easier if she could stay in Boston a couple days at a time."

"As long as you're not harboring a fugitive or a hooker, there's no problem. You know I'm leaving Wednesday, so why don't we meet for lunch today at the Beer Garden around twelve-thirty. I'll give you my spare key and a parking card, along with all the codes 'your friend' will need to get in. I know you don't want to, but you'll also have to furnish me with a name. I have to register my 'mystery guest' with security."

"I'll be there. I owe you, my brother."

"And, one of these days, I'll collect. See you in a few."

Chapter 32

The image of the Raggedy Ann doll kept popping into my head. I closed my eyes and tried to visualize it sitting in the corner of baby Carleen's crib. "If only the doll could talk," I whispered, then rubbed my eyes and the vision was gone.

Until, and if, I get new information from Sam, I'd have at least one name to research. I actually didn't ask Sam to run Gerber's name, just to get me the names attached to the old crimes. I had to go back to the Tribune and do more digging.

"Jamie, it's me again. Is Chuck around?"

"He is, but he's getting ready to leave. I'll put you through."

"Mornin' boss."

"I wish," said Chuck. "What's up?"

"Can I stop over in about a half hour? There's a couple of things I forgot to check the other day and, until I do, I'm at a standstill."

"I won't be here, but I'll let Jamie know you're coming. By the way, we're getting an exclusive on whatever it is you're working on." He hesitated. "Right?"

"That's the deal—you help me and I'll write you a front page, sell-a-newspaper story."

"That's my girl. I've got to get going. We'll be in touch."

Doesn't hurt business to keep my name in print.

I held a plastic bag over my hair and took Watson outside for a quick walk around the building, then set him up with fresh water and a bowl of *Kibbles 'n Bits*. "Hey, boy, you're in charge. I'll be back soon."

It was still a drizzly, drab day—typical for spring on Cape Cod. I didn't care. My snooping kept me inside and dry.

Jamie was on the phone when I walked into the Tribune's reception area. She handed me the spare key to my old office and mouthed she'd talk to me later.

I nodded and headed down the corridor.

I fired up my computer—I mean my former computer—readied myself with paper and pen and continued my research on the Boston 'bad boys'. I connected to the DMV first and plugged in Martin Gerber. He had a strip of wallpaper—mostly speeding, traveling the wrong way on a one way street and parking violations. I get the wrong way and parking, but speeding in Boston—really. He had two suspensions. Both times his license was reinstated only after a brief period of having to bum rides. One of the suspensions was a DUI. It was dated after Charlie's death, so they weren't involved together on that one. Mostly what I was looking for, was information on Gerber after Charlie's death—the man between the pages, not the Photo Shopped picture on the cover. I jotted down his home address, then sent the DMV history to the printer.

While I was in the DMV site, I checked a listing for Elaine Gerber. She may have been married to a bad boy, but her record didn't show any problems. I wasn't surprised. Her stepfather was a Dorchester cop. I'm sure that's why her husband didn't lose his license. While printing the copy of her DMV history, I noticed her address was different from Martin's. I highlighted both of them. Either they never updated their information or they didn't live together anymore. On my next trip to Boston, maybe I'll check the current census records at City Hall.

There wasn't anything more to do. I packed up my findings, locked the office door and went back to reception to visit with Jamie before heading back to the Village.

"This phone hasn't stopped ringing since you came in. Don't know what's happening out there, but I've gotten some crazy calls."

"Maybe it's a full moon." I moved my eyebrows up and down trying to create an eerie spirit, then laughed. "Watson's waiting for me back at my office, so I've got to get going. I'll catch you later."

Jamie answered her phone, then put her hand over the mouthpiece and whispered, "Here we go again. We'll talk."

Chapter 33

Watson was sitting in front of the door waiting for me. "Let me make a coffee, then we'll take a walk around the building." I gave him a pat.

The drizzle had stopped and it had warmed up some, so I sat at the bistro table with the boy curled up beside me. I looked up at my shingle, moving slightly in the afternoon breeze reminding me to get back to work.

I was in the process of opening *googlemaps* when my phone rang.

"Hi Casey, it's Big M."

"Good afternoon. I figured I'd hear from you today."

"I don't have any words of wisdom or any new information, but I do have something that might interest you."

He sparked my curiosity. "Well, I'm waiting."

"One of my best friends is leaving on an assignment in Europe on Wednesday. He has a condo in the Harbor Towers. I thought while you were skulking around Boston, it would be easier if you didn't have to drive back and forth from the Cape, so I talked to him today about letting you stay there a few nights."

"You've got to be kidding me. Don't the Harbor Towers sit on Boston Harbor near the North End?"

"That's the place."

"And, you're sure it's okay for me to be there?"

"I'm sure. I have his spare key, the parking card and the codes you'll need. Tomorrow he'll give your name to security, so you can park in the garage."

"I don't know what to say. I appreciate it more than you know. I'm not fond of the Route 3 drive and more than half of my investigation is going to be in Boston. Can I come up Wednesday or should I wait until Thursday?"

"His flight leaves from Logan at eight-thirty in the morning, so you're golden. Let me know what time you'll be here and I'll meet you."

"I'll call you tomorrow." I hung up without saying good-bye. The Harbor Towers—that's like living a dream.

If I'm going to Boston on Wednesday to play super sleuth, I'd better have a plan. I went back into *googlemaps.com* and plugged in the address the DMV showed for Martin Gerber. Since I didn't know Boston all that well, I'd need all the help I could get, especially if I was traveling alone. I typed in the Alimeda Street, Dorchester address, then clicked the street view symbol. The image showed a three family house with lots of trash both at the end of the driveway and on the front porch. The small patch of grass in the front needed mowing. The empty lot to the right surrounded by a broken chain link fence shared the same unappealing curb-side view. If this was, in fact, Martin's address, I'd have a hard time doing surveillance without being seen.

I repeated the process for Elaine Gerber. Her address was listed as 2601 Beckman Boulevard, also in Dorchester. Her neighborhood was a mixture of multi- and single-family houses, not as close together as the ones on Alimeda. They appeared to be well maintained—a nice area.

I didn't want to spin my wheels for nothing, so before I scoped out the two houses, I wanted to make sure Martin and Elaine were still listed as residents.

I made a note to check with Big M about Gerber. He may or may not know much about him. I wanted to know where he worked or if he worked at all. If Big M didn't know, Jim Kelly might.

It was four-fifteen. There wasn't anything else I could do until after I talked to Sam. I hoped he was able to get me information on the unknown juveniles. Tonight was a work night. If I was going to

98

be productive Wednesday and Thursday, I had to have a plan. Sam could help me put it together. I packed up my briefcase, and Watson and I headed to the car.

I didn't want to go out for supper, so I visited Stop and Shop and picked up a rotisserie chicken, potato salad and a can of green beans. The thermometer on the bank sign next to the market read sixty nine degrees. I cracked the window slightly so the boy had air, then scurried inside to pick up the food.

The table was set and the chicken was warming in the oven when Sam walked in the door. "Something smells good. My little domestic goddess has worked her magic."

"You get the drinks. Wine for me." I folded my arms. "Enjoy supper, because if you want 'dessert', you're going to have to work for it." I gave him a little wink accompanied by a smile, then put the food on the table and motioned for him to sit down.

"I did my homework today. I was able to get ahold of my friend in Boston. Didn't go into details, but told him I needed names in any old arrests that involved an eighteen year old named Charles Davis and Martin Gerber and possibly three juveniles. I gave him the information and the dates you provided me. He did make a comment about how old the cases were and said it might take a little extra time."

I set my fork down and gave Sam my undivided attention. My chicken could wait. "Well, did he find anything?"

"He did. It took him a couple hours, but he called to tell me he found reports. He faxed me copies. After supper we'll set up shop."

I wanted to clear the table immediately, but knew Sam wouldn't go for it. He didn't mind working at home, at least most of the time, but, he didn't want work to take over our lives completely.

Fifteen minutes later I loaded the dishwasher and Sam emptied his briefcase of what I presumed to be the copies of the Boston PD reports.

"My buddy, Jimbo, sent more than I asked for. There are ones that are just Charlie Davis and others that are just Martin Gerber. Then, there's the reports that involve Charlie's little band of merry men, or should I say kids." Sam put them into their respective piles. "Jimbo also researched the juveniles after they became adults. I owe him big time and in turn, you owe me." He leaned over and gave me a kiss.

"You're the man." I made us a cup of coffee, got out my red pen and two different color highlighters and settled in for a long night's work. "The sooner we get this done, the sooner you get your dessert." I batted my eyelashes in a flirtatious flutter and blew him a kiss.

Chapter 34

I skimmed the reports and highlighted Charlie's name in yellow, Martin's name in pink, and any additional names in red. I made a color-coordinated list of the names and set it aside.

"We're going to be late into the night. Want some Oreos?" Sam asked.

I nodded and kept writing.

After twenty minutes, I took a break. "Forgot to tell you the best part of my day."

"Pray tell, I can't imagine what it might be."

"I got a call from Big M."

"You were expecting one, weren't you?"

"I was, but not for the reason he called. A friend of his, who's going to be out of town for a while, is letting me stay at his condo. Big M thought if I had to be in Boston two or more days in a row, it would be better if I didn't have to travel back and forth from the Cape."

"I agree with him. I didn't say anything, but I didn't like the idea of the two-way Route 3 run."

"You'll never guess where the condo is."

"I'm not playing that game—where?"

"Harbor Towers."

"Say what!" His face came to life. "You might need a body guard or a city guide. Just saying—I'm available."

"And, if you're good to me, I may take you up on your very generous offer. For now, what I will need is for you to either stay here with Watson or take him to your place."

"I'll stay here. And, I'm sure Marnie will take him if I join you in Boston."

"That can be arranged—if you join me." I looked at him. "Let's get back to work."

"Start with the drug bust. Charlie was the only one over seventeen. Martin Gerber was sixteen, same age as the one that got killed. The other two were fifteen. Their names are Henry Smalls and William Brogan. I took the liberty to run them through the DMV. Smalls lives in Revere." Sam took a pen from his pocket and circled the address. "Brogan's moved around. He has six listed addresses in the Boston area." Sam circled them too. "According to the DMV, he's been at the one in South Boston for the last eight years. His rap sheet actually shows two more older residences than the DMV does."

"You have a copy of the rap sheet?"

Sam handed it to me. "You'll notice that, still as a juvenile, Brogan was arrested for breaking and entering, but nothing ever came of it. It was a church in Revere. Charges were dropped."

"Was anyone else named?"

"Davis, Gerber, and Smalls."

"Do you think Charlie Davis' stepfather waved his magic wand and made things go away?"

"Unfortunately, I do."

I picked up the rest of the reports piled beside Sam. "I need a minute to read the charges against Gerber, Smalls and Brogan." I took a sip of coffee and grimaced—it was cold.

Sam didn't ask, he just got up and made us a fresh cup.

"Looks like all of Brogan's incidents, except for a couple of traffic problems, happened as a juvenile and he cleaned up his act after the church break-in. He's not off my list, but right now he's on the bottom. Charlie was thirty when he died. It appears that Gerber and Smalls didn't stop after their 'leader' left the picture, instead they continued to broaden their bad boy image."

"Some missing person investigation." Sam leaned back in his chair. "There are days I wish you'd stayed with the Tribune."

"Well, I didn't." Even though I told Sam about the condo at the Harbor Towers, I didn't tell him I planned on going up Wednesday and maybe staying until Friday. This time I was going solo—no Sam and no Marnie.

"What's running through that pretty little head of yours?"

"The drug bust. Why wasn't there more information about it? If one person was killed, this wasn't just a group of kids being picked up for having a few bags of weed. And, if my assumption is correct, there wasn't just one episode. You've been in this business for a long time. What do you think? Was this an isolated incident? Am I over-reacting?"

"There is a problem here."

"And further, I'm positive there's a connection between the fire at 18 Buzzy Lane and the Boston bad boys."

"There's no doubt you could make a case tying the two together, but that's not what you were hired to do. You were hired to find a baby who presumably went missing twenty-five years ago, when her family's house was destroyed in a fire. Actually, missing isn't the word. She was declared dead. The fact that they found no verifiable remains of the baby can lead to reasonable doubt as to her demise. To further reinforce that doubt, a stuffed Raggedy Ann doll bearing the child's initials on the foot was anonymously delivered last week to the home of the maternal grandparents."

I drew in a deep breath and let it out hard enough to blow out a candle two feet away. "I don't believe baby Carleen died in the fire at 18 Buzzy Lane, but if I don't figure out who else was at the Sandwich address the night of the fire, it will be impossible to find her. Somebody had a problem with Charlie, and possibly Megan. That somebody also had a twinge of compassion for the baby. Where, and with whom, Carleen has lived for twenty-five years is the mystery." I picked up the pile of reports and threw them back on the table. "There's pages missing—no, not missing, never written." Somebody knew the real story and I intended to find out who, but I couldn't push my luck much further with Sam.

We sat silent for about five minutes.

"Let's put this to bed for tonight. How about we have a nightcap and watch the news?" Sam didn't wait for my reply. He got a couple glasses from the cabinet, filled them with ice, then took a bottle of white crème de menthe and one of Amaretto Disaronno and poured each of us a drink.

I swirled the minty liqueur over the cubes, then took a sip. "I love you, Sam Summers. You know exactly how to cool me down."

Chapter 35

Tuesday

I rolled over, only to get blinded by a penetrating stream of light coming through my bedroom window. I closed my eyes as tight as I could, but it didn't work. I'd forgotten to pull the bedroom shade all the way down when we went to bed. There were twenty-two minutes before the alarm was set to go off. Sam was still in la la land. Even Watson was snoring.

I slowly slid to the edge of the bed, so as not to disturb the boys, but it didn't work. Sam whipped around and pulled me back against him. "And just where do you think you're going?"

"It's morning and a work day."

He glanced at the clock on my nightstand. "Looks like we have time for a quickie." He smiled and kissed my neck.

"You mean I didn't wear you out last night?" I kissed him back, then squirmed under his arms and jumped up. "Save that energy for tonight." As I scurried down the hallway to the bathroom, I yelled, "First in the shower."

"Make it quick."

Coffee and a bowl of strawberry mini-wheats were waiting for me.

Sam rinsed his bowl and put it in the dishwasher. "You were so slow, I already ate mine. But, *I'll be back*, for a second cup of joe."

"Okay, Arnold."

Since today was an office research day, a pair of black jeans and a light gray turtle neck fit the bill. I pulled my hair back in a ponytail, then wrapped it into a bun and checked myself out in the

105

mirror. *I'm presentable in case I have company.* I rejoined Sam in the kitchen.

"Nice work attire."

"I don't plan on going anywhere. Maybe meet Marnie for lunch."

"So what else is new?"

"Oh yeah, speaking of new. I forgot to tell you. Chief Lowe called Maloney to offer him the detective slot and he took it."

"Great. He'll be an asset to the Barnstable PD. We'll have to celebrate."

"That's not all. He'll be moving in with Marnie."

"I didn't bother to ask, cause that's a given." Sam looked around, didn't say anything else, just smiled.

I tried to climb inside his head to figure out what he was thinking, but the wall was too high. "Anyway, I'm happy for the both of them."

"Me too."

"Plan on eating at home tonight. I picked up burgers, rolls and curly fries when I got the chicken last night. That way we can have another bullshit session. Maybe I'll get something useful out of it."

"Anything else you want from me?"

"Nothing at the moment, but that doesn't mean I won't call you during the day."

Sam laughed. "Since I know you'll come up with something, I'll expect a call. Meanwhile, I've got to get going. Are you taking Watson with you?"

"No. It's supposed to be warm, so he can stay outside on his run."

Chapter 36

Traffic in the Village was a little heavy for a Tuesday morning. Most of the cars were pulling into the parking lot for the superior courthouse. Marnie was working on a case for Mike. Maybe, the influx of people and the case were related. I'd wait until at least ten o'clock before I gave her a call.

I emptied my briefcase onto my desk, looked at the pile of papers and shook my head. "Lots of trees were killed to create these reports." There was no time to dilly-dally. I had information about a number of incidents involving a lot of people, and a good portion of it was bound together with invisible thread.

I made myself a coffee, then settled in to generate a plan that would allow me to verify data I'd extracted from my research sources. Most of it included people and locations in Boston. Since Big M said the condo was available starting Wednesday, I knew I'd be meeting the doorman at Harbor Towers some time tomorrow morning.

I picked up the phone and called Big M. "Morning Sergeant. It's Casey."

"Top of the mornin' to you."

I laughed. "I'd like to take your friend up on his offer. I can only do so much over the computer. It's time to pound the pavement."

"When do you want to come up?"

"Tomorrow."

"What time?"

"Say around ten o'clock?"

"That works for me. I'll meet you at the Harbor Towers' garage. There's a pull-off just before the entrance. I'll be there in an unmarked at ten."

"Thanks, see you then." I hung up. It was time to tell Sam.

I wasn't about to drive around Boston proper, so I planned on getting a Charlie Pass and use the MTA. Out of the city, I'd be able to navigate with the help of the GPS lady. I checked my purse for cash—twenty-three dollars. A credit card was good for most things, but I needed at least a couple hundred in small bills. First on my list—stop at the bank.

My camera was in the car, so I was all set there. A couple of clean notepads and a few new pens. Probably wouldn't be a bad idea to take my laptop. Big M's friend must have Wi-Fi, otherwise it's a trip to Dunkin's or Mickey D's.

For the next three days it would be life in the fast lane. I pulled up the WhitePages.com and ran Martin Gerber and Elaine Gerber. The addresses in the White Pages were the same as the ones I got from the DMV. I red-checked them. I planned to visit City Hall to check the city directories, but would check with Big M first because I don't know how current they'd be. When I did genealogy years back, the printed books I found were old—fine when you're researching your ancestors, but no good when you are investigating the living. Face-to-face was going to be the most productive, and dangerous. All the people I want to talk to have some connection to Charlie and Megan Davis—some maybe more than others. I'm sure my visit will bring up old memories, be they good or bad. It'll be my job to use my intuition to sort them out. I knew it wasn't going to be easy.

I was deep in thought when Marnie walked into my office. She may have knocked, but my mind was so engrossed I didn't hear anything happening around me.

"I have a few minutes and know you have a supply of coffee." She walked to the kitchen and popped at K-cup into the machine.

A wave got her attention. "Make one for me."

"Coming right up."

It was a welcome break.

"You must have been involved in some heavy thinking. You only drank half of your first one. That's not like you." Marnie set the fresh one down in front of me.

I cupped my hands and lifted my mug to take a sip. "Ah, like a glass of a fine liqueur."

She smiled. "What are we doing?"

"We? I'm planning a trip to Boston and, I guess, we're planning on what to do for lunch in two hours."

" Boston? When are you going?"

"Tomorrow."

"Want company?"

"Not this time. I'm meeting Big M around ten o'clock and won't be back on the Cape until sometime Friday."

"What? Explain, please."

"Big M has a place for me to stay in Boston while I'm doing some leg work."

"You're being very evasive. Are you going to tell me more?"

"Not right now. At lunch, I'll tell you the *rest of the story.*" I took another sip.

Chapter 37

Sam already had the grill fired up and the burgers on the counter. The table was set and an empty wine glass signaled the identity of my beverage. He knew about the condo in Boston, but he didn't know my first night in a strange bed was going to be tomorrow.

"Hmm, I could get used to this." I put my briefcase on the floor and gave him a hug.

"So could I."

I froze. I wasn't sure what to say next, so I changed the subject real quick. "I could use something in that empty glass."

He poured my White Zin over a handful of cubes and got himself a frostie. "Let's take this conversation out on the deck."

"And, how was your day?" I asked without looking up.

"Slow. Working on the classes for the academy." His sentences were short. He knew I was about to drop a bombshell. "Since I didn't hear from you, I figured you were playing Farm Heroes on the computer or deep into reading about places in Boston you'd like to visit."

"The barn door was shut all day. I had too much work to do." I looked out over the backyard.

"And." He could read me like a book, but he'd come to a page he couldn't turn.

"I'm heading to Boston tomorrow morning and I'll be back some time on Friday."

"You going alone, or is Marnie traveling with you?"

"Sam, I love you dearly—you know that. And, whatever cautions you're about to share with me, I'll respect. But, this is my

110

business now. I don't just sit behind a desk anymore. It's my job to move stones, maybe even mountains, to find clues to help me get answers for my clients. The work I've done in the past has helped me immensely, but I was working for the PDs. Now I'm working for Casey Quinby, and she's a broad on the move trying to make a name for herself." I raised my glass to offer a toast. "Will you join me?"

Sam hesitated, then clinked his mug against my glass.

"To us," I said.

"Those two words said it all." He smiled. "To us."

An iceberg that had started to form between us suddenly melted. "I'll get the burgers."

He nodded. "Can you bring me another beer?"

"Aren't you going to ask me what my plan of attack is?"

"I'll exercise my patience. I figure you can't keep it inside much longer. Yeah, of course, I want to know how Sherlock is going to coerce 'Boston' into spilling the beans."

"I'll just tip over the pot and go after the ones that try to get away." I laughed.

"What's first on your agenda?"

"The kid—William Brogan? His last address was on Greenbush Street in South Boston. He's first on my list. Harry Smalls is second. I'll run Brogan's name and address by Big M. Hopefully, it sets off warning lights. If not, I'll pay him a visit. He may be working, so if there's no answer, I'll go back after six. Smalls is out in Revere—the opposite side of the city, but a straight drive on Route 1."

"I have a friend, Mike Mastro, in the Revere Police Department. He's a fellow detective. If you need him, call me and I'll give him a heads up." Sam slid the burgers onto the grill. "In fact, he lives somewhere near the North End—not far from where you're staying. Good guy. Been with the Boston PD for thirty-two years—twenty-two in the North End and ten in Revere. His contact information is in my desk at the station, I'll give it to you tomorrow morning before you leave."

Chapter 38

Wednesday

I stared out the window at what looked like an iffy day. The weatherman predicted a forty percent chance of rain by noon—not a day to leave Watson outside. Sam said he'd be home around four and would stay at the house while I was gone. I got the boy set up with food and water, then finished packing my new Vera Bradley cargo bag. I only needed a couple changes of clothes, a tee shirt, my Joe boxers, an extra pair of comfortable shoes and several sets of underwear, along with my toiletry bag. The last thing I packed was an unopened bottle of White Zin and, just in case, my cork screw.

Once everything was in the car, I gave Sam a call.

He answered on the first ring. "You ready to travel?"

"I am. I'll give you a call when I get to Boston. If something comes up and you have to stay in Bourne, give Marnie a call. She'll come by and take care of Watson. She's got a key."

"I don't anticipate a problem," he said. "I've got Mike's information. Let me know when you're ready."

"Go ahead." I cradled the phone between my shoulder and ear, while trying to hold a napkin taut enough to scribble on. "I got it. Thanks."

"The Chief's buzzing me. Later." The connection ended.

I looked at the phone. "Sam Summers, you're slipping. You didn't tell me to be careful." I actually missed his words of caution.

I didn't have coffee before I left the house, so I pulled into the Dunkin's on the Cape side of the Sagamore flyover. It was my day to be different. I ordered a large mocha iced coffee with cream, two

Splendas and an extra shot of mocha. A poor little jelly donut sitting on the tray called my name. I had to take him along for the ride.

Traffic wasn't bad on Route 3. I wasn't in a hurry, so I took my time. It was nine forty-five when I pulled off by the Harbor Towers' garage. Big M was outside leaning against his car waiting for me. I parked behind him.

He walked over to my window. "I've already talked to the attendant. Here's your pass. Keep it until you're sure you won't be coming up again."

I looked up at the condos. "Do I really have to turn it in?"

"Someday." He smiled. "I'll go up to Shamus' with you, get you settled, then we'll head over to the Black Rose. Jim Kelly is meeting us there around eleven."

"Works for me."

Big M got back into his unmarked. I followed him into the garage and pulled into a space beside him. He took my Vera from me while I gathered up the rest of my stuff, then we headed towards the elevator.

"Shamus lives on the twelfth floor, overlooking the harbor."

I stopped dead in my tracks when we walked into the condo. I died and went to heaven. "In my past life I was a reporter for a newspaper. I never would have left if I thought I could have it this good." I was still gripping my briefcase, computer and toiletry bag as I stumbled past the leather furniture toward the floor to ceiling windows with its majestic views of the harbor, cargo and pleasure ships making their ways to and from the ocean and airbus activity around Logan Airport. "What newspaper did you say your friend works for?"

Big M laughed. "The Boston Globe."

"Where did I go wrong?"

"I'll let you ponder that question later." He grinned. "Let me give you the five dollar tour, then the key and list of codes you might need so we can get going."

I ran my finger across the polished granite countertop in the kitchen. "This place is amazing."

113

"Enjoy it while you're here."

Instead of just taking a notepad, I took my briefcase so I had names and addresses handy if I needed to present them for consideration. "I'm ready."

"It will be easier for us to walk to the restaurant. It's almost impossible to find a place to park. I'd be okay because of the cruiser, but most of the parking spaces are by permit only. The City makes lots of ticket money because people tend to ignore the signs posted almost every ten feet."

Jim Kelly got to the Black Rose five minutes after we did. He joined us in the backroom. "Good morning, Casey. It's nice to see you again." He looked at Big M. "Top of the mornin' to you Sergeant Maloney."

Big M rolled his eyes. "And, to you."

"What's on the docket for today?" Jim lifted his arm to get the attention of the server. "Anyone else for coffee—Irish or otherwise?"

"Yes, please," I said. "Just regular."

"Nothing for me." Big M checked his cell and put it on vibrate. "Casey is staying in Boston for a few days to do some people checking. I'm going to let her run some names by you. Stop her if any one of them sounds familiar."

"As far as I can determine, the addresses I have are the most current. They came from DMV records, which we all know aren't always the most accurate for one reason or another. One of the guys, William Brogan, has a laundry list of addresses, but the last one is 229 Greenbush Street in South Boston."

"I think I know Bill. A guy around fifty-three . Been in a little trouble now and then."

"Your Bill and mine are one in the same."

"He frequents my bar. Pretty quiet, except during a Pat's or Red Sox game. Never any trouble though."

Our server brought our coffee. We waited until she was out of earshot before we continued our conversation. "According to the DMV he's been at the same address for the last eight years."

"What do you need to know about him?"

"He used to run with Charlie Davis." I knew I had to be very careful what I said even though Big M had given me the okay to confide in Jim. "I'm checking background on some of Charlie's bad boys."

"Wasn't he younger than Charlie?" asked Jim.

"He was. Brogan was a juvenile, as were all of Charlie's little band of followers. Brogan never did or, should I say, never got caught doing anything illegal after he turned eighteen. And, he never did any time in juvenile hall. It's almost like his charges were written with invisible ink." I waited for a reaction. There was none. "Brogan may have cleaned up his act. What about the name, Harry Smalls? Again, the address info comes from the DMV. His last known is Carter Lane in Revere. I have a contact there, who might be able to help me on this guy, but I thought I'd run it by you anyway."

Big M shook his head. "Nope."

"Not familiar with me either," said Jim.

"Okay. I have one more name—Martin Gerber."

I saw Jim and Big M exchange glances, then nod in recognition.

"A nod isn't going to help me. What's the story on Gerber?"

"He was Charlie's brother-in-law. A real cocky, son-of-a-bitch." Big M's face went cold. "I had dealings with him. In fact, my whole family had dealings with him. My nephew, Tommy Darcy, my name sake, was a Boston cop. He was my sister's boy. He was killed when he responded to a domestic violence call in Dorchester. It was rumored that the wife was screwing around with Martin Gerber, but it was never proven. The husband came home, caught the asshole leaving out the back door and went ballistic. The wife claimed it was an intruder. A neighbor made the call. The husband heard a noise, said he didn't hear the cop identify himself and thought it was the 'intruder' coming back. He emptied his gun in the direction of the noise. Three of the bullets hit Tommy. He was pronounced dead at the scene. So, do I know Martin Gerber? I do."

I fidgeted with the papers in front of me, then looked at Jim. "Does anyone want lunch?"

"I could go for a fish sandwich." Jim got up to find our server.

I put my hand on Big M's arm. "You okay?"

"I will be. That name triggered a bad memory. Believe me I kept an eye out. If I saw Gerber anywhere in or around Southie, he wouldn't be walking around today." Big M shrugged. "And I'll deny I just said that."

"I didn't hear a thing."

Jim came back with the server right behind him. "She's ready to take your order. I already gave her mine."

"I'll have a corn beef on rye with fries and a Diet Coke."

The server looked at Big M. "For you?"

"The same as she's having. Thanks."

"Casey, this Gerber guy is a dangerous dude. He should be in jail. His father-in-law, Robert Cushing, was a cop in Dorchester. He died about fourteen or fifteen years ago." Big M's face was cold.

"Sam already told me about Cushing. Do you know if Gerber is still married to Elaine?"

"I don't, but I'll find out."

"All right, I'll leave him alone for now."

Our food came.

I looked at Big M. "Do you think I'll be able to meet Mrs. Maloney while I'm here?"

"That can be arranged. She'd like that." He smiled. "Maybe we can do lunch on Friday before you go back to the Cape."

"On a happier note, everyone's excited for Maloney," I said.

Jim gave me a puzzled look.

"I forgot you call him Rusty."

"So what's the news?"

I stuffed a bite of sandwich in my mouth, so Big M would answer.

116

"My son is now Detective Rusty Maloney with the Barnstable PD. He starts in two weeks."

"That's great. You should be so proud. Bring him by the bar the next time he's home."

"I will."

We finished eating.

Jim checked his watch. "I've got to get back to L Street. Tomorrow night is dart night. Brogan is a sub on one of the teams. He usually shows up in case they need him. You can call me or just show up around seven."

"Thanks. I'll be there."

"And, I'll be with her."

Jim nodded his approval for me to have an escort, then turned and left.

"Where are you off to now?"

"Revere. I'm going to do a ride by. Hopefully Smalls' address from the DMV is valid."

"Are you planning on stopping?"

"I'm not sure. Time to get a move on. I'll call you later." I put a twenty on the table.

"Put it back in your pocket. Jim already took care of it."

Chapter 39

I got into my Joe boxers and Mickey Mouse tee shirt, poured myself a glass of White Zin and curled up on the oversized chair in front of the picture window that faced out onto Boston Harbor. The beam from the full moon projected a walkway across the water. Flashing beacons from several channel buoys warned an incoming boat which side of the waterway provided safe passage. I took a sip of wine, leaned back and closed my eyes. *Sam would love it here.*

No sooner did I get that thought out, my cell buzzed. "Good evening, Miss Casey is busy observing the tranquility that rolls in across the harbor every night at this time."

"You're supposed to be working. How much have you had to drink?"

"I heard that muffled laugh. If I have to come up and stay over again, you definitely have to come with me. This is a little slice of heaven, for sure." I sighed. "And, to think it all belongs to a newspaper reporter."

Sam smiled into the phone. "Do they allow dogs?"

"I don't know—probably not."

"Then that leaves us out. Not going anywhere without the boy."

I shrugged. "You've got that right."

"So, how did your day go?"

"Interesting. I met with Big M and Jim Kelly. I told you about him?" I got up and poured myself a half glass of wine. "I asked about William Brogan and Harry Smalls. Seems like Brogan frequents Jim's bar in Southie. Wednesday is dart night and Brogan is usually there. This afternoon I had planned to ride by the address

118

you got from the DMV, but I can do that before I go to Boston Blackie's tomorrow."

"Are you going there alone?"

"No, I have an escort."

"Okay, smart ass, who?"

"Big M's meeting me. Know what's scary—he's just like you. He insisted on comin' along. So, let me assure you, you have nothing to worry about." I kissed the phone.

"I'd know that sound anywhere. Right back at you."

"What I did do is take a ride to Revere. That was the last address we got on Harry Smalls. He lives in a two family house a few blocks back from the beach. It's no Taj Mahal, but it's nice. If, in fact, he still lives there, he must bring home a decent paycheck to afford the location."

"I'd say it would be a smart move to get ahold of Detective Mastro. I know Mike would be more than willing to share any information he has on Smalls." Sam hesitated. "Do you want me to give him a heads-up call? I won't fill him in on anything, I'll leave that up to you."

"Yeah, I'd like that."

"I'll introduce Casey Quinby, private investigator and you can take it from there."

"That works. First thing in the morning would be great ?"

"You've got it. That didn't take up your whole day. What else did you do?"

"Rode by the Dorchester addresses for Martin and Elaine Gerber. Elaine's was nicer than it showed on Google Street View, but the residence listed for Martin was a pig sty—much worse than the picture. I didn't stop. I've got to figure that one out." It wasn't the time to repeat the Martin story Big M had lamented over at lunch. "I drove from one side of Boston to the other, so the rest of my time was spent maneuvering the one-way streets of the City."

"I know one thing you left out."

"What?"

"Did you venture to Hanover Street?"

119

"Well, yeah. I ate at Pagliuca's, then walked down to Mike's Pastry for a cappuccino and a cannoli. I'm in Boston and in the North End to boot. Did you think I'd order delivery from Pizza Hut and eat double-stuffed Oreos for dessert?"

"That's my girl."

"I'm going to type my notes into the computer and watch a little television before bed. Give me a call in the morning after you talk to your buddy at the Revere PD."

"I will. Hey, Sherlock, Watson and I miss you."

"You and Watson, huh. Love you both."

"Love you, too."

I didn't want to admit it, especially to Sam, but I wasn't sure of my next step. Right now I have a meeting scheduled with Big M at Boston Blackie's for tomorrow night. I plan to talk to Brogan, if he shows up. It would be much easier if I could hold a Philo Vance *chair-in-a-circle* bullshit session with all the players in attendance. Tomorrow will be dicey on some level. Maybe I'll be wrong, but I wish Sam would be hiding in my hip pocket.

Chapter 40

Thursday

It was eight-thirty. I was coming out of the bathroom when my cell rang. I was sure it was Sam and I didn't want to miss his call. "Mornin.'" I tried to sound perky. It didn't work.

"You just get up?" Marnie chuckled. "I talked to Sam last night. You better not get too used to that lifestyle."

"You should see this place. Absolutely beautiful and it's not even decorated like a man cave. He must have hired a professional." I looked out the wall of glass at the boats maneuvering in the harbor like well-planned choreography. Their wakes moved across the surface forming patterns as they headed towards the open water.

"Hello. You there?" Marnie asked.

"Yeah, just taking in the sights." I sighed. "What's up?"

"Figured I'd give you a call. Is there anything I can do to help while you're away?"

"Not at the moment, but ..." My call-waiting beeped. "Somebody's on the other line. Later."

It was Sam. "I almost hung up."

"I was talking to Marnie. Did you talk to Detective Mastro?"

"Just got off the phone with him. He's expecting your call."

"Did you give him any details?"

"No, I told him I'd leave that up to you. After all, it's your case."

"Smartass. Let me get ready and I'll fill you in later."

Sam laughed. "Watch out for Mike. He's one eligible bachelor."

"Does he have a condo like Shamus?"

"Far from it." Sam was gone.

It was fun to tease him, but in reality I wished he were here with me.

*****

Benny, the doorman, smiled as I headed for the garage. "Can I give you directions?"

"I'm all set today, but I'm sure I'll take you up on that before I leave the Towers."

"I'm like a GPS, only live and far more accurate. Lived in Boston all my life. Can't imagine living anywhere else." He smiled. "If you stick around, I'll give you a list of must-see places or things you should do."

"I'd like that. Thanks. Right now, I better get to work."

"Have a good one, ma'am." He nodded as he held the door open for me.

"I hope to."

Detective Mastro suggested I meet him at the Dunkin Donuts on Beach Street near Revere Beach. *A man after my own heart.* He said it was quiet this time of the year and we'd be able to talk. I plugged the address into my GPS. I wasn't meeting him until ten-thirty, so I had plenty of time in case it directed me to make turns onto one-way streets or instructed me to take several 'legal' U-turns. Staying at the Towers was unbelievable, but driving around Boston was a nightmare.

After only two wrong turns and almost running a red light, I spotted my favorite orange, brown and white sign two blocks ahead. There were only a couple cars in the lot, but I had no idea if one belonged to the Revere PD. I parked and went inside. A 'police-looking' person stood up as I walked in. Apparently, Sam had described my car—a lime-green Mazda Spider with the license plate CQ007. "Detective Mastro?" I reached forward to shake his hand.

"That's me. You're just as Sam described you—lime-green and a great vanity plate."

122

"That's Sam. Now I know why you two are friends." I smiled.

"First of all, call me Mike. Sam didn't tell me why a private investigator was scouring my town. He said you'd fill me in. But, before we start, I'm getting a coffee. Can I get one for you?"

"Dunkin's provides me with my drug of choice. I'd love a French Vanilla."

"Be right back."

My briefcase was in the car, but I wanted to get acquainted before I went into details. So far, so good.

"Here you go, little lady. One sissy coffee for you and a manly black for me."

"Just fine," I whispered.

"What was that?"

"Nothing." I smirked.

"Let's get down to the business part of this meeting. Like I said, Sam didn't say much, so you need to start from the beginning."

"I've been hired to find a missing person. It's not your typical runaway, or parental abduction, or car crash where the victim didn't have any identification. Twenty-five years ago, there was a horrific house fire in Sandwich. That's a town on Cape Cod."

"I know it well."

"The occupants were a young couple and their month-old baby girl. The parents' remains were found, but not the child's. The fire was so intense on the side of the house where the baby's bedroom was located, the authorities declared the baby deceased. That's the abridged version. I've been hired to find the, now twenty-five-year-old, girl."

Mike lifted his coffee and took a drink. "I'm puzzled. She was ruled dead?"

"Yes, then last week her maternal grandparents found a shopping bag with a Raggedy Ann doll wrapped in a towel on their front stoop. The doll belonged to their granddaughter."

"They believe she's still alive?"

"They do. And, they're paying me to prove them right."

The look on Mike's face produced an invisible thought bubble. He leaned back in his chair and folded his arms over his chest.

"That's the story."

"Somehow it involves Revere or you wouldn't be here looking to answer questions pertinent to the case."

"Detectives are so smart."

He gave me a sideward glance. "Question number one."

"Does the name Harry Smalls sound familiar?"

"Hmm." Mike smiled. "Harry's a bad boy trying to be good. I have to admit, his name hasn't come up for the last couple years. But, given your timeframe of twenty-five years ago, that's when he was honing his image. He ran with a nasty crowd. He was one of the younger kids."

"What do you know about him now?"

"He's worked in lots of different places. Most recently, he was driving truck for a local delivery service. He's more than likely still there. I pulled up beside him a couple months ago at a traffic light. When he looked at my car and realized it was me, I could see his hands tighten on the wheel. When he was running the street, I chased that SOB—he was fast—real fast. I caught him every time but one. How does he fit into your missing person investigation?"

"If I did my homework right, one of his mentors, those many years ago, was Martin Gerber."

"You did your homework. Martin was a no-good bastard. He was tough, but not tough enough to hang with the big boys." Mike noticed the puzzled look on my face. "The boys, you know, like the Winter Hill Gang or the Angiulo brothers."

Of course I'd heard of them, but only from reading the papers or listening to the news.

"Okay, now you've thrown two names out—Smalls and Gerber. They're Boston boys and your crime scene was on the Cape. What's the connection?"

"The young couple found dead in the fire was Charlie and Megan Davis. The baby's name was Carleen."

"Charlie Davis. You don't have to go any further. Now, you have a name I can talk about. He was the 'bad-boys' fearless leader. You're bringing back old memories. His stepfather, Robert Cushing, was a Dorchester cop. He died fifteen years ago."

"Sam filled me in on him."

"And Sam probably doesn't know the half of it. When I worked out of the North End, I had cases that overlapped with Dorchester. Cushing was involved in several of them. I could never prove it and I was a rookie, so I didn't want to jeopardize my job, but I'm sure, to this day, he was crooked." Mike fist punched the palm of his left hand. "Let's run by Smalls' house. I doubt if he'll be there. It's almost lunch time. I've seen his truck parked at Millie's many times. If he's not home, he may be at the luncheonette."

"I appreciate what you're doing for me, but ..."

"Don't worry. I know this isn't a police matter, at least not yet. I'll introduce you, then sit back and listen, unless you'd rather I stayed in the car."

"Not at all. I might get more out of him if you're riding a silent shotgun." I smiled. "Let me throw out another name, William Brogan. He's originally from the Dorchester area. Now, he lives in Southie."

He shook his head in disgust. "He was another one of Charlie's boys, wasn't he?"

"He was," I said. "Do you remember the break-in at the Saint Paul's Church in Revere?"

"I do, but I was still in the North End and wasn't involved in the investigation."

"Seems as though Brogan's name didn't appear much after that. Sam read over the rap sheets, many of them from juvenile, and said it looked like Brogan tried to straighten out."

"It happens, but not often."

"I'm meeting with Tom Maloney tonight at Boston Blackie's in Southie."

"Big M? I haven't seen him in years. How's he doing?"

"Great. He's the reason I'm here. He recommended me to a friend of his. Actually, it was to Megan Davis' father."

"He's the one who found the Raggedy Ann doll on his stoop?"

"Yep."

Mike's eyebrows went up. "What's his name?"

I leaned toward him and lowered my voice. "Patrick O'Malley."

"O'Malley. If I had a dollar for every O'Malley I've met, I'd offer to buy you lunch."

"You know him?"

Mike shrugged. "Depends on which Patrick O'Malley you're talking about."

Chapter 41

There was no answer at the address I had for Harry Smalls, but Mike assured me it was the right house. His name was in the window of one of the mail boxes fastened to the wall just outside the front door.

"Next stop, Millie's."

Since Mike volunteered to be my chauffeur while I was in his neck of the woods, I left my car at the Dunkin's off Revere Beach Boulevard. I never would have found my way around using all the short-cuts he took me on.

"Sam didn't come up with you?"

"Not this time. Big M arranged for me to stay at a friend's condo. The friend is away in Europe on business."

"Where is the friend's condo?"

A man of many questions. "At Harbor Towers."

"Welcome to Boston." He laughed. "An exquisite place to stay and easy access to the North End. What more could you ask for?"

"To find my missing person."

"The luncheonette is just ahead on the right. We're looking for a white panel truck with *Smith's Package Delivery* painted in red and green letters on the side. It's an outfit out of the North End, hence the colors. They only have three trucks, so if one's there, we stand a one out of three chance Smalls is taking a lunch break."

Mike was right. Two trucks from *Smith's Package Delivery* were parked beside the restaurant.

"I might be in luck." I noticed the two drivers immediately when we walked inside, since they had the name of the company plastered across the back of their shirts. I didn't know which one was Smalls, but Mike did. And when Smalls saw Mike, I knew which one he was. We took the empty table beside the two guys.

"Good afternoon, Harry. I see you're still working for Smith's."

"Seven years now," Smalls said. "I've changed my ways."

"Or haven't gotten caught." Mike glanced at the food on their table. "Looks like you're getting ready to leave."

"Yep. Got to get the rest of the deliveries done before end of shift."

Mike looked at Smalls' buddy. "Why don't you get going. He'll catch up with you."

The other driver didn't say a word, left a tip and headed to the counter to pay his bill. We waited until he left before I pulled my chair closer to Smalls.

"Harry Smalls—my name is Casey Quinby. I'm a private investigator working on an old case that happened on Cape Cod."

"Okay, so what's that got to do with me?"

"Do you know or, should I say, *did* you know Charlie Davis?"

"What's going on here?"

"I asked you a question. What part of it didn't you understand?"

Mike didn't say a word, just sat back in his chair and watched.

Smalls looked at Mike, then back at me. "I did know a Charlie Davis, but he died in a fire."

"Exactly—you get an A for not lying. You and Charlie used to be good friends. Isn't that right?" I asked.

"Yeah, I guess you could say that."

"I have a couple more names for you. How about Martin Gerber and William Brogan?"

Smalls' breathing showed signs of anxiety. "Martin married Charlie's sister, Elaine, and Brogan is no relation, just one of the guys."

"Are Martin and Elaine still married?"

"I don't think so. I haven't seen him for years, but they were having their troubles back then." Smalls hesitated, then continued, "she didn't like the line of business he was in."

"What business was that?" I asked, while Mike watched Smalls' reaction.

Smalls didn't say anything, only took a drink of his soda.

"Let me try to refresh your memory." I leaned closer to his face. "Could that business have something to do with drugs?"

He looked around the room, then back at me. "Look, I don't want to cause any problems. I've been clean and, like I said before, out of trouble for seven years. If Martin finds out I'm talking to you about him and Charlie, I could be an anchor for one of those boats in the harbor." He stood up. "I gotta go. I'm behind on my route."

Mike, who hadn't said a word until now, stood up beside Smalls. "You're not going anywhere. The lady asked some questions and I didn't hear you give answers." He put a hand on Smalls' shoulder to indicate he should sit back down.

"If you help me out, Martin Gerber will never know. I'm not investigating you or him or Brogan. I'm working on a missing person case."

Smalls was clearly rattled. His eyes scanned the restaurant. "Who's this missin' person you're lookin' for?"

"You'll know in due time, but right now, it's better you don't. Just give me answers and you can be on your way."

Smalls looked at Mike. "You ain't gonna hold any of this against me, are you?"

"Just answer Ms. Quinby's questions. I'm here as her escort."

"Okay. You want to know about the drugs? Charlie and Martin were dealers. Brogan, me and Eric Towers were runners. Towers got killed in a bust. We were juvies. I will tell you, though, Charlie and Martin had a partner. We were sure of it, but never saw him and those guys didn't mentioned his name in front of us."

"You have absolutely no idea who this mystery man or woman was?"

"Not a clue. I asked once and was told to mind my own business."

"I'll probably want to talk to you again. You're not planning on skipping town are you?"

"No, but next time, if there is one, can we do this after I get out of work? I'll give you my address and cell phone number."

"I have your address, just the number will do." I slid a piece of paper and a pen in front of him. "Don't mention our conversation to anyone. Do you understand?"

"Here's my number and don't worry, I won't tell anyone I talked to you or Detective Mastro." Smalls stood and left fifteen dollars on the table to cover his tab.

"It's on me." I handed him back his money.

"Later," he said as he left the restaurant.

"Why did you do that?"

"Because I could."

Mike shook his head. "I've got an idea. Since it's going on two o'clock, why don't we skip lunch and I'll pick you up for dinner."

"I told you I was going to Boston Blackie's tonight."

"You said you were meeting Big M there, but didn't say what time."

"Darts start at seven, so I want to be there between six and six-thirty. I've got to call Big M with the time."

"What if I pick you up and we do dinner somewhere, then I'll go with you to Southie. I haven't seen the big guy for years. I'd like to say hi."

"You guys are all full of shit. Big M doesn't want me to go there alone and now you want to play bodyguard, too. Don't you think I can fend for myself?"

"A little feisty, aren't we?" He smiled. "Of course you can handle yourself—you're one gutsy broad. If you were a cop you'd understand. We all watch each other's backs. So, do I want to take you to dinner? Yes. But, do I also want to watch your back? Double yes. Unless there's anything else you want to do right now,

130

I'll take you back to your car and pick you up in front of the Harbor Towers at four."

"Where are we going for dinner?"

Mike wrinkled his face, then rubbed his chin. "How 'bout *Mickey 'D's?*"

"Yeah, right." I laughed.

"Legal Seafood sound better? I can't let Sam think I wasn't taking care of you, now can I?"

Chapter 42

I touched Mike's arm. "Thank you. Dinner was excellent. I'll report back to Sam later tonight."

"Glad you enjoyed it."

The hands on the clock were straight up and down—six o'clock. We had plenty of time before the dart players arrived at Boston Blackie's. "I hope I get lucky tonight."

Mike started to laugh.

"You're a dirty old man." I enjoyed my choice of words.

"There's a parking spot just down from the joint." He maneuvered into the tight space.

"Glad you're driving. I couldn't have gotten into there."

"If you lived in the City, you'd learn how."

I knew this would be different from Smalls' interview earlier in the day. Brogan, if he showed, would be surrounded by friends or acquaintances. He'd probably recognize Detective Mastro, but I'm not sure about Big M. I glanced at Mike. "If there's a darker area at the bar, that's where we should sit."

He laughed. "I haven't been here for years, but if I remember correctly, the whole place is dark. They light up the dart area, but other than that, you need a flashlight to get around. If Big M is here, casually walk over towards him. We don't want people to sit up and take notice of a couple newbies."

I nodded. "Especially if they recognize two of the three of us as Boston cops. Do you know what Brogan looks like?"

"Depends on how much he's changed. He was a kid when I had dealings with him."

"Jim Kelly will let us know."

Mike came up behind me when I paused to open the door. "It's show time."

Boston Blackie's wasn't crowded. A thin layer of smoke drifted in from the open back door. As we walked to the end of the bar, I checked out faces.

Jim saw me and motioned us to take two of the six empty stools. We took the second and third ones, leaving the first one for Big M. "I talked to the big guy this morning. He said he'd be here around six-thirty. Brogan isn't here yet, but he usually doesn't drag his sorry ass in until quarter of seven."

Mike reached over the bar to shake hands. "Since she won't introduce me, I'm Mike Mastro."

"Jim Kelly."

"Men—no patience whatsoever. I was just about to do that."

None of us noticed Big M come in until he tapped Mike on the shoulder. "A fine surveillance team you three make." He walked by and sat on the stool I had designated for him. "Mike Mastro, you old dog—long time no see." His voice low enough for only us to hear.

Jim piped in. "If you want to be incognito, which probably won't last long, you're in a bar, so you should have a drink in front of you."

I got my usual White Zin with a side of ice, both guys ordered Sam's Summer Ale on draft.

"I thought that beer didn't come out until summer?"

"Just got it in." Jim walked away to fill our drink order.

There were some guys and a couple girls starting to fill the tables in the dart area. Big M casually glanced at the group. "I don't see Brogan."

Mike didn't turn around, instead he studied the reflections in the mirror.

Jim returned a couple minutes later with our drinks. "Brogan just walked in," he said softly. Then to keep things on the norm, he asked just loud enough for the benefit of the guy three stools away, "You guys want to start a tab?"

133

Mike nodded, then took a drink of his beer as he glanced back into the mirror.

Brogan approached the dart players. After he spoke to one of the guys, he came up to the bar, ordered a draft, and went back to the lit corner of the room. He set his glass down beside a girl who looked barely old enough to be in Blackie's, then took a case from his jacket pocket.

Jim came by and pretended to get something from the cooler across from us. "He's playing tonight, so he'll be around for a while," he whispered.

I turned towards Mike. "Does he look familiar?"

"If I was in here just having a beer, I wouldn't recognize him, but since Big M pointed him out, I can see some of the young Brogan."

"You're out of your area, so he probably won't spot you," said Big M. "If he sees me, he knows I'm a cop. I'm sure he knows I live in the area, so he won't think anything of me being here. You— you're here with one of us and since I'm married, we'll pretend it's Mike."

"I assume this is a beer league. Looks like they have ten players. Must be two teams of five. I used to play a little—to pass the time after I got divorced."

I raised my glass in tribute. "Brilliant deduction. Were you always good at math? Mirror, mirror on the wall, what's the next detective's call?"

Mike hands, all except for his two middle fingers, were wrapped around his glass of beer.

"Birds are flying." I wanted to laugh, but didn't want to draw attention, so I just smiled.

Mike resumed his knowledge of the dart game. "Anyway, what I started to say was—it should take about forty-five minutes for them to play a game. Usually, they play three. So, that's over two hours."

I glanced at the dart corner. "Too long. Do they take a break?"

"Sometimes." Mike caught Jim's attention.

"What's up?"

"Do these guys take a break between games?" Mike asked.

"About ten minutes—if that."

"Thanks. Now we know whatever we have to say has to be done quickly. And, we have no idea how he's going to react. He might just leave."

"If I'm going to find the truth about this little girl, that's a chance I've got to take."

Big M checked his watch and looked at Mike. "Let Casey make the first move. We're not here as cops. This has nothing to do with a case either you or I are working on. If she has a problem, then we can step in. But, once she starts to talk to him and he sees who she's keeping company with, he'll either be cooperative or shut up tighter than a clam."

"Point well taken."

My cell rang. It was Marnie. "Hi." I used my quiet-in-the-bar voice.

"Where are you? I've been waiting for you to call."

"Well, I'm sitting in a bar in South Boston and can't talk right now."

"Should I be concerned?"

"No, I'm in very good company. Can't talk. I'll call you later, if that's okay?"

"I don't care what time—call me." And she was gone.

I looked at Big M. "That was the son's girlfriend. She's like a mother—tries to keep me in line. I emphasize the word *tries*."

Mike looked puzzled.

"My son, Rusty, is dating Casey's best friend, Marnie. That's how I met this girl." Big M patted my back. "My son worked for the Provincetown Police Department and Casey helped them with a case that had background in Boston." Big M smiled. "I was so impressed by her investigative abilities that when my friend, Patrick O'Malley, needed a private investigator, I referred him to Casey."

"She's got two great escorts and is staying in one of Boston's finest condominium residences. I should take my retirement and go into private investigation work?"

"Face it, Mike, once a cop always a cop."

"You're right. When I needed five more years to make a decent pension, I couldn't wait. Now, I'm years past that date and I'm not ready to go. Funny how that works. But, trust me, when I do make the move, I'll be basking in the sun and drinking frozen strawberry daiquiris or pina coladas on a beach in Florida. I've got a lot of friends in Sarasota and Naples. It's like the retirement home for Boston cops."

"Sarasota and Naples sound good, but what's with the sissy drinks?" asked Big M.

"They're refreshing and I don't get drunk so fast. You'll have to come visit me and have one."

"Yeah, right."

Jim acknowledged a short, heavy-set man walk in through the back door. "My night bartender just came in, so I can take a break."

"Just came in? I'd like a job like that," I said.

"Been with me for ten years. He's usually here at four, but he had some family issues so I told him to get here whenever he could. When you have somebody you can trust and doesn't play the piano with the cash register, he's worth his weight in gold."

Big M turned just enough to watch the teams shake hands. "Looks like they're ready to take their first break."

"That's my cue to introduce myself to Mr. William Brogan."

He was on his way to the bar, I assumed to get another beer. It was his third—I'd been counting. I moved in beside him as he slid onto one of the stools.

"Hi."

He gave me a puzzled look, then returned the greeting.

"Aren't you Bill Brogan, the champion dart player?"

His expression didn't change. "I'm Bill Brogan, but I'm barely a Wednesday stand-in here at Blackie's."

136

"That's too bad, I was going to ask for your autograph." I hesitated, then continued. "Bill Brogan, let me introduce myself. My name is Casey Quinby. I'm a private investigator and I've got a few questions I'd like to ask you." I'd already used three minutes of the ten he got for a break between games, so I had to kick this conversation into overdrive.

"I don't know you and I have no idea why you'd want to talk to me, so unless you want to tell me, I suggest you find another place to sit."

I shrugged. "I'll get right to the point. Let me throw out three names for your consideration, Charlie Davis, Martin Gerber and Harry Smalls."

His head snapped around. The eye contact was piercing. I wasn't going to be the first to blink. "Lady, whatever your name is, I've got nothin' to say to you." He glanced around, but stopped when he saw Mike and Big M.

Mike gave him a little Three Stooges wave, then gestured him to walk down to where he was sitting.

Brogan looked at me and shook his head, but followed Mike's directions.

"Bill, long time no see." Mike folded his arms over his chest and nodded. "But that's a good thing—means you're keeping your nose clean. I see you've met my friend, Casey Quinby. I believe she has a few questions she'd like to ask you. And, I also believe you just might have some answers to give her."

"Look, Detective Mastro, I've been minding my own business for a long time. I don't know what this is about, but Charlie's dead and I haven't seen, nor do I want to be in the company of Gerber or Smalls." Brogan glanced towards the dart corner. "The next game's about to start. I gotta go."

I stepped forward, putting him between Mike and me. "You play your game. I'm not going anywhere. During your next break we'll finish our conversation. Fair enough?"

"Yeah, sure." He walked around me, took his beer from the bar and headed back to join his buddies.

Big M ordered a pickled ham hock and another beer.

"What the hell is that?" The smell penetrated my nostrils.

"It's good. Want a bite?"

Mike laughed.

"Absolutely not." I turned my head to keep an eye on Brogan. Since he was closer to the door than we were, I didn't want him to sneak out.

Big M took a bite of his ham hock. "What's your plan for tomorrow?"

"I'm going to try to get ahold of Elaine Gerber. I don't think she and Martin are living together because I have a different address for him. Both are in Dorchester, but in different areas."

"They were separated for a while and I thought they filed for divorce, but I don't know if they went through with it. She's not a bad person. Martin's just plain no good. I was working in the North End when he got nailed for the church robbery. They should have hung him by his balls. Instead, the priest gave him, all of them, a lecture and didn't press charges." Mike shook his head. "He'd walk the back streets in the North End and terrorize the old Italian men sitting in their doorways smoking and drinking espresso. He'd grab their smokes and dump their drinks in their laps." Mike tightened his fists. "He was a real punk, but assholes like Smalls and Brogan idolized him."

"How'd he get away with doing this stuff?"

Mike did his routine 'mirror watch' to make sure our boy was having fun. "People were afraid of Martin. He'd instill the fear of God in them. Some people called him 'little Whitey'."

"You mean Bulger?"

"The one and only."

Chapter 43

Game two ended and, as instructed, Bill Brogan walked over where we were waiting.

I got up from my stool. "Let's sit at a table to talk." I pointed to one near the end of the bar, next to Big M. Brogan didn't say a word, just followed me.

"Here's why I'm here." I pretty much repeated what I said to Smalls. "I've been hired to find a missing person. Your name, along with Gerber and Smalls, was mentioned. I really don't care what you've been up to for the last eight, or whatever, years. I have questions about your past and the past of a couple of your former acquaintances." I emphasized 'former' so he didn't have to remind me again that he didn't hang with them anymore.

"I don't understand."

"Listen carefully and you will. You were a juvenile when you first met Charlie Davis. I know this to be true, so you don't have to agree or disagree. He was the leader and you were a follower."

When Brogan started to say something, I held up my hand.

"Let me finish, then you'll have your turn." I took a sip of wine, then continued. "Was Martin dating Charlie's sister, Elaine, when you first met him?"

"I believe he was."

"What was Elaine like?"

"Nothing like Charlie. She was quiet and stayed in the background. In fact, she didn't talk much at all when us guys were together. Martin wouldn't let her get a word in edgewise."

"Did you ever see Martin hit her?"

Brogan snapped to attention in his chair. "No. Charlie would never let him hurt her."

"So, he protected his sister?"

"Yeah."

"Did Charlie and Martin get along?"

"For the most part."

"So, they did have their moments?"

"There were a few. Smalls and me knew when to stay clear of them."

"Did you know Charlie's stepfather?"

Brogan took a deep breath. "I knew who he was, but I didn't know him personally."

"Are you sure about that? Didn't he help Charlie's little band of thugs stay under the radar? You know, off the books—no filed charges when they kinda *broke the law*."

"I don't know what you're talking about."

"Let me give you a couple examples. First, the church in Revere. I don't think it was the priest that pardoned you. Father Michael was visited by his friend, Robert Cushing. The same Robert Cushing who married Charlie Davis' mother and the same Robert Cushing who was a lieutenant on the Dorchester Police Department. And, I believe it was the same Robert Cushing, who managed to get the drug charges stemming from a bust dropped. A bust where one of your buddies was killed. Did I refresh your memory enough or do you want me to go on?"

Brogan leaned on the table and cradled his face in his hands. "You don't have to go on."

I looked at the dart corner. They were getting ready to start the next game. "You've got one more game. Think about what I've said while you're trying to get a bull's eye. We'll finish our conversation when you're done."

Brogan got up, picked up his beer and slowly walked towards the corner.

I went back to my stool between Mike and Big M and filled them in. "We made progress. I told him we'd finish our conversation when he was done playing."

"I heard the whole thing," said Mike. "You'd make a good detective."

"That was my career of choice, but circumstances changed." I didn't feel like going into my tale of woe, so I changed the subject. "I gave Brogan something to think about. We'll soon find out if he's going to talk."

Big M stood up and walked behind us. "If you guys don't mind, I'm going to head home." "Mike, nice seeing you again. And Casey give me a call in the morning?"

"If I don't get pulled into a Southie alleyway on my way out of here I will."

Chapter 44

"Looks like your team won," I said as Brogan sat down at the table where Mike and I were waiting.

"We did."

Mike looked at Brogan. "I'm getting a beer. Want one?"

"Sure. Thanks."

"Casey, how about you—wine?"

"No, I'm good."

"Bill, I'd like your help. I told you I was looking for a missing person."

"Who?" he asked.

"You'll be on a need to know basis and right now you don't need to know." I gave him a head shake. "Understand?"

He shrugged.

"Were you friends with Charlie up until his death?"

"We all still hung together. That was a long time ago, like twenty-something years."

"Twenty-five to be exact." I watched for any change in his facial expressions. "So if you were friends, you must have visited him, Elaine and baby Carleen at their house down the Cape?"

"Yeah, lots of times. Me and Smalls helped when he was building. Charlie had a contractor, but he still did a lot of the work himself. I don't know why. He had money, so why not just let somebody else do it?"

"What did Charlie do for work?"

"I'm not sure. He said he did consulting work. I know he came to Boston a lot. Sometimes Megan would come, but most of the time she stayed in …" Brogan stopped to think. "I believe it was the town of Sandwich. Their house was way off the road. Nobody around. Too remote for me. I could never live there. I like people. Charlie liked the fact there wasn't anyone around to bother him. He said he didn't like nosey neighbors poking into his business. I didn't know what business he was talking about and he didn't want me to know. That was fine with me."

I looked hard at Brogan, but kept my voice soft. "You told me what you thought, now let me tell you what I think. You had just enough time tonight to put together a story I might buy. But guess what, I'm putting my money somewhere else." I leaned back in my chair and narrowed my eyes. "What you're telling me is Charlie had lots of money and didn't work. If I take those two ingredients and mix them with his history, I come up with a perfect recipe for drug trafficking."

Mike smirked.

Brogan twitched. "I don't know what you're talking about."

"Yes, you do. Let me ask you about the fire. If you close your eyes can you see the flames surrounding the house? Can you hear any screams? Can you imagine a baby's cries?"

Brogan thumped his fist on the table. "If you think I had something to do with that, you're crazy. I heard about it two days after it happened. Charlie might have been a piece of crap, but he was my friend and Megan and the baby were in the wrong place at the wrong time. It was horrible. I wasn't there physically when it happened, but me and Smalls rode down a month later. My imagination drew me a picture. A picture I can't shake off. For years after, I got sick to my stomach every time a damn fire truck rode by." He sighed. "Are we done here?"

Mike, who'd been quiet for almost a half-hour, spoke up. "If you're so adamant that you had nothing to do with Charlie's death, then I'm sure you'd like to help Casey find out who did."

Brogan looked at me. "I thought this was a missing person case?"

I made sure I didn't lose eye contact. "It is, but everything I've talked to you about tonight is a key part of it and you can be a key player."

"I do have a question. If you wanted to talk to me, why didn't you come alone? Why were you flanked by two guys I go way back with?"

Mike swiveled around. "She's a friend, and friends don't let friends drink alone."

Jim came by our table. "Does anybody need another drink?"

"I'm leaving," said Brogan.

"We'll keep in touch," I said and extended my hand to shake his.

He reluctantly acknowledged my gesture.

Jim went back to the other end of the bar.

Mike watched as Brogan turned and walked out the front door. "You might be able to tap Smalls and Brogan for more information, now that you've got them thinking. Gerber isn't going to be so easy. He could still be in the drug business. When Cushing was alive, Charlie and Martin knew they had an ace in the hole. Charlie died or was murdered, then Cushing died. Martin is running solo."

"Or is he?" I asked. "There's another explanation. Lieutenant Cushing was in on the drugs, but he wasn't alone. There are just so many times he could keep his kid and his son-in-law out of trouble."

"The Lieutenant was well liked within the department. From what I understand, he did a lot in the community too. Are you saying he, and one or more others, stepped over the line?"

"Did you ever see Cushing's house or know what he drove? Did he own vacation or income property? Did you know anything about his personal life?"

"I don't. But, he's gone, so that's all moot."

"It may be, but if he wasn't the only one calling the shots, there may be others who know exactly what happened twenty-five years ago in Sandwich."

"You're treading on thin ice. You're an outsider coming into a City with a bunch of old-boy networks."

"The Cape is the same way."

"Maybe the term 'old-boy', but here the word 'network' takes on a whole different meaning."

"I hear you."

"I hope you do." He got up and went to the bar to settle up, then came back and stood beside the table. "You done for the night?"

"I am."

It was a quiet ride back to the Harbor Towers. Mike was like Sam and I didn't want to get into a discussion that had no end. We pulled up just past the front doors.

"It's been nice. You've done a great job so far. I have no doubt you'll find Carleen Davis. If there's anything you need me to check into, you've got my number, give me a call."

"I appreciate all you've done. I'll be back. Next time I'll drag the old guy with me. Instead of *Two Men and a Baby*, it'll be two dicks and a PI.

Chapter 45

I wasn't back in the condo ten minutes, when my cell rang. It was Sam. "Do you have long distance x-ray eyes? I just walked in the door."

"I've been trying to reach you. Did you shut your phone off?"

Oh shit. There were three unanswered calls all from Sam. "I put it on vibrate, but it was in my purse and I didn't hear it. Now that we've cleared up that problem, can you say 'hi, how was your day' in your best smiley voice?"

"Now that I know I don't have to drive to Boston to rescue you, I suppose I can handle that."

"I had an eventful day. Your buddy, Mike Mastro, was with me when I interviewed Harry Smalls. Then, tonight, Mike was on one side and Big M on the other when we sat at the bar in Boston Blackie's. I was Julie Barnes, the girl in the *Mod Squad*. I'm not sure which one of them was Linc—neither one fits his description. Anyway, that's where we caught up with William Brogan."

"Did you accomplish anything?"

"I believe I did. Tomorrow night I'll run everything by you."

"Are you doing more digging tomorrow before you head home?"

"I'll try to talk to Elaine Gerber. She doesn't know it yet, so I'm not sure if I can catch up with her. Her input could be beneficial. I'm going to have two different sets of questions—one if she's alone and one if Martin happens to be there."

"I hope Brogan and Smalls didn't contact Gerber to let him know you're snooping around."

"They didn't. I believe they've changed."

"That remains to be seen. Is Mike going with you to Elaine Gerber's house?"

"No. I'm sure he would, but it isn't necessary. I don't foresee any problems. He told me to call, if I needed him."

"Now that I know you're in for the night, I'm going to walk the boy around the yard, then turn in. Figure out where you want to go for dinner. Miss you Sherlock. Love you."

"See you tomorrow afternoon. Love you, too."

My mind was swirling, bouncing from side to side trying to figure out what to do with the information I'd pulled from Brogan and Smalls. I poured myself a White Zin, dropped in a few cubes, and curled up on my favorite chair overlooking the harbor. It was eleven o'clock. I didn't feel like talking to Marnie tonight. She'll be mad, but she'll get over it.

Chapter 46

Friday

The shower felt like a warm, gentle chute of spring water cascading over my body. I could get used to this. Living in Boston, well, that's another story. Today was more than a jeans kind of day. I slipped on a pair of light gray ankle length pants, a black and gray check sweater, wrapped a silver scarf around my neck, then finished the look with a pair of black Coach Loafers. I pulled my hair back into a ponytail, securing it with a black scrunchie, then checked myself out in the full length wall mirror. My image and I looked very cosmopolitan. One of my journalism professors always said to *'dress for success'*. Today I did.

The condo was readied and my stuff was waiting beside the door when my cell rang. "Hello," I said without looking at the ID.

"What happened to my call last night?"

"It was late and I didn't want to wake you."

In my mind Marnie stood with her hands on her hips and a scowl permanently affixed to her face. "I waited up."

"Sorry. Next time come to Boston with me."

"Just may do that." Marnie's voice remained in scold tone. "What are you doing today?"

"I'm going to attempt to interview Elaine Gerber, Charlie's sister. I have mixed feelings on how to approach her. She and Martin are divorced or at least separated. They're not living together. She's nice and he's an asshole."

"What time are you going there?"

"I'm ready to leave the condo now, so I'll head towards Dorchester, grab a coffee, then see if she's home. After that, I plan on seeing Big M. If it's close to noon, we'll have lunch, talk a little, then I'll head home before the Friday night migration to the Cape starts."

"Call me when you leave her house."

"How about I call you when I leave for home?"

"Fine."

Marnie needed a time-out for an attitude adjustment, but I didn't want to get into a pissing match on the phone. Something was going on, and a conversation with sixty-five miles between us wasn't going to fix it. "Is Maloney coming up this weekend?"

"No, he has to work. He's breaking someone in to take his place."

"Then I've got an idea. Want to go shopping for a few hours, then we'll meet Sam at Seafood Harry's for supper?"

"It's in my calendar as we speak."

"Let me get going. I'll call you after my meetings." I pushed the red end button.

Benny was in the lobby when I stepped off the elevator. "Miss Quinby, are you leaving us?"

"I'm meeting with a few people, then heading back to the Cape. I may be back the beginning of next week." I smiled. "It's great here."

"See you next time around." He lingered in the partially opened garage door, watching me until I got to my car.

Chapter 47

I pulled up the addresses for the Dorchester Dunkin's on my cell. There were four on Dorchester St. in Dorchester. The one closest to Elaine's house was number 2100. I set my GPS and pulled out of the garage.

It took me less than a half hour. The morning coffee bunch had left, so there were plenty of places to park. I ordered my usual number one—French Vanilla and two jellies—and headed for a small two-seater in the corner by the window. It was nine o'clock. I hadn't written down any pre-rehearsed questions for Elaine. I'd wait until I could assess the climate. Besides, I'm more comfortable with extemporaneous probing. It gave me a more credible impression with the person on the answering end of my interview.

Big M's cell rang five times before he picked up. "Casey, you still there?"

"I'm here."

"I was on another call."

"I'm near Elaine's house having coffee at a Dunkin Donuts in Dorchester. I was going to give her a call, but changed my mind. I'm just going to stop over. If she works, she might not be home, but I'll take the chance."

"Did you rule out the possibility that Martin might be there?"

"I didn't, but if he is living there, with any luck, he works and should have already left."

"You're dreaming. I don't think Martin Gerber has ever worked at a legitimate job in his lifetime."

"I didn't say legitimate. I just said work. He could be on the road promoting products from the 'back seat drug store'. I'll take my chances."

"You're the boss."

"I'm glad somebody thinks so."

"Are you coming back to Southie for lunch?"

"If you're going to be around, I'll be there."

"I'll be here all day. Park at the station and we'll take my car. It makes finding a parking spot at a restaurant much easier. I talked to the O'Malleys earlier and they can't meet us today. Pat said to let them know the next time you're going to be around. So, it's just you and me. Call me when you leave Dorchester."

"Will do."

Elaine's house was a small, two-story, single-family on less than a quarter acre of land. It was maintained, but still had the lived-in look. The door to the one-car garage was down, so I couldn't tell if it was occupied. The shades in the front windows on both floors were raised half way—an indication someone was home. I'd stuffed a notepad into my purse, so I didn't look like a reporter or somebody taking a survey when I rang the doorbell.

Here goes.

Her doorbell was a frog. I shook my head, then pressed its backside. I half expected a ribbit, but instead muffled sounds from movies scores announced my presence. There was no response. I tried again. Nothing. Instead of pushing Mr. Frog again, I opened the screen door and knocked. Nothing. The frog was so intriguing, I had to try it one more time. When the theme from the Godfather started to play, I closed the screen door and turned to walk back to my car. Half way there, a female voice called to me.

"Hello, can I help you?" A woman in her mid-fifties stood in the doorway—her hair wrapped in a towel. "The water was running, and I didn't hear the bell."

I walked back to the door. "Are you Elaine Gerber?"

"I am. What can I do for you?"

"My name is Casey Quinby. I'm a private investigator doing research on a missing person case. May I ask you some questions." I handed her one of my cards.

"Please, come in," she said without emotion.

I was hesitant. Did somebody give her a heads up about my impending visit? I'd never let a complete stranger into my house. Was I walking into a trap? I followed her into her living room.

"Seat?" She motioned to a wing-back just inside the door, then sat in the matching one across from me.

I studied Elaine before I began. Fortunately, from where I sat, I could see if anyone tried to sneak into the room unnoticed. It appeared we were alone. Elaine's passiveness bothered me.

"I have a meeting at noon. You said you have questions for me, so why don't you ask and I'll see if I can help." She smiled. "Who are you looking for?"

"It has to do with your brother Charlie."

Now there was emotion. She grew stern. "My brother died in a fire twenty-five years ago."

First question and I was already treading on thin ice. "I know that. I understand his wife and infant child also perished."

Elaine's eyes shifted from a piercing stare to an uncommitted roam of the room—looking for something else to focus on. "It was a tragic accident."

I had to be careful. "That was the ruling from the Fire Marshall's office. I understand it was questioned, but no evidence could be obtained to change it to something other than accidental."

"What do you want from me?" She snapped.

"Your husband, Martin, was Charlie's close friend. Is that correct?"

"My ex-husband," she said with authority. "We've been divorced for eight years. It was never a match made in heaven. I have to use both hands, and then some, to count the times we were separated before we finally got divorced. And, as far as being Charlie's friend, he was. My brother had his problems and Martin was one of them. They fed off each other. Their minds worked in unison."

"I know they were 'bad boys'—did some breaking and entering, had numerous DUI's, were involved in an assault on a police officer, provoked street fights and engaged in various drug related activities." Elaine had no reaction, so I continued. "To use a lame cliché, they did the crime, but not the time. That's what confuses me."

When Elaine checked her watch, I took the opportunity to glance at mine.

"You've made a lot of statements and filled me in on stuff I already knew. You said you had questions. What are they?"

I bit the inside of my lip. It was now or never. "Why weren't criminal charges filed against Charlie and Martin?" Now for the big one. "Did your stepfather, Robert Cushing, take care of them?"

"You better leave." Elaine stood, walked to the front door, opened it and moved to one side. "Now." She pointed towards my car.

I tried to hand Elaine my business card, but she refused, so I left one on the small console table next to the door. "If you'd like to talk, or think of anything else I should know, please give me a call."

Again, she silently raised her hand and pointed emphatically at my car.

Her eyes welled up. I'd hit a nerve or dug up a long-buried memory. She had information, but wasn't about to share it. At least not today. My concern was, her sharing our conversation with anyone, especially Martin. She expressed a hatred for him, but at one time she loved him. After all, she'd been married to him.

She and I weren't through.

Chapter 48

"Good afternoon, Sergeant Maloney speaking."

"Ready for lunch? I'm hungry."

"Hey, Casey. You're a welcoming voice right now. This morning was crazy. Where are you?"

"Still in Dorchester, but heading in your direction. I just left Elaine Gerber's house. I pulled over at the end of her street to call."

"Come to the station and we'll go from here."

"Be there shortly."

"I'll meet you in the back lot in a half hour. Gotta go, another call coming in."

*****

JJ's was crowded. I would have had to wait, but Big M was escorted to a table near the kitchen door.

"It's a perk of the job."

"I know this place. You brought Maloney, I mean Rusty, and me here when we were working the Jane Doe case for P-Town. I had a corn beef sandwich." I looked at a few of the adjacent tables. "Looks like it's on the menu today. That's what I'm having."

"My son always has one when he's in the City. Rusty's a true Irishman. Can't live without his corn beef." Big M ordered our lunch. "Now that that's taken care of, how did your meeting with Elaine Gerber go today?"

"It had its moments, but all in all, it went as well as could be expected. At times it was a little strange."

"How so?"

"When I first got there, she was pretty mellow—almost like anxiety drugs had kicked in. She invited me in without knowing why I was there, except that I was investigating a missing person case. Believe me, I looked around to make sure nobody was hiding behind a curtain or lurking in the shadows." I shrugged. "Nobody, just her and me."

"The makings of a movie." Big M laughed.

"Seriously, would you let a complete stranger into your house without knowing why?"

"I don't let people I *know* into my house without a reason."

"Police mentality—what's her excuse."

"Okay, now you're inside—what next."

"I mentioned her brother's name. It was as though Charlie slapped her upside the head. Her attitude changed. She told me about the fire and emphasized that it was an accident. When I mentioned Megan and Carleen, emotion number three kicked in. She became distant."

"I can relate to her change. You named two innocent people who were reported as victims of the same fire—especially one being a one-month-old baby. That would trouble anyone."

"I understand that, but when I mentioned Martin, number four came out with a vengeance. She didn't disagree with any of the goings and comings of the 'bad' boys. What triggered her demand that I leave was when I asked if her stepfather, Robert Cushing, had anything to do with 'unreported' or 'dismissed charges' against Charlie and friends."

"You do have balls." Big M rolled his eyes. "Big ones at that."

"I've been told that before. Girls have balls, we just wear them on our chest to prevent chafing." I smirked.

"What about Martin? Is he still in the picture?"

"According to Elaine, she has nothing to do with him. She said they've been divorced for eight years. I believe her."

"Do you plan on talking to her again?"

"Hopefully. Before I was escorted to the door and told to leave, I left one of my cards on the table just inside the foyer. After she has time to consider our conversation, I expect I'll get a call. She doesn't know who the missing person is." I leaned on the table and moved closer to Big M. "She didn't ask and I didn't tell."

Chapter 49

Boston proved interesting, but I was glad to be on my way home. My cell rang, but my hands were frozen to the wheel, so whoever it was would have to wait. This Friday afternoon Route 3 traffic was like a reverse evacuation route heading to the Cape rather than leaving.

Only once do I remember an impending hurricane forecasted to be so bad that it was recommended people seek shelter on the mainland. It was in the summer when I was vacationing in West Dennis with my parents. We left, along with five million others—at least it seemed like that many. After we finally got over the bridge, the threat had lessened, so we turned around to finish our two weeks. But, the traffic jam was one I'll never forget. Today brought back that memory.

By the time I got to the Sagamore flyover, traffic was back to normal and the Dunkin's at Exit 1 called my name. Besides, I needed the rest room and wanted to check who called me as I was maneuvering through Quincy.

Before I had a chance to check the message center, my cell rang again. "Casey Quinby, Private Investigator." I put my coffee into the holder in the center console.

"It's only me." Sam's voice was welcoming.

"Did you call me about forty-five minutes ago?"

"I did. Figured you'd be on your way home."

"I was on Route 3 dodging the finger-slinging assholes. It's like a living puzzle. The cars are the pieces trying to move into spaces where they don't fit, but they try anyway. I couldn't do that day in and day out."

Sam laughed. "So, my little country bumpkin sees a nice cold glass of White Zin in her immediate future?"

"You know it," I tittered. "By the way, I talked to Marnie earlier and invited her to go to Seafood Harry's with us. Maloney isn't coming up this weekend, so I knew she'd go. I thought I would be home sooner, so we were going to do a little shopping first, but I'll call her with the change of plans."

"I'm home. I'll see you whenever you get here."

"Later." I hit end, then speed dialed Marnie.

"On your way?"

"I'm at Dunkin's at the Sagamore flyover. Since I'm later than expected, can we reschedule the shopping and meet you at Harry's around five-thirty?"

"I'm still at the office. A few things came up, so that works for me. See you then." Never a good-bye, just a click.

My visit with Elaine Gerber kept replaying in my mind as I drove the sixty-three miles to Hyannisport. I couldn't figure out the reason for her mood swings. There was something I had missed, but without another meeting, I was stymied. Ideally, I'd like to talk to her again before trying to meet with Martin, but doubted if that was going to happen. And, if she talked to Martin before I did, I'd be treading water just to keep the case alive. I had some serious planning to do before I made my next move.

Sam's car was in the driveway, but neither Sam nor Watson were bouncing around the front yard. I pulled up beside his car, gathered my stuff and headed for the door. It was locked. *Strange.* By the time I fished my key out, my boys were scurrying up behind me.

"We took a short walk. Figured you'd rather relax on the deck when you got home."

"You're a good man, Sam Summers." I leaned over and gave him a kiss. Watson looked on. "Oh yeah, you're a good boy, too. I missed you both." I got down on my knees and tussled with him for

158

a bit. "How about a treat for my favorite little guy?" Instantly he let me up. "If nothing else, he knows what treat, walk and beach mean."

We laughed and headed inside.

It didn't take me long to put my stuff down, fill a bowl with peanut butter stuffed pretzels and bring Watson out to the back yard.

Sam followed with our drinks.

"Harbor Towers was wonderful and the view was spectacular, but nothing beats Cape Cod." I lifted my glass to propose a toast.

Here's to it
Those who get to it
And don't do it
May never get to it
To do it again.

We clinked and took a sip.

"I'm glad my girl is home." He smiled. "What time are we meeting Marnie?"

"Five-thirty. She said she was working late, so she'll leave from the office and meet us there."

"We've got plenty of time."

I knew what was coming next.

"So, how was your trip to Boston? Was it productive? Do you have to go back?"

"Too many questions without a break, but to answer you, my trip to Boston was great. I feel it was productive and, yes, I'm going back." I took another sip.

"Are you going to elaborate or are we going to keep playing fifty questions?"

"I kinda like the fifty questions."

Sam sighed, "I figured you would."

"I told you about Brogan and Smalls and you know I paid Elaine a visit. Without getting into details right now, I expect all three again will contact me. I've left the best, and worst, for last—Martin Gerber. I'm trying to decide how to approach him. He's a ruthless piece of shit with the emphasis on ruthless."

Sam's face went into thinking mode. "Sometime back, didn't you mention something about a partner?"

"Smalls said he and Brogan were sure Charlie and Martin weren't acting alone, but had no idea who the other person was."

"Martin might be ruthless, but the unknown character could be dangerous, too." Sam gave me a stern look. "Do you understand what I'm saying?"

"It's the same thing you always say. And, I'll give you the same answer. I can take care of myself. If I need your help, I'll let you know."

"Okay, Sherlock, I'll try to behave." He changed the subject. "Can you believe the weather? Seventy degrees in April. If this keeps up, the bridge traffic will start earlier than usual and Patti Page's Old Cape Cod will again be a thing of the past."

I got up, walked behind Sam, cuddled up close and wrapped my arms around his shoulders, then kissed him on his thin spot. "You need to have the doctor check your head. There's definite damage up there." I smiled. "But, I love you anyway."

He reached around his chair and patted my thighs. "Can we cancel our dinner engagement with Marnie?"

"No. There'll be plenty of time to return my kiss, and then some, when we get home."

Chapter 50

Marnie's car was in Seafood Harry's parking lot. She waved from the window as we walked up the ramp to the door.

"She got here early."

"Hi guys." She slipped her Kindle into her purse. "I finished up at the office and didn't feel like staying there, so I figured I'd catch up on my reading while I waited for you."

"Let me know what you want, and you girls can talk while I place the order."

"I'll have the usual, whole belly clams, fries and coleslaw." I looked at Marnie.

"The same."

"Three Coors lights?"

"If you ever lose your job at the police station, you'd make a decent server," I said.

Sam walked away shaking his head. "See what I put up with?"

"What's this thing about quiet time?" I asked.

"Maloney called me earlier to tell me he'll be done in Provincetown next Friday. He's got two weeks' vacation time on the books. He'll use one of the weeks to move to Yarmouthport. He mentioned something about us taking a few days and going away."

"Your life is about to change, but it sounds like for the better. He's a great guy and he's getting a great girl."

"I'm back, better stop talking. I might hear something I'm not supposed to." Sam set the beers down and handed one to each of us. "I assume from the statement you made just before I went to the counter, it involved Maloney. Must be making the big move."

I wonder if Sam ever thought about relocating to Hyannisport. On one hand, we complemented each other, but on the other hand we had our own distinct idiosyncrasies that would require some work.

"You're thinking too much. I can see smoke coming from the top of your head."

I watched him look from me to Marnie, then back to me.

"You better wipe that shit-kickin' grin off your face and start eating, otherwise you might get into trouble."

"Enough of me. How was Boston?" asked Marnie.

"I'll give you the abbreviated version."

"Why spare the details?"

"Because I'm sitting with my best friend and my boyfriend trying to enjoy a basket of fried clams and an ice cold beer and not think about what I left three hours ago." I took a drink, then doused a clam in tartar sauce and stuffed it into my mouth.

"Okay, I'll settle for the basics."

I could tell by the look on Sam's face, he knew I was going to just skim the highlights. He'd already heard them, so he listened with only one ear. Marnie's ears were like little antennas, zooming in on whatever I had to say.

"I spoke with a couple of Charlie's 'bad boys', then to his sister. They all seem to be running single now, having nothing to do with each other, and that's fine with me. My interest in them dates back thirty plus years when they were tight. On my next trip to Boston, I want to speak with Martin Gerber, the sister's ex-husband. He might not be so accommodating."

"Do you know where to find him?" she asked.

"I checked out an address. It appears to be good. I don't want to knock on his door halfcocked, so this weekend I'll plan my strategy. I'd like to find out where he works, if he works at all. When I was at his ex's house, I left a business card. She demanded I leave, but I hope once she reflects on my visit, she'll call me. She definitely knows more than she let on, which wasn't much."

"What if she contacts this Martin character?"

"I don't think she will."

Sam picked up the empty bottles. "Another Coors?"

Marnie and I nodded.

"When are you going back to Boston?"

"Probably Monday."

"To complicate things, Charlie's stepfather was a lieutenant on the Dorchester PD."

"Can he help you at all?"

"The 'was' means he now patrols the street in heaven, or works the hot corner down under. He's been dead fifteen years."

"So, you're no closer to finding Carleen Davis than you were when her grandpa, Patrick O'Malley, first knocked on your door."

I've got some ideas I'm not ready to share.

"That's about it."

"You know, if we work in the same office, you're going to have to share everything." Marnie grinned.

"I don't know if Cape Cod is ready for the *Cagney and Lacey* tag team. Sherlock 'Quinby' Holmes is bad enough." Sam took a drink of beer and didn't look at the girls for their reaction.

"Sure they are." Marnie straightened her back and gave a proper little shake of the head.

"Maybe Cape Cod is, but are you two ready to deal with the Boston 'bad boys' or the ghost of Lieutenant Cushing?"

Chapter 51

It was only seven-thirty when we pulled into the yard. My mind still fixated on baby Carleen. Sam poured me a glass of White Zin and got himself a bottle of Coors. I needed to put things into perspective. He took Watson outside and I took my wine and his beer from the counter and sat down at the kitchen table. I closed my eyes and leaned my face into the palms of my hands to create a darkroom, hoping to develop the pictures I had stored in my mind. I'd never seen a photograph of Cushing, but a fully uniformed cop appeared, then disappeared just as fast. I was sure he held the key to my investigation. Unless I could figure out who he passed that key to, I was quickly approaching the barrier at the end of a one-way street.

My cell rang, as Sam and Watson walked through the door. I didn't recognize the caller ID. "Hello. There was no reply. The call disconnected.

Sam held his bottle by the neck and pointed the butt toward me. "Who was that?"

"I don't know. Probably a wrong number."

"A hang up. At a time like this, it's suspicious, but maybe just an innocent wrong number.

"Let me see your phone." Sam pulled up the list of recent numbers. "The last person, the one who just called, had a Boston area number. I'm going to call the station and have them find out who it belongs to." He put my phone on the table and used his to make the call. "Hi, Sonny, it's Sam Summers. I have a phone number I want you to run." Not ten seconds later, Sam had an answer. "Thank you."

"Well, who was it?"

"Elaine Gerber."

My stomach turned over. "I knew she'd call, but why'd she hang up?"

"It was Elaine's number. I didn't say it was Elaine that called." His voice reflected the concern that masked his face.

The silence that followed was deafening.

"Bring your beer over here and sit with me. Look, I don't intend to read anything else into this, other than she got cold feet and hung up. She'll call me back when she's ready."

"Write that number down so when she calls back, if she does, you'll see it on the caller ID and know who's supposed to be on the other end."

"I've got a question. We know that drugs were a major bond between Charlie and Martin. And, it's pretty clear Robert Cushing was more than a father and father-in-law to those two. The question is how much more? Do you think the Lieutenant could have been the ring leader or at least a major player?" I took a breath. "What groups were vying for position thirty or thirty-five years ago?"

"Are you talking about the Winter Hill Gang or the Patriarca crime family or the Angiulo Brothers?"

"That's exactly who I'm talking about."

"Now you're talking stupid. Charlie and Martin were two bit thugs, not puppets for organized crime. And, as far as Cushing goes, he doesn't fit the bill either. I'm not saying he's squeaky clean, but I don't think he worked for anyone—maybe with someone, but not for someone."

"That was the reaction I was looking for. There is another person, other than Martin, who's still in the picture. This other person has kept a low profile for years. If I talk to Martin, the shadow is going to find out I'm snooping—probably from Martin himself. I don't even think Elaine knows who our mystery man is."

"That remains to be seen."

"When Elaine calls me back, I'll set up a meeting with her for Monday."

"Don't you mean 'if' Elaine calls you back?"

"I believe that was her that called. Never doubt a woman's intuition. You'll see."

"What do you plan on doing about Martin?"

"Introduce myself, but only after I know more about the man." I didn't want a lecture, so I didn't tell Sam about my plan to follow Gerber—see where he has coffee, watch who he talks to, and try to get close enough to eavesdrop on a conversation. I might even play tourist and, if I catch him keeping company next to a historical site, start taking pictures. "I'll share my findings with you."

"Are you planning on staying in Boston Monday night?"

"Depends on how far I get with my inquiries and the time. I'll pack a bag, just in case. If I do, will you stay here with Watson?" I looked down at my boy lying quietly on his bed, gnawing on a new chew toy. I knew Sam wasn't thrilled.

"You know I will. What about asking Mike to accompany you when you try to talk to Gerber. You might find he'll cooperate more."

"I've got Mike's cell phone number. If I stay over, I'll be home early."

"There's no need for more discussion, let's enjoy the rest of the night. *Blue Bloods* is on at ten. Maybe you can get some pointers."

Chapter 52

Saturday

I woke in Sam's arms. Molded as if we were one. Neither of us wanted to get out of bed. I thought about Marnie and Maloney and wondered if I should broach the subject about Sam and me moving in together. Sam spent most of his time in Hyannisport anyway. It was just the idea, on both our parts, of making a commitment. Rather than jeopardize what we had, I tabled the thought and closed my eyes.

"Mornin' Sherlock," he whispered softly.

I shivered with the series of warm, gentle kisses across the back on my neck.

Watson jumped off the bed and walked toward the kitchen.

"The boy has a sixth sense."

"Either that or he has to go outside." I turned to Sam's waiting lips.

"He'll wait."

A half hour later, Watson jumped back up on the bed. "He's letting us know we've had our fun and it's time to pay attention to him." I tussled with Watson while Sam got up, slipped on his joe boxers and gave the boy the high sign.

I pulled my nightshirt over my head, slid out of bed, slipped on a pair of flip-flops, then went into the kitchen. I needed a cup of coffee to get the cobwebs out of my head before I could function like a human being.

"You're up." Sam took a cup, set it on the tray in the Keurig and pushed the brew button.

"I opened the back door. The sun sent fingers of warmth beckoning us. It's a 'have coffee on the deck' day."

"Works for me. I promised Watson a treat. Go ahead. I'll be out in a minute."

Just as Sam came through the door, a baby frog shot up onto the table, took one look at me and leaped back off onto the deck.

"You didn't even flinch when the little green guy did a record breaking high jump and almost landed in your coffee. Is that the latest thing, frog flavored coffee?"

I still had a smile on my face. I added a raucous laugh.

"What's so humorous?"

"Elaine Gerber had a frog doorbell. The first time I hit it, tunes from Showboat, Hello Dolly and Phantom of the Opera played a few notes on a rotating basis. When she didn't answer the door, I knocked, but I wanted to be serenaded again, so I pushed the frog's button a second time. That's when she answered." I leaned forward and stared at Sam. "It's a sign. The frog reminded me of Elaine. That was her that called last night."

"Where did I ever find you?"

"I don't recall, but you can't give me back." A wink and the distant ring of my cell ended our conversation. I scurried inside to grab the it before the caller hung up. "Hello."

"Is this Casey Quinby?" came the voice from the other end.

I put the caller on speaker and went back outside. "It is."

"This is Elaine Gerber. I tried to reach you last night, but got cut off."

I looked at Sam and shrugged my shoulders.

"Keep her talking," he mouthed.

"You took me by surprise yesterday when you showed up at my house unannounced. The memories you stirred up were ones I've tried for years to forget. Last night, when I snapped on the table lamp by the front door, I found your card. Even after I took a sleeping pill, I didn't sleep much. We need to talk."

"I plan on being in Boston on Monday. Does that work for you?"

"It does. It'll give me time to write stuff down. Like I said, I've been trying to forget things for years, now I have to remember. I don't know if it's better to meet at my house or at the Dunkin Donuts near me." Her voice was strained, probably from lack of sleep.

Sam formed a D with his fingers.

I nodded. "Let's start at Dunkin's. I'll be there at ten."

"Thank you." She hung up.

"This could be the break you're looking for." Sam rubbed his chin, then took a drink of coffee. "Just don't ignore the fact you're walking on eggshells. Keep your back to the wall and the radar on to detect any unwanted company."

"Yes daddy." I got up and gave him a kiss. "Want a fresh cup?"

"Which one—the right or the left?"

"Of coffee, asshole." I shook my head and looked at the sky, then went inside to get fresh cups of joe.

Sam's eyes were shut when I returned.

"For you." I set his down and went back to my seat.

He leaned back. "You know you're dealing with people whose mind gears are missing some teeth and don't function normally. It appears Elaine wants to come clean, but don't get blindsided by her."

"Once a detective, always a detective."

"But, I'm your detective and you're my Sherlock."

I jokingly waved a finger at him. "And it better stay that way."

"Did you tell me you had a friend in the Dorchester PD?"

"Yep, he's the one I called to inquire about Lieutenant Cushing."

"How well do you know this friend?"

"We go way back—to Academy days." He cocked his head to one side. "Why?"

"Do you think he'd be willing to do some probing within the department? I have a feeling that Cushing's partner is still on the job or connected to one or more persons that are."

"That's a tough request. The brotherhood is tight. For a cop to investigate another cop, especially one as decorated as Cushing, can be like signing your whole life away. If your fellow officers find out what you're doing, there's no doubt you'll be ostracized. If you're right, they may come around to trusting you ninety percent, never back to a hundred. And, if you're wrong your life as you knew it won't exist. "

"So it's much like a whistleblower. Even though it's proven that information or activity is deemed illegal, dishonest, not correct or a threat to public interest, the person making the allegations can face stiff reprisal or retaliation."

"Unfortunately, you're right."

"If push comes to shove, I'll see what I can do. You've got a few things in the works, so let's see how those pan out first."

"Fair enough."

"Not to change the subject, but what do you want to do today?"

"I have an idea."

"Should I be afraid of what you're going to say?"

"Not at all. If Marnie is going to be around, I can ask her if Watson can have a sleep-over, then we can go to Boston for the night. I have the use of Shamus' condo for at least three more weeks."

"I believe it was to use if you were in Boston working on the case."

"Technically, yes. We could make that happen—a scouting tour of Dorchester or maybe meet up with Detective Mastro and/or Big M." I smiled. "What do you say?"

"Call Marnie."

Chapter 53

"Hello, Miss Quinby."

"Benny, you're here again?" Don't you ever take a day off?"

"Yeah, but my counterpart who works weekends is on vacation, so he asked me to fill in for him. I don't mind." He rubbed his thumb across his first two fingers to display the universal sign for money.

"Well, glad you're here." I turned towards Sam. "I want you to meet Sam Summers. We'll be staying tonight and leaving sometime tomorrow afternoon. I may be back on Monday, but don't know if I'll be staying over." I grinned. "I can't get too used to this, after all, Mr. Flannigan will be home the end of the month and I'm sure he doesn't want a permanent roommate."

Benny gave me the once over, then laughed. "He might."

"I'll loan her out," said Sam.

"All right, now that you've both arranged for my future, I'd like to get going while I'm still in control—lots to do, you know."

The look on Sam's face was priceless as he walked through the door into Shamus' twelfth floor condo. I walked over and opened the blinds covering the glass wall that over-looked Boston Harbor.

"He's a newspaper reporter?"

"For the Globe."

"Wow. That's all I've got to say. Wow."

"You look around while I put our snacks away and the beer and wine in the fridge." When I came back into the living room, Sam was sitting in *my* chair taking in the view.

"I'm surprised you left this place at all. I've ridden by Harbor Towers many time, but never imagined how beautiful they were inside. If we hit the Power Ball, we can have the best of both worlds—a condo on Boston Harbor and a house at a beach on the Cape."

I folded my arms across my chest. "That's true, but you have to play to win."

"Well, then, we should start today."

"Why don't you give Mike a call? We can meet him somewhere for dinner. That'll give us time to take a ride around Dorchester. I'll show you where Martin's and Elaine's houses are. And, you can show me where the police station is."

"We're not stopping there."

"I know. I'd like to know where it is, just in case."

Sam alternated his lower and upper lip between his teeth and moved his eyes randomly around the room. He wanted to say something, but didn't.

"Here." I handed him my cell with Mike Mastro's number highlighted.

He looked at me, then hit the green button. Sam was ready to leave a message, when Mike answered. "Hi Casey. Did you dump that boyfriend of yours and decide to come live in Boston?"

"You're not my type and I prefer the Cape." Sam laughed. "You should be careful what you say. Sometimes the caller ID lies."

After a couple seconds of silence, Mike answered. "You got that right. Did you kidnap Casey?"

"She abducted me. We're in Boston. I'm taking advantage of her 'condo-on-loan' setup. If it were up to me, I'd just sit here, drink beer, eat pizza and gaze out over the harbor. But, my better half, said to call Mike and find out where you want to meet for dinner?"

"I like her way of thinking. Anywhere is all right with me."

"How about Abe and Louie's? We're going on a 'private investigator's sight-seeing tour' in Dorchester. We should be back here around four."

Mike laughed. "I'll pick you up in front of the Towers at five. I've got preferred parking at the Mandarin across the street from the restaurant."

"Of course you do," said Sam. "We'll be ready." He pushed the end button.

"Let's get going, so we can be back in time."

The first thing Sam and I did was drive by the police station.

"It's easy enough to get to." He slowed as we passed.

"I don't think Elaine lives too far from here. I know I saw a McDonalds with Burger King just across the street and a Marylou's Donut Shop next door. Also, CVS and a Rite-Aid on opposite corners."

"That same set-up is probably in six places around Dorchester."

"Whatever, this looks familiar." I put Elaine's address into the GPS. Immediately the obnoxious GPS lady came on to let us know we were five miles away from our destination. I knew there was nothing remarkable about her house or neighborhood, but because I had a chauffeur, I didn't have to concentrate on the road and could look around.

"No camera?"

"That's all I'd need, someone questioning why I was taking pictures."

"I'll tell you what, there's something in front of the house up the street from Elaine's. It could be a FOR SALE sign." Sam crept up the street and came to a stop in front of a nicely manicured small white house with seafoam green shutters and trim. The front lawn, on the property owner's side of the walk, sported a Century 21 placard. "Now you can pretend you're interested in the house, look around and take your pictures. No one will suspect you're just being nosey."

I snapped a bunch of pictures of the area, then got back in the car. "You're hopeless. I need to know my players and this is one of my ways of doing it. You call it nosey, I call it being observant. Besides, there are always little crimes that hide the big crimes and my type of sleuthing could expose some of those little ones."

"Yeah, I know. Al Capone got caught because of tax evasion. I learned that during my academy days too."

"I'm being paid to find a missing person, not to dig up dirt on Charlie, his band of 'bad boys' or his stepfather. But, if they were involved in Carleen's disappearance, got into the saddle willingly and all enjoyed the ride, then I'll turn over whatever I uncover on them to the proper authorities."

"Fair enough. If you're done here, put Martin's address into the GPS and we'll do the same thing there."

Once we got close to Alimeda Street, I recognized the house I'd identified last week as Martin's. "There it is." I pointed, 4802. As we rode by, the front door opened and a man carrying what appeared to be a fully stuffed briefcase emerged. Since he lived in a three family house, I had no way of knowing if this person was Martin Gerber.

"Keep him in you sight. I'm going to turn around and pull over far enough back so as to remain unnoticed."

I jotted down any physical features I could determine from fifty feet away. Sam was six two, so I judged Martin to be about three or four inches shorter than him. He had a ball cap on, so I couldn't determine if he had hair or not. He was a medium to heavy build— nothing that would make him stand out, other than a slight limp. "He's turned around a couple times. Do you think he realizes someone is watching him?"

"He hasn't changed his pace. He may be waiting for a ride and checking to make sure whoever it is, sees him. We'll give him another twenty feet, then move up a little closer. If we stop too close to his house, he'll see us and, if he's smart enough, he'll know something is wrong." Sam waited a few more seconds, then started to move slowly in Martin's direction.

"Take a look at the briefcase." I didn't take my eyes off it. "It must be on the heavy side. He's changed hands three times and each time it appears he's weighted down on the side holding the case."

"The speed limit on this street is thirty, so if I drive past him slowly, it shouldn't cause him any reason for concern. Did you bring a copy of the Facebook picture of Gerber?"

"It's in my briefcase."

"Without making it obvious, try to get more distinguishing features you can use to id him."

Just as Sam was going to pull out, a black Chevy Camaro pulled by us. "Shit," said Sam. "I don't want to be right behind him. Two cars close, even though we're not together, may cause Gerber to be uneasy, especially if he's carrying something of interest in that briefcase."

"You've got to be kidding me." The Camaro pulled over to the curb beside Martin. He opened the back door and got in.

"Pull down your visor. I'm going to pull up behind them, but only for a minute, then I'm going to turn onto one of the side streets. Take down the plate number and note anything else that might be of significance."

I prepared to write. "The car has a Cape and Island plate and there's an ACK bumper sticker. Nothing else distinguishing, but I might not need anything else. Those two things are like having a magnetic sign attached to the side of your car. Chances are the car's owner lives on the Cape and, to narrow it down further, the ACK suggests Nantucket."

"I'll run that plate later. Do you think you'd be able to identify Martin if you saw him in a picture?"

"I'm not sure. Unlike his house, he appears neat and well put together. Since he's already left, he won't notice if we do another ride by."

"You're assuming that person we observed is Martin Gerber. It's a three family house, it could very well be another resident."

"I don't think so."

"Woman's intuition again?"

"Stop it. I know he had a Red Sox hat on. There was a pair of embroidered red socks on the back—dead giveaway. When I see Elaine, I'll ask her to show me some pictures of her ex."

"More than half the residents in Boston own a Red Sox hat." Sam gave me a quick glance. "I thought you were meeting at Dunkin's?"

"We are, but if things go right, I hope to be invited back to her house."

Sam glanced at the digital on the dash. "We should head back to the Towers. It's two-thirty and Mike's picking us up at five. I'd like to sit for a while and take in the view."

Chapter 54

There was still a half-hour wait at Abe and Louie's. I saw empty tables, but the hostess said they were reserved—a ploy to get people to go to the bar for a before dinner drink. There were two stools, a single man sitting in the third one, then another empty one. I sat down next to the loner. He didn't budge. "Excuse me sir, could you please move down so we could sit together?" Without a word or eye contact, he moved.

"Thank you." Something was familiar about the silent man, even though I couldn't put my finger on it. I tried to study his face in the mirror behind the bar, but he didn't look up. My observations didn't go unnoticed.

Sam nudged my arm. "Knock it off."

"Be careful, your object of observation can do the same thing you're doing," Mike whispered.

Just as our drinks came, the silent man picked up his briefcase, put on his baseball cap, left a couple bucks on the bar for a tip and headed towards the front door.

"That's him," I said without trying to draw any unwanted attention. "It's the same briefcase as I saw earlier, only not as heavy. I didn't see the front of his hat, but the back has the red socks embroidered on it, just like the one the man on Alimeda was wearing. And, this guy also has a slight limp."

"That's who?" Mike asked.

"The man Sam and I did mini-surveillance on earlier."

Sam's head immediately turned in the direction of the door. "Mike, did you see him at all?"

"Not really. He only lifted his head up to take a drink of whatever was in his glass, then went back to studying the bar."

"Casey thinks the silent man was Martin Gerber."

"You've got to be shittin' me?" Mike leaned back in his chair and took a deep breath. "No wonder he was so uncomfortable. He recognized me."

"You haven't seen him for years and according to police files, he's stayed out of trouble. So why would seeing you make him nervous?"

"Maybe because he's a slimy bastard and I know he'll never change." Mike took a mouthful of beer. "I'm surprised he's drinking here. This place is way out of his league, unless he's upped his game."

The guys had be right on. Still, what bothered me was if I could id him, then, if he had to, he could id me. And, if he recognized Mike, he knew I was in the company of a cop he had dealings with years ago. My gut feeling told me I had to step up my investigation. If I moved to far one way, I could jeopardize my life, but if I stepped too far the other way, I could do the same to Carleen. At this point, I didn't want to share my concerns with Sam and Mike.

*****

"Dinner was wonderful. I'm glad you talked me into the prime rib. I love seafood, but living on the Cape, I can get it anytime I want to." I finished my last sip of wine.

"Does anyone want an after dinner drink?" Mike looked around for our server.

"Sure, I'm not driving. I'll have an Opal Nera with some ice on the side," said Sam.

Mike turned to me. "How about you?"

"A glass of White Crème De Menthe over ice sounds good."

Mike ordered for the three of us. "Are you guys going to be around a few days?"

"We're going back tomorrow, but Casey's coming back Monday."

"I'm going to meet with Elaine Gerber again. This time she called me and wants to talk, so I'm meeting her at the Dunkin's near her house. At some point I'll head over to Martin's. He may or may not be home and if he is, he may or may not talk to me. I don't think Elaine told him about me, but won't know that until I see him face to face."

Mike remained cautious. "Do you want me to take you to his house?"

"No, I'll be fine. I'll check the area before I start poking. When Sam and I went by his place today, we saw him get into a black Camaro. I got the plate number. I want to know who owns that car before I decide if I'm going to knock on Martin's door."

"I'll run it when we get back to the condo."

"I can call it in now."

"Later's okay."

Our drinks came. Mike raised his glass up for a toast. "To old friends, to new friends."

Chapter 55

It was eight-thirty when we got back to Harbor Towers. I was exhausted, but not ready for bed. "Are you going to call Bourne tonight to run the plate?"

"I am." Sam pushed number two on his cell. "Officer Whitman, Detective Summers here. Please pass me through to dispatch."

I took a pen and notepad from my briefcase. "If you put it on speaker, I'll write down the information."

"Officer Travers here."

"Danny, it's Sam Summers. Why are you working tonight?"

"The officer on duty went home sick. I was next on the list, so here I am. What do you need?"

Sam took a slip of paper from his pocket. "I want you to run a Cape and Island plate for me." Sam gave him the number.

"Hold on."

It was quiet, except for the clicking of a keyboard.

"It belongs to Blake Myers. Mr. Myers lives at 116 Madison Avenue, Nantucket." Officer Travers hesitated. "The name sounds familiar, but I can't wrap my brain around why."

"If you figure it out and think I should know, call my cell. Run him through our data base and, while you're at it, check the state police files, too."

"You got it. I'm working Monday, so if I don't talk to you later, I'll see you then."

"Thanks, buddy."

"This is why we should've brought the laptop." I was chomping at the bit. I wanted to google map the address where this guy lived.

Sam went into the kitchen and came back a couple minutes later with a glass of wine for me and a bottle of Coors for him. "There's nothing more we can do tonight. Let's take advantage of the condo and just relax."

I checked the listings for HBO and CINEMAX. "The movies suck. How about we watch *48 Hours*?"

"How about we make our own movie?" Sam took the glass from my hand and put our drinks down on the coffee table.

Chapter 56

Sunday

The friendly rays of sun peeking through the shutters rallied my senses. I got up and moved towards the sound of running water. The master bath was an extension of the bedroom. There wasn't a door that separated the two rooms, just an oversized archway, so there was always an image created, be it someone sitting on the throne or, in this case, my man lathering up his perfectly proportioned body while humming a tune from *Rocky*. His back was to me, so he didn't realize I was standing in the doorway. I smiled, went out to the living room, opened the curtains and curled up in my harbor-watching chair. Ten minutes later, a shirtless, shoeless Sam joined me.

"Morning Sherlock."

I bent my head back enough to offer choices as to where to plant a kiss.

"We forgot to play the *Power Ball* last night."

"They pull it again on Wednesday."

"I should have taken a few days off, then we wouldn't have to go back to the Cape today and I could help you with your case."

"First of all, the only reason I'm in a condo at Harbor Towers is because of my case. There's no doubt it's beautiful, but I'm here for work, not a vacation. And ..."

"If you need my help, you'll ask." Sam threw his arms up and rolled his eyes. "I've heard it before—many times."

I gave him my best 'you're finally learning' look, even though he'd never commit it to memory.

Sam knew when to change the subject. "You should give Marnie a call. Besides, I'm sure Watson could use a dose his mommy's melancholy voice."

"I've got an idea."

"Here we go again."

"Shut up and listen. We can grab a coffee and hang around Boston for a while, but leave early enough to get to Marnie's around three. Since the weather is nice, we can take her to Chapin's for late lunch, early supper. Watson will be okay at her house for a few more hours."

"Good idea."

Marnie answered on the second ring. "Hi, guys. How's Boston?"

"This little dream bubble is going to burst one of these days, but for now, it's beautiful." A yacht was making its way through the harbor. "Is Watson being a good boy for Auntie Marnie?"

"He might want to stay. We've been having fun. Does he have a brother or sister?"

"We'll have to check that out. Then we'd really be related."

"You're weird."

"We're trying to get motivated. This place makes me think I need to clean it before the maid gets here. There's a coffee somewhere close calling my name. I'm going to call Big M and catch him up on my plans, then we'll decide if there's any other places Sam needs to introduce me to. We should be at your house by three. How does that sound?"

"I'll be ready."

Sam made an eating motion.

"Oh yeah, would you like to go to Chapin's?"

"You have to ask?" There was a smile in her voice. "See you then." The call went dead.

"That girl never says good-bye, sometimes 'later', but never good-bye."

Sam checked the condo before we left. "You'll be back tomorrow in case I missed anything."

It was Sunday. I looked around, but didn't see Benny anywhere in the lobby. We left the car in the garage and walked over to Hanover Street to grab coffee and a pastry at Mike's. Being so close, it wouldn't be fair to deprive Sam of the best Italian pastry in the North End.

What a good excuse.

Mike's was crowded with people picking up pastries to go, so there were a couple tables available. We chose one toward the front of the store away from the bakery cases. A little Italian lady, probably in her sixties, asked us, in broken English, what we wanted. Sam got regular coffee and an elephant ear and I got cappuccino and two white cherry macaroons.

"I'm puzzled. Somebody associated with everyone I've talked to, short of Gerber, knows exactly what's going on. Why don't they just come forward and tell the O'Malleys where their granddaughter is? This game of hide and seek sucks."

"Did you ever consider that Carleen could be involved?"

"That would be cruel." I spooned the foamed milk from the top of my cappuccino.

"Maybe she just found out and doesn't know how to deal with it."

"I don't accept that theory."

"Just throwing things out for you to ponder." Sam checked his watch.

"Find something else, 'cause that one doesn't work. Why don't I call Big M and tell him we're heading to the Cape, but I'll be back in Boston tomorrow."

"Keep in mind, you never called him yesterday to tell him you were here."

"You're right. Forget that call." I shrugged. "Let's start back. You can stop in that little corner 'everything' store we passed and get a couple power ball tickets. Maybe the luck of the Italians will rub off."

"Isn't that the luck of the Irish?"

"I don't care who does the rubbing, the Irish or Italians."

184

Chapter 57

Watson and Marnie were sitting on the front steps when we pulled into her driveway. The boy was so happy we were home, he literally pulled Marnie to her feet. "Hey, boy, slow down before you choke yourself."

Sam ran over and took the leash. "Did you have fun at Auntie Marnie's house?"

Marnie reached in her pocket, took out a handful of treats and handed them to Sam. "I didn't spoil him—much."

"Likely story," I said.

"So did you accomplish anything on your little mini-vacation?"

"Well, let's see, we ate at lot, drank a lot, talked a lot, screwed a lot, but didn't really get much resolved regarding the case. I'm going back up tomorrow to talk to Elaine and try to meet with Martin. She knows I'm coming. He doesn't."

"Wish I could come with you, especially if you're staying overnight, but it seems like Maloney's dates have changed. The person taking his place won't be able to work with him this week. Instead of taking his two weeks starting next Saturday, he has to take this week off, then work a week, then take off the following week. After that he's done in P-town. I have to go into work Monday and Tuesday, then I'm gone for the rest of the week and we're heading for New York. My father has already made dinner reservations for Wednesday night at Rao's."

"I've heard you say that name before. What's so special about Rao's?" I asked.

"It's a really good, high-class Italian restaurant with lots of authentic ambiance. The Rao's family has owned it for over a hundred years. I've know them since I was a kid—nice people. Their food is outstanding. You can only get a seat there if you're a regular and have 'table rights' or if you're an invited guest by someone who does."

"Your father has 'table rights'?"

"Yep."

"Can I be an invited guest someday?"

"Me too?" asked Sam.

"That can be arranged. In the meantime, I'm starved." Marnie cupped her hand around the back of her ear. "I hear a lobster pot pie calling my name."

Sam sat down beside Watson and bribed him with another treat. "You be a good boy. We won't be gone long, then we'll head to the homestead. If you're lucky, maybe, we can find some doggie ice cream in the back of the freezer."

Chapter 58

Monday

I'd packed my Vera Bradley duffel last night, so I didn't have to think about anything this morning other than my drive to Boston. The sun wasn't smiling, and the fully packed clouds spread a mist that helped bring the temperature back to its seasonal sixty degrees. Boston was usually warmer, but I stuffed an extra sweater and a pair of jeans in with the rest of my clothes just in case.

Sam had a meeting with the chief, so he left early. I turned on the television to catch the weather report. The Cape and Islands showed a thirty percent chance of rain around noon with a high of sixty-six degrees. Boston only had a ten percent chance of rain and the temperature was almost ten degrees higher. I was fine with what I'd packed.

Watson paced in front of the door to let me know I had to tend to him before I left. We took a mini-walk up the street, then headed back home. "You're keeper of the castle today." I reached down to mess his hair. "I won't be home tonight, but Daddy will be. You be good. I'll see you tomorrow." I gave him a hug and just before I left, I put a few treats beside his food dish.

It was eight-thirty when I started out. I figured if the drive-thru at the Dunkin's Sagamore flyover didn't have a long line, I'd swing in and get a French Vanilla. By the time I get to Quincy, the inbound traffic should have slowed.

I was surprised, the traffic wasn't bad. People still have to go to work. If I worked in Boston, days like this I'd leave early. Maybe they did. The way the assholes drive on Route 3, they don't care if it's raining, snowing or dry as a bone. I don't know which causes more accidents—weather or cell phones.

Fortunately, the obnoxious GPS lady was awake and brought me directly to the Dunkin's where I was meeting Elaine. There were five cars in the lot, but I didn't know what she drove. I slipped my notepad into my purse while hoping our shared coffee time would lead to an invitation back to her home. She had been in a helpful mood when we spoke on the phone, but sometimes things change.

Elaine was sitting at a table against the far wall. She waved. "Good morning. How was the traffic coming up Route 3?"

"Actually, it wasn't bad. Could I do it every day—absolutely not."

"I've grown up with it. There are days you want to pull your hair out, but after thirty-seven years, I'm used to it."

"I'm going to get a coffee. Are you ready for another one? How about having a donut so I don't feel so guilty eating alone?"

"I'm good on the coffee, but I'll have a chocolate glazed."

"Be right back." I was fourth in line.

We got into our donuts before our conversation. For Elaine, it was like a security blanket; after a few bites it appeared she was more comfortable.

"Our unexpected meeting last week opened up a Pandora's box. All the bad things in my life, no matter how insignificant they seemed, flew out to haunt me. I was afraid if I didn't get the lid back on, and quickly, I would suffer the consequences—even though I had no idea what they would be." She went silent. I watched her eyes study the top of her coffee cup. "Am I making any sense or do I sound like a crazy who lives alone and makes up stories so I don't have to face reality."

"I understand. There are things in my past I don't ever want to talk about, but there are times when I have to." I reached over and laid my hand over hers. "Whatever you tell me today will stay with me, unless you want it to go further. Years ago, I had a friend who was a great listener. Maybe I can be your listener."

She looked up and smiled. "Want another coffee?"

I nodded. "Dunkin's French Vanilla is my drug of choice."

"I don't do the flavors, but the regular Mr. Dunkin is my best friend. They know me here, so refills are always on the house."

"We're going to get along just fine." I watched her walk to the counter.

She put the fresh cups on the table and sat down. "Let's start our conversation here, then go over to my house. I have some pictures and newspaper clippings I'd like to show you."

"That'll work for me." I took my notepad from my purse. "I'm going to take some notes to be sure I get it right."

"If you're anything like me, I have to write things down or a half-hour later I've totally forgot what I was thinking."

"In my past life I was a newspaper reporter, so old habits never die. I could wallpaper a room with notes I've written, be it in regards to a story I was working on or my weekly grocery list."

"Let's get started." Elaine leaned forward and rested her arms on the table. "By the way, you haven't told me who you're looking for."

"You have to trust me. When the time is right, you'll know."

Elaine reluctantly agreed.

"The best thing to do is start at the beginning and not jump around. That way I should be able to piece things together and create a more effective timeline to follow. If my questions get too painful, or I hit on something you need to think about before answering, please let me know."

"Casey, I called you. You wouldn't have shown up on my doorstep if you didn't need my help. I'm here to help, so let's get on with our conversation."

Her reference to showing up on her doorstep brought back the image of Raggedy Ann in the Macy's bag that was left on the O'Malley's stoop. I couldn't write my thought down in front of her, so I filed it in my head for future consideration. "Ready?"

"As ready as I'm going to be."

"This is going way back, so bear with me on dates and times. Feel free to insert them if you think they're necessary. First we'll talk about when you and Charlie were growing up."

"Did you know there were five of us kids—two girls and three boys."

"I read it in Charlie's obituary. It also listed a father and stepfather."

"My parents were divorced when we were young. My sister was the youngest—she was only seven when that happened. When she was old enough, she moved away and I haven't seen her since. I have no idea where she is. My oldest brother was killed in an automobile accident when he was sixteen and my youngest brother died of an overdose of drugs. You know what happened to Charlie. So, not including my sister, I'm the only one left. As far as my parents, my father was a drunk—a mean one at that. My mother had enough, so she divorced him. That wasn't a fun time. He finally drank himself to death. Frankly, not many people cared. She met Robert Cushing—a policeman on the Dorchester PD. I surmised they knew each other long before my mother filed for divorce, but I never asked. When he came into the picture, our lives changed."

"How so?"

"We didn't get beatings, we had food on the table, my sister and I had new clothes and my mother was happy. We were young and impressionable. It took the boys longer to accept Robert—that's what we called him—Robert. After a time, Charlie became very close to our stepfather. Sometimes the rest of us were a little jealous, because Robert would take Charlie with him to meet his friends or to go fishing or even to the Wonderland dog track in Revere. It was always Charlie."

"I understand Robert was a lieutenant in Dorchester?"

"A well liked one, too. He worked his way up through the ranks. He had help along the way, but a lot of cops do."

"Did he come from a police family?"

"Robert's grandfather was a patrolman in Revere. But, I never knew him. In fact, I didn't know much about his family."

190

I wonder if Detective Mastro heard of him?

"Did Charlie finish high school?"

"We all did, except Matt, my brother who was in the car accident and my brother, Timmy, who liked the white powder. School was a biggie in our house, although none of us went on to college. I waitressed for a while, went to work at Macy's on Washington Street and finally ended up as a secretary at a now defunct company in the North End."

Macy's, another coincidence?

I noticed a black car pull out of the street next to Dunkin's and slowly drive by. I wasn't sure if it was a Camaro. It looked like the car Sam and I saw Martin Gerber get into on Saturday, but without seeing the license plate, I couldn't be sure.

Elaine gave me a puzzled look. "You okay?"

"Just thinking. The brain told me I was trying to push too much in and to take a break." I grinned.

"Why don't we continue this back at my house? That way I can show you pictures that correspond to the timeframes we're talking about."

"I'll follow you."

We cleared the table and headed to the parking lot. I did a quick look around to make sure there wasn't a vehicle waiting in the blind spots of the building. There wasn't. Still, I wasn't about to let my guard down. I checked my watch. It was ten-forty-five.

Elaine pulled into her driveway and I followed.

"I'll put the car in the garage after you leave."

We went through the back door into the kitchen. It was retro style with white major appliances and turquoise counter ones. The valance on the window over the sink was a turquoise, white and black plaid to match the curtains on the window beside the table. I smiled when I saw the cat clock with its tail wagging back and forth marking cadence to the passing seconds. A braided rug on the floor and placemats and plastic flowers on the table completed the décor.

A room from 'Happy Days' or 'Leave it to Beaver'.

"You like the cat?" Elaine asked.

191

"I do. I haven't seen one of those for years. It brought back memories. My great aunt had one."

"A lot of things in my house were my mother's and her mother's before that. I do like antiques or at least the antique look. You likely got that impression the last time you were here. Have a seat, the albums and boxes of 'memoirs' are in the other room. I'll be right back."

It was almost eleven when we started looking at pictures. None of them meant anything to me and some meant more to Elaine than others. I surreptitiously watched her reaction to certain ones. Her stepfather was not only a tall man, he was big. She had lots of pictures of him—some in uniform and others in casual home attire. I didn't see any of her real father and didn't see a need to ask.

"I miss Charlie. I'm sure you know he was married to Megan O'Malley and less than a month before the fire they had a little girl, Carleen." Tears formed in Elaine's eyes as she reminisced over a picture of her brother and his family.

"Can I see that one?"

She handed it to me. "It was taken right after Carleen was born."

"Do you know anything about the fire?"

"Just that it started in the wood burning stove in the family room. My brother had two ATVs, a riding lawn mower, a regular lawn mower, a snow mobile and God only knows what else used the gasoline housed in his garage. I never saw the house, but they said the family room shared one of the garage walls and Carleen's room shared another one. The baby didn't stand a chance, nor did my brother and sister-in-law."

"I have a real tough question to ask you. Do you think the fire could have been anything other than an accident?"

Elaine rubbed her face, leaned on the table and folded her hands as if to pray, then whispered, "I've always thought there could have been a possibility it was set, but I didn't want to believe it, so I never said anything. I hinted about my suspicions to my ex, but he never took the bait. And there was no way I was going to ask him outright."

"Speaking of Martin, what was his association with Charlie?"

"They were inseparable. They were trouble. They were nasty. Some people feared them. I could go on and on, but you get the picture. I never knew why Megan hooked up with my brother. Megan and I weren't close, but she was a good girl. She came from a nice Southie family. I'd met them a couple times. They didn't like Charlie and I can't say I blame them. The more they downed Charlie, the more she distanced herself from them. Then came Carleen. The O'Malleys, Megan's parents, were in seventh heaven. That baby girl seemed to bring them back together." Elaine took a deep breath. "I'm going to have a glass of water. Want one?"

"Sounds good."

Nothing was said as Elaine filled two glasses with ice and some bottled water, then set them on the table.

"Thanks."

"Martin Gerber. He was a couple years younger than Charlie and a year older than me. He was handsome." She flipped a couple pages in the album and showed me a picture of herself and Martin standing in front of the European Restaurant. She smiled and touched his face in the picture. "You probably don't remember the European. It was on Hanover Street. They had the best pizza around. I don't know why they closed, but it was a shame."

I didn't want to rush Elaine. I didn't need a story to go with every picture. But, if she thought I wasn't interested in what she was saying, she might just stop talking and that would defeat my whole purpose of being here. "Tell me more about Martin."

"Charlie was very protective of me. At first, he didn't want to have any part of Martin and me dating. He finally gave in. They were both very protective, almost too much. I don't really know what happened, but Martin started to get edgy—you know, jumpy. It made me nervous. I'd ask questions. Sometimes he'd answer, sometimes he wouldn't. Once I asked something about drugs. That was the first time he hit me. I cried for days. He didn't care. Told

193

me to mind my own business. When I said I was going to talk to my stepfather, he became furious and suggested I drop the subject because Robert wasn't going to do anything about it."

"Did you ever wonder what he meant?"

"I didn't have to wonder. My brother and my husband and possibly my stepfather—the well-respected lieutenant, had dirty hands. After that encounter, any relationship I had with Martin was over. He had a girlfriend—or should I say several. I just went to work and stayed away from him as much as I could. Finally, I couldn't stand it any longer and filed for a divorce. He didn't contest it, but his parting words were 'I'll give you this, but I'll give you this if you open your mouth.'"

I knew what she meant, but I wanted her to say it. "Explain."

"With the first 'I'll give', he held a pen in his hand—meaning he'd sign the papers. The second 'I'll give' was represented by a clenched fist. The worst part was how hard he laughed when he finished. I was petrified. He knew he had me."

"What about Robert?"

"He's dead now. There were years when I expected him to rise from the grave to haunt me. I never said anything about my suspicions, but I didn't have to. He knew I surmised stuff involving him, my brother and my ex was going on, when in reality, I didn't have any proof at all as to what was happening. He didn't know that and I kept it that way."

Elaine's phone rang. She checked the caller i.d. then put it back on the counter. "It said caller unknown. I don't answer them."

"I wish I could do that, but my other half is a cop and he's always unknown. If I didn't answer he'd send the militia out to find me." I smiled. The cat clock purred at twelve o'clock. "How are you holding up?"

"I'm all right. It's hard though. Maybe we can finish up another day if that's okay with you?"

"Not a problem."

"One thing I'm pretty sure of, there was, and maybe still is, a band of people making beaucoup bucks selling, dealing, whatever you call it, drugs. I suspect that Robert was the ring leader, but he had a partner. I'm not even sure if anyone but Robert knew who that person was. That partner must have taken over after Robert died. I wish I could give you a name." Elaine shrugged and threw her hands up. "Another thing, after Carleen was born, my brother wanted to go straight. That little girl changed him. The problem was, he knew a lot about what was going on and who was involved. If Charlie and Megan's house was arson, you'll discover your arsonist, actually your murderer, if you find out who took over the 'business' after Robert."

"Do you think Martin knows"?

"He might, or at least know who does."

"Thanks for your help. Let me get this in the works and I'll get back to you within the next few days."

"Now that we've talked, let me ask you a question. Who's the missing person you're looking for?"

I hesitated. "You've been up front with me. If I tell you, you'll have to promise me you won't share the information with anyone. And, if you think of something I should know, you'll call me immediately—day or night."

"Our conversations are between us and only us. You'll have to trust me."

"I do. I'm looking for Carleen O'Malley."

Chapter 59

My next stop was Martin Gerber's. It was confrontation time. I contemplated calling Sam or Big M to let somebody know where I was headed, but banished the thought as I pulled onto Martin's street. Since it was a three family house, I parked in front to avoid blocking the driveway. I loved my little lime-green Mazda, but it certainly did announce I was there.

I sat for a minute to compose my thoughts. It was twelve-twenty. The pad of paper I'd used at Elaine's was under my purse on the passenger side. I tore off my pages of notes, leaving a fresh sheet to record what I hoped to get from Martin. Before I got out of the car, I perused the area in front of me and around the house, then checked in my rearview mirror to make sure no one was following me.

Here goes.

I pushed the buzzer next to Martin's name. It was loud. I could hear it from the street. There was no doubt. The person inside the apartment heard it too. Nothing. I waited thirty seconds. I pushed again.

"Yeah, yeah, I heard you. Whatever you're sellin', I don't want none."

"I'm not selling anything, Mr. Gerber."

"Then why you botherin' me?"

"My name is Casey Quinby. I'm a private investigator and I have a few questions for you."

"Who you investigatin'?"

"You don't want this over an intercom. Let me in. I'll explain."

I waited, but nothing. Two minutes. Then three. After four, I started to walk toward my car. The door to the three-decker opened.

An older version of the man in Elaine's photo album glared at me. "Where you goin'"?

I turned around and moved back to the bottom of the steps. Closer. He crossed his arms, revealing sweat moons on his wife-beater tee shirt. I stopped at the bottom of the stairs. He widened his stance, staring down at me. His shiny blue gym shorts tried to decide whether to continue clinging to his gut or become warmers for his bare feet. A Yellow Cab entered my peripheral. It stopped four houses down to my left.

"Here I am, so talk." His width blocked my view of his front door.

"Like I said, I'm a private investigator. I'm working a missing person case. I have questions. You have my answers."

"I don't know no missin' nobody'." He reached behind himself and opened the door, stepping back inside.

I moved to the top step. Without consciously deciding, I made my foot a doorstop. "I think you do." I gripped the edge of his door, as if I could stop him from shutting it. "Let me in. You don't want me saying this stuff outside."

"I'll give you fifteen minutes. I'm a busy man." He held his gaze on his watch.

He wanted me to notice he was wearing a Rolex.

Dressed like a street person, wearing a Rolex. And, he wanted me to know it. Why?

We walked up two floors. He pulled a key from his pocket. I crossed my fingers he didn't have to dig too deep. With the slightest bit of assistance, those gym shorts would fall off.

The furniture in his apartment didn't match his person. Actually, his end and coffee tables were the same ones I had. Except for a few magazines scattered around the room, a jacket thrown over the end of the couch and a couple closed Chinese food containers that I hoped were empty, the room wasn't in bad shape—and didn't smell. There was no indication he had a roommate.

Sam's imaginary presence sat on my shoulder whispering in my ear not to let my guard down.

He pointed to a chair on the opposite side of the room and motioned for me to sit down. Fortunately, it faced the door leading out. He sat in the chair next to me, separated only by a lamp table. "Your fifteen minutes begins right now." Martin sat back and crossed his legs, not concerned that one of the side of his gym shorts had slid up to his crotch.

"I understand you were a friend of Charlie Davis'."

Martin's body didn't move, just his head. His eyes pierced mine. "Charlie's dead."

"I know that. He died, along with his wife, twenty-five years ago when his house in Sandwich burned to the ground."

"Three people died—Charlie, Megan and their baby daughter, Carleen." Martin spoke with no emotion. "Where is this goin'?"

"Maybe nowhere—maybe somewhere."

"Listen, Kelly, or whatever your name is. You got somethin' to ask me, you better do it. I'm not playin' a game."

"The name's Casey and believe me, this isn't a game." I took a deep breath. "You want me to get to the point, then I will. Who burned the Davis' house down? And, why?"

Martin turned away. A troublesome look replaced the surly, rigid expression. I'd hit a nerve.

His character suddenly changed. He slid forward in his chair, positioned his elbows on his knees and rested his chin in his hands. "He was my best friend. We been through a lot together."

"Was that 'a lot' what got him killed?" I moved slightly closer.

"I don't know." His voice was soft, almost inaudible.

"I think you do and I need your help. I told you I was working a missing person case, but I didn't tell you who that person was."

"So, tell me."

"Carleen Davis."

Martin jumped up and turned to face me square on. Now he was talking, not only with words, but with his hands. "The baby died in the fire."

198

I held my position. Our faces closer than before. "No, she didn't. She's alive and I intend to find her with or without your help."

"Get the hell out of here and mind your own business before you get yourself or someone else hurt."

"Just hear me out. You and Charlie were involved in drugs. I believe you were dealing and you got caught, but you never did time. Either evidence was tainted or eliminated, or paperwork just happen to disappear. Robert Cushing—or should I say, Lieutenant Robert Cushing—name sound familiar?" I stopped for a minute to let everything I said sink in, then continued. "You don't have to answer, because I already know. He was Charlie's step-father and the leader, or one of the leaders, of a very successful drug ring."

Martin's face tightened.

"Whether you want me to continue or not, I am. Who was his partner? And, who is the guy who drives the black Chevy Camaro with the Cape and Islands license plate?"

Martin didn't say anything, just walked to the front window and scanned the outside in front of his house.

"Looking for someone?"

"No. Your fifteen minutes is long gone. I don't know nothin' about none of that. You made lots of accusations. I don't like it. So, I'm gonna politely ask you to leave."

I hesitated, then stood up. "I'm sorry about your memory lapse. If you feel the need to talk to me, all my contact information is on my card." I set it on the lamp table, then held out my hand.

He didn't return the courtesy, just opened the door and pointed to the stairs.

"By the way, nice Rolex," I said trying to irritate him a little more. It worked. As soon as I cleared the door, he slammed it as hard as he could without loosening the hinges.

As I got into my car, I glanced up at the living room window in Gerber's second floor apartment. He was watching. I wanted to wave, but thought I'd irritated him enough, besides he had

199

information I wanted, so it wasn't in my best interest to push the envelope.

No sooner had I pulled away from the Alimeda Street address, I caught sight of a black Camaro parked a couple spaces in on one of the side streets. I checked the time. It was twelve-forty-five. An uneasy feeling came over me. I took my cell phone from my purse and punched in Big M's number, then put the phone on speaker and set it on the passenger seat.

"Lieutenant Maloney, how may I help you."

"Big M, it's Casey. Can I swing by your office?"

"Of course. I didn't know you were in town."

"I decided to come back up for a day or two. I was going to give you a call later tonight, but I need to talk to you now." I glanced in my rearview mirror. The black Camaro was about fifty feet behind me. "Actually, I might already have a problem. I'm being followed."

"Where are you?"

"I just turned off Alimeda Street onto Lincoln in Dorchester. I already plugged in your address. My GPS is sending me to Morrissey Boulevard."

"I'm going to keep you on the phone. What's the next street you're coming too. The GPS lady said in two miles make a turn onto Gallivan Avenue."

"Do you still have your tail?"

"Yep. They're keeping a safe distance and trying to stay obscure by using a few cars for camouflage."

"Morrissey is a direct route to Southie. I'm going to have an unmarked stationed somewhere along your route. Fortunately, lime-green sports cars with a CQ007 plate stand out. He'll follow you into the station. Pull into the back lot, but stay in your car and I'll come out to get you."

"Are you going to stay on the line, at least until you know your guy has spotted me?"

"Just to err on the side of caution, I am."

"Thanks."

"Question—were you at Elaine Gerber's house today?"

"I met her at the Dunkin's on Dorchester Street, then we went to her house to talk. Why?"

"A report just came over the air that a female identified as Elaine Gerber was being transported from 2601 Beckman Boulevard to Boston Medical Center."

I checked in my rearview mirror. The traffic had gotten heavier, so I had to pay more attention to where I was going instead of where I'd been. "I don't see the Camaro," I said to Big M. "Did the report say what happened to her?"

"No, but I'll check on it as soon as my guy has you covered."

"Wait, the Camaro, it's still behind me. There's two cars between us."

"Hold on." Big M called his undercover for his location, then came back to me. "What's the next cross street showing on the GPS?"

"Dominic J. Bianculli Boulevard."

"My guy is almost right next door to that. He's in the Boston College High School parking lot. Don't look for him. He'll see you and your buddy. Let me know when you see the school."

"I just passed BC High."

"You're golden. I'm going to hang up. See you in a few."

My breathing slowed to as close to normal as it could get. I was worried about Elaine. I turned on my right blinker and pulled down the driveway to the back lot of the South Boston Police Station. I was two car lengths off the street when I saw the Camaro drive by. Big M was standing beside the back door waiting for me.

"You okay?"

"I am now."

"We need to talk. We pass by the breakroom on the way to my office, want a coffee or a soda?"

"I could use a glass of wine, but a coffee will do."

We fixed our coffees, then headed down the hall to his office. "Have a seat." He closed the door behind me.

"Did you find out anything about Elaine?"

201

"She's not in good shape. They don't know if she's going to make it."

"What happened?"

"She was beaten, stabbed and left to die. If one of her neighbors hadn't seen a car speed away from her house, then gone to check on her, she'd probably be dead."

"Do they have any leads?"

"Only that it was a black car."

"No make or model?" I shrugged.

"Nope. You were at her house earlier. Was she alone?"

"She lives alone and there wasn't anyone else there when I was. I asked her questions about her brother and her ex-husband. She pretty much confirmed that her step-father, Robert Cushing, was a crooked cop. She showed me lots of family pictures. We talked about Charlie and his family, then about Martin. Elaine was attacked because she talked to me."

"Did you tell her what you were working on?"

I nodded. "A missing person case."

"Casey, you know exactly what I'm talking about. Did you mention Carleen Davis?"

"I did."

Big M crossed his arms over his chest, then leaned back in his chair and studied the ceiling. "Somebody got wind of your conversation. Do you think she called anyone—maybe Martin?"

"She hates Martin. I don't believe she'd call him."

"Here's the problem. Presumably you were the last person who saw Elaine Gerber alive and well. I know she's not dead, but she's in a coma, so at this point, she can't communicate with anyone. The Dorchester Police will want to talk to you. My friend, Dan Wilson, is the lead detective in that department. I'm sure he's at the scene right now. I'm going over there with you."

"I thought you didn't want to or couldn't get involved in the case."

"This started out as a missing person investigation. Now it's an about-to-be reopened closed case and a new attempted murder investigation with possibly more repercussions to follow. And, you're no closer to finding Carleen for the O'Malleys."

I held my hands up in front of me. "Are you saying I've opened up a can of worms that caused the attempted murder of Elaine Gerber?"

"Not at all. I'm saying your investigation has caused things that were suppressed for many years to surface. Things could get nasty fast, especially if it involves a bad cop—a high ranking one at that. It doesn't matter that he died fifteen years ago." Big M took a drink of his coffee. "Finish yours. I'm going to call Dan and tell him we're on our way to Beckman Boulevard."

All I could think of was Elaine lying in a hospital bed. I waited for Big M to get off the phone and we were in the car on our way to Dorchester before I asked more about her. "Are they going to have a cop stationed outside her door?"

"I would imagine they are. Why?"

"You know I was also at Martin's today. I went there right after I left Elaine's. There's no way he was the one who tried to kill her. First of all, he doesn't have a valid driver's license, so I don't think he has a car and second of all, I was at his house at twelve-twenty, twenty minutes after I left Beckman Boulevard and didn't leave until twelve-forty-five. My concern is the person in the black Chevy Camaro. Today wasn't the first time I saw him."

"When did you see him before?"

"Sam and I came up Saturday and stayed overnight at the Towers. We did some riding. When we went by Martin's house, we saw him get into the backseat of the Camaro. He was carrying a briefcase."

"Who was in the front seat?"

I shrugged, my hands getting into the gesture.

"Do you think they, whoever they are, saw you then?"

"No, I don't. Sam was doing his thing. If it was me, then that's a different story. There is one thing though, Sam ran the plate. It's registered to Blake Myers. He has a Nantucket address."

"Do you have that information with you?"

"It's in my briefcase. When we stop I'll get it. Somebody should go by Martin's house."

"I'm sure they've got that covered. They're well aware of the relationship between the Gerbers. The PD probably has a file full of domestics they've answered at both addresses over the years. Besides, Martin, himself, isn't a stranger to the department. When we talk to Dan, you can tell him about your visit with Elaine's ex earlier today."

Marked and unmarked Dorchester police department vehicles filled the driveway and lined the street in front of Elaine Gerber's house. The front door was open and a handful of uniforms and suits were standing on the walkway at the bottom of the stairs. We parked in front of the house next door. I walked beside Big M as he held out his badge to the three officers assigned to keeping onlookers from getting anywhere close to the scene.

One of the suits broke away from the group and headed in our direction. "Tom, nice to see you, although I wish it was under different circumstances."

Big M reached out to shake hands. "Detective Dan Wilson, I'd like you to meet Casey Quinby."

"My pleasure." He extended a welcoming hand shake. "I understand you were probably the last person to see Elaine Gerber alive."

"Alive?"

"Yes, we just got word she died."

My head dropped to my chest. I was unable to speak. My eyes puddled up and as hard as it was going to be, I had to keep my composure.

Big M put his arm around me and guided me away from the others. He didn't say a word until we were out of earshot. "I'm sorry."

I appreciated the fact he didn't get fatherly. This wasn't the time to second guess my change in careers. It was my time to prove myself. I cleared my throat, "I'm ready to talk to Detective Wilson."

"You sure?"

"I'm upset, but I'm angry. Whoever did this needs to be found, and soon. I want to help put the puzzle pieces in the right spots, and that's what I intend to do."

"Your call." Big M looked back at the house. "Detective Wilson's still outside."

I wiped my cheeks. "Let's do it."

Chapter 60

Police were combing the inside of the house for anything that could provide a clue. There had definitely been a struggle. The kitchen chairs we sat in only hours before were overturned and pools of blood had been marked with yellow plastic tents. There was splatter on the pantry door as well as on the cabinets next to the sink. One thing that struck me as odd, the photo albums Elaine had shown me were still on the kitchen table right where we left them. Apparently, whoever did this wasn't concerned with their contents or had seen them before. I found that interesting enough to mention it to Detective Wilson.

We caught up with him in the living room, but before I had a chance to mention the photos, he started talking. "According to the neighbor, Elaine didn't have many visitors. The neighbor knew Martin and said she hadn't seen him in years. She told us a girl in a lime-green sports car was here twice—once last Friday and again earlier today." He crossed his arms over his chest and gave me the raised eyebrow look. "I'm assuming that was you."

"It was. Our talk last Friday didn't end well. She escorted me to the door and, without speaking, pointed to my car to indicate I should leave. I did, but on my way out the door I left one of my business cards on her hall table. Apparently after my visit, she needed to talk because she called me Saturday morning. That's when we made arrangements to meet this morning at the Dunkin Donut's near here."

"Why didn't you go to her house?"

"Since our visit on Friday was somewhat hostile, I wanted to meet on neutral ground. I suggested Dunkin's. We were there for forty-five minutes. Things went well, so she invited me back to her house to continue our conversation and take a look at pictures she thought I might find interesting. The photo albums are in the same spots on the table, still opened to the last pictures we looked at."

"Before we go any further, I know you were talking to Elaine. And, you were looking at picture albums, I'm assuming, of her family. My question is why?"

"I'm working a missing person case and she was a possible player or had some knowledge about it that could help me."

"All this you're telling me, I need to get it down on paper." Detective Wilson glanced around the room, his eyes stopping on a uniformed, female officer armed with a clipboard. "Be right back." Two seconds later, he returned. "Casey Quinby, I want you to meet Officer Carla Regan. She'll be working with you to get your story on record."

Officer Regan shifted the clip board to her left hand and reached out with her right to shake mine. "After I finish here, I'll meet you at the station." She looked at her watch. "It's one-fifteen. Why don't we plan on meeting at two-thirty? Do you need directions?"

Before I could speak, Big M stepped forward. "I'm Sergeant Maloney, Southie division. I'll see that she gets there."

Officer Regan nodded. "See you at two-thirty." She rejoined her fellow officers.

Detective Wilson stepped forward. "Is there anything else I should know before you leave?"

"Yes. There was a black Chevy Camaro. It pulled up in front of Martin Gerber's house on Saturday. The person inside never got out, so I can't confirm it was a male or female. Gerber got in the back seat and it drove off. He had a briefcase with him."

"I'm going to be at the station when you talk to Officer Regan. I know there's more to your story."

"Dan, do you mind if I sit in?" asked Big M. "In fact, I'd like her to talk to you before she officially talks to Officer Regan. There's background here you should know about."

"There are a few more things I need to do here. If something new comes up after I leave, they know how to get me. I'll meet you at the station." He walked back to converse with the investigation team.

"Unless you see anything else that looks out of place from when you were here this morning, we should get going. Let's grab some lunch at Mickey D's. It could be a long afternoon."

I wanted to call Sam, but knew I couldn't tell him what was happening—not until I knew myself. Elaine was dead and the Dorchester PD thought that, other than the killer, I was the last person to see her alive. There was a sick feeling in the pit of my stomach and a McDonald's hamburger and fries wasn't going to help. But Big M wanted to stop, so we did.

"When we meet with Dan, you have to tell him how you got involved in this case. He needs to know your missing person investigation spilled into, and is now part of, a murder investigation. Elaine or Martin Gerber, although related to the missing Davis baby, were not the subjects of your probe. Your questions may have prompted other people to react, but you had no idea it would end with a murder. The worst part is you're no closer to getting answers for the O'Malleys than you were when you started."

"I don't know what to say except that I feel I've made progress. You might not think so, but look at it this way. Whatever happened twenty-five years ago was kept a secret. Over those years no feathers were ruffled—no questions were asked. Not until now. Not until I came along. Somebody thinks I know more than I do and that's a good thing. They're not going to hurt me until they find out what it is they think I know, how much of that information I've shared, and with whom."

"That puts you in harm's way."

"It's too late to change it. Whether I'm here in Boston or at my house in Hyannisport, whoever's back I put against the wall is going to find me. That leaves only one option. I have to find him or her first." I wrapped up my half eaten burger and most of my fries in the bag they came in and threw it in the trash. I kept the drink.

"You ready?" asked Big M.

"Before we go, I want to run something by you. It's possible Robert Cushing had a partner. Elaine thought so too. She told me whoever the person was might be still running the operation, so I got to thinking. Cushing's been dead for fifteen years. If, in fact, he and a partner were involved in a successful drug trafficking operation and Martin and Charlie were his main men, when two of them died, the partner and Martin kept it going. Since Martin doesn't appear to have a regular job, but sports a Rolex, he's making money somewhere. We know Cushing covered for Charlie and Martin when it came to the law. Cushing's gone, so somebody else is doing the covering."

"Are you saying you think there's at least one, if not more, cops involved?"

"I am."

"That's a dangerous path to take."

"I know, but right now it's the only one. Think about it. Elaine was murdered and not by Martin. Who would want her dead?"

"Somebody who thought she knew too much." Big M leaned forward and stared at the table.

"Exactly," I said. "How well do you know Detective Wilson?"

"He's one of my best friends. We went through the academy together. We've helped each other out with cases. His family, like mine, has been involved in police work for generations. He's not your missing partner."

"We need somebody we can trust. Do you think he'd listen to my theory?" I waited for an answer.

"Since you have to tell him your whole story, you need to include your theory. I don't know how he'll take it. It's best if I'm with you. I'll call my desk sergeant and let him know where I am and my radio's on if he needs me."

"You realize, of course, I'm scared shitless right now." I took a deep breath. "But I'm okay. I want whoever killed that baby twenty-five years ago, and earlier today, killed a good woman who lived scared too long."

Chapter 61

Ten minutes after we left Micky D's, we were sitting in the lobby of the Dorchester Police Department waiting for Detective Wilson.

"In case I forget later, thanks so much for all your doing. You're a real sweetheart."

"Are you staying at Harbor Towers tonight?"

"I originally planned on staying until Wednesday. Now, depending on what happens here, it may be extended. I wanted to meet with the O'Malleys and fill them in on my progress to date, which isn't much. Tonight's television news and tomorrow morning's newspapers aren't going to help me explain things to them. With any luck my name won't show up in print, but don't bet on it." I looked away.

"From one reporter about another."

"You talkin' to me?" I forced a grin. "In fact, I'm surprised there aren't a few news trucks outside the station now."

"Believe me, once they clear the scene, they'll be here. That's why we parked out back in the cruiser only section."

"Thanks, I appreciate that."

I was at the lobby showcase reading commendations that had been awarded to the Dorchester PD, when Detective Wilson came into the room. Big M stood up and I walked over to join him. We followed the detective through the inner sanctum to his office. Without saying anything, he motioned us to the two empty chairs in front of his desk. He closed the door before he took his seat across from us.

Detective Wilson didn't waste any time. "We sent a car to Martin Gerber's house. The lady on the first floor told my officers that Martin left almost an hour before in a fancy black car."

I leaned my left elbow on the desk and cradled my face in my hand. "That would be the Camaro."

Big M crossed his arms, then nodded. "That's why I wanted Casey to meet with you before she meets with Officer Regan."

I reached down into my briefcase and pulled out the information Sam had gotten on the Camaro. "Here's the name and address to go with the license plate attached to that car." I handed it to Detective Wilson.

"Where did you get this?"

"From the DMV."

"You know what I mean. Who gave you the information?"

"One of my sources."

"Dan, could we talk about that later?" asked Big M. "Right now, she has more to tell you about how she got involved."

"I'm a private investigator with an office in Barnstable Village across from the Courthouse." I looked at Big M.

He nodded for me to continue.

"I was hired to work a missing person case that makes the town of Sandwich and the City of Boston kissing cousins."

Detective Wilson studied my face before speaking. "If you give me the name belonging to the missing person, will I be surprised or will it be familiar?"

"You probably won't recognize her name, but you definitely know her family." I pulled in my top lip and held it between my teeth trying to buy some time before I spoke again. "The name is Carleen Davis. She, along with her parents, Charlie and Megan Davis, died twenty-five years ago in a fire at their house on 18 Buzzy Lane in Sandwich. Something has surfaced indicating that the child, one month old at the time of the fire, was alive. Obviously, that would make her twenty-five now." I waited for the detective to absorb what I had said. "You knew the family."

Wilson held up his hand to stop me from going any further. "That's Lieutenant Cushing's stepson, daughter-in-law and granddaughter you're talking about. The lieutenant was my boss. I was in the office the day the state police came in to tell him what happened. When they left, he closed the blinds in his office and locked his door. He didn't want to talk to anyone." The detective sighed. "He didn't come out for hours."

"Dan, I'm sure you knew his stepson, Charlie Davis? He and Martin Gerber ran together."

I could tell by the look on Big M's face, he wasn't quite sure how to continue.

"You're telling me, the baby didn't die." Detective Wilson repeated what I had already told him.

"It appears she's still alive."

"Who hired you?"

"Megan Davises' parents, Patrick and Mary O'Malley."

He looked at Big M. "Don't they live in Southie?"

Big M nodded. "They do."

Detective Wilson hesitated, then turned towards me. "How come they contacted you, instead of somebody in this area?"

"Because I gave them Casey's name." Big M bobbed slightly in affirmation.

The detective's attention went from me to Big M and back to me. He took a deep breath. "So that's why you met with Elaine and Martin. Now Elaine is dead and Martin is who-knows-where? What time are you supposed to meet with Officer Regan?"

"Two-thirty."

Detective Wilson glanced at his watch. "If Officer Regan is back, I'll have her conduct the interview in my office. There's no need to go over the background story twice. She's only been on the job a few years, but she's sharp—that's why I want her to talk to you. Tom, I'd like you to stay. You might have to fill in some backstory."

Chapter 62

Big M and I stood up when Detective Wilson came back into the office accompanied by Officer Regan.

"Have a seat. Casey, you met Officer Regan at the crime scene. She's going to ask you questions regarding your relationship with the deceased. I don't have to remind you that we believe you were the last person to see her alive, so your answers will be extremely important in the development of a timeline the department will need to investigate her death."

"I understand."

"Officer Regan, before you begin, Casey has information that may help the investigation establish a motive. There's backstory. You're conducting this interview in my office because what you're about to hear is sensitive information and is to remain within these walls. Once it's determined what's pertinent to the case, I'll hold a briefing. After Casey is finished, she'll answer your questions related to the murder." Detective Wilson leaned forward on his desk. "Since you've only been on the job a few years, there's one thing you need to know before we start. Elaine Gerber was Lieutenant Robert Cushing's stepdaughter. You may or may not know the Lieutenant died fifteen years ago. But, anyone working in this department is familiar with his legacy. So, I'll re-emphasize my earlier directive that nothing leaves this room without my permission."

"I know of Lieutenant Cushing's reputation."

He must have put on a good front.

Detective Wilson gave me the high sign. "Why don't you get started?"

"I'm a private investigator. My office is on Cape Cod, in Barnstable Village. My clients hired me to find their missing granddaughter. Twenty-five years ago, it was presumed she died in the same fire that took her parents lives. A couple weeks ago, some evidence surfaced that may prove otherwise. Her parents were Charlie and Megan Davis. Elaine Gerber was Charlie's sister. That's why I'm in Boston asking questions."

Big M sat quiet. His head didn't move, but his eyes shifted between Officer Regan and me.

"During the course of my research, I've uncovered some things I find unsettling. Things that lead me to believe the fire in Sandwich wasn't an accident started by an overheated wood-burning stove, as was reported. The O'Malleys tried to get the Sandwich Police Department to do further investigation, but without any evidence to change the finding, they deemed the case closed. The new evidence that surfaced two weeks ago is a strong indication their granddaughter is alive. And, from my conversation with Elaine Gerber, I agree with them."

Big M spoke up. His face showed no emotion. "The O'Malley family and mine were, and still are, very close. Twenty-five years ago Patrick was sure foul play was involved in his daughter's and granddaughter's deaths. He literally hated his son-in-law because of the life Charlie subjected his daughter to. A brief history for Officer Regan—Charlie Davis was known to the PD, and not as an upstanding citizen. He ran under the radar and the rare times he got caught, the charges disappeared."

Detective Wilson spoke without looking away from the table. "Are you saying a member of this department was involved in making things vanish?"

"I'm afraid that's exactly what I'm saying, Dan." Big M looked from the detective to Officer Regan, then at me. "Casey's missing person case may furnish information that proves the Sandwich fire was arson. And, that the fire was set to possibly cover up the murders of Charlie and Megan Davis."

"The whole thing hinges on finding baby Carleen. Whoever took her was involved in starting or helping cover up what actually happened at 18 Buzzy Lane. She's the biggest missing piece of the puzzle. In my opinion, find her and we'll find the murderer or murderers." I took a deep breath and sat back in my chair.

"You're traveling a dangerous route here. You spoke to Elaine Gerber and now she's dead—murdered. You spoke to Martin Gerber and now he's missing. What's to say someone might come looking for you?" The detective leaned forward and folded his hands. "Are you traveling back and forth from the Cape or are you staying in Boston?"

Big M answered. "She's staying at a friend of mine's condo in Harbor Towers. He's away on business, so he loaned it to me. She should be safe there."

"She'll be fine at the Towers. My concern is when she's not at the Towers. Cape Cod is nothing like Boston." Detective Wilson made a few notes, then turned to Officer Regan. "When Casey's in Boston, other than at the Towers, I want you to be with her. So as not to draw attention, wear street clothes and take an unmarked."

"I don't think that'll be necessary," I said. I knew from the look on Big M's face, he wanted to kick me under the table. I ignored him and kept talking. "I'm staying until Wednesday, then heading back to Barnstable."

"Here's what's going to happen," said Detective Wilson. "Officer Regan is going to be your best friend as long as you're running solo in the City. She'll check in with me during the day. This will begin immediately. Understood?"

"Yes sir." I knew better than to push the issue.

"Now that we've settled that, I believe you have information on a vehicle that was seen several times on your visits to Elaine's and Martin's houses. You said it was a black Chevy Camaro. Elaine's neighbor said a black car sped away from her house. Then, when we went to talk to Martin and he wasn't there, the lady downstairs said he left in a fancy black car. I don't think there were three cars. You've already given me the plate information from the DMV. Have you tried to reach this person?"

"No."

"Don't. We'll check it out and I'll keep you informed."

"I'd appreciate that. He could be a link to my missing person."

"Is there anything else I should know?"

"Yes, I should fill you in on who I've already talked to and what I've already done. I feel partially responsible for Elaine's death. Maybe my interviews will help find her killer. I'll get them together tonight and see that you have copies tomorrow morning."

"Regan will pick you up in the morning and bring you to the station. You can make the copies here."

I didn't want a nursemaid. I was used to flying solo—except for Sam or Marnie. When it came to actual investigative work though, I did better without a tag-a-long. I did some of my best creative thinking in my office on wheels. *Guess I'll have to make the adjustment.*

"Regan, I want to talk to Sergeant Maloney. Why don't you and Casey get some coffee and make arrangements for tomorrow. "He motioned us towards the door. "See you in fifteen."

Chapter 63

Fortunately, there wasn't anyone in the breakroom. We got our coffee, then sat at the table furthest from the door.

"I notice you're married. Do you have children?"

"Just changed my name four months ago, so not yet." She smiled. "We do want a family, but in time. My mom was never married. She was engaged, but her fiancé died in a car accident. As I understand it, I showed up a month later. Strange how things happen. My husband, Andrew, and I live with my mother." Officer Regan wrapped her hands around her cup and stared away from the table. "She's sick, so we try to help as much as we can."

"I'm sorry."

"I shouldn't burden you with my problems. Today was a bad day, not only here at work, but at home." She took a deep breath. "My mother has cancer and was given bad news when she went for her appointment this morning."

I didn't know what to say, but knew she needed someone to talk to, so I let her continue.

"Detective Wilson knows the situation. That's why he assigned me to you rather than have me work the streets on patrol. It's just for a few weeks."

"And, he thinks I'm safer to be around?" I let my mouth form a half smile.

"I guess so."

"I appreciate the company and an extra set of eyes. Tomorrow morning I'll fill you in on what I assume Sergeant Maloney is telling your detective, then I'll show you my reports to see if something pops out at you."

"What time do you want me to be at the Towers?"

"If you're there at seven, we'll grab a coffee at Dunkin's before we head into the station."

"I'll be there." She looked at her watch. "Since we've got five minutes, why don't you tell me about yourself."

"I grew up in Shrewsbury. Do you know where that is?"

"Next to Worcester. We've got a couple guys in the department from that neck of the woods."

"Anyway, I have a Master's Degree in Criminal Justice from U Mass and an Associates in Journalism from Cape Cod Community College. What you're doing now is what I dreamed of doing. While I was in the academy, I fell during a training exercise and broke my leg—bad. Because of the injury, I couldn't finish. Instead, I became the head investigative reporter for the Cape Cod Tribune and worked on cold cases for various Cape police departments."

"I'm confused. I thought you were a private investigator."

"I am now. About a year ago, I made the decision to leave a job that provided stability and a more than adequate salary, to hang my shingle. That's when Casey Quinby, private investigator emerged. And, here I am, working anything but a boring missing person case."

Regan raised her eyebrows. "You've got that right."

We walked back to Detective Wilson's office. Whatever they had talked about was finished.

Big M watched as I walked in the door. "We're done here for now."

"For now is the operative word." Detective Wilson sat on the corner of his desk. "Regan, what time are you picking Casey up tomorrow?"

"Seven."

"Print those reports when you get to the station and if I'm not in my office, leave a copy on my desk."

"Detective, I've got some things to do tomorrow regarding my case."

He stood up and folded his arms across his chest. "If they intertwine with the Elaine Gerber murder, I want to know about them. Not now, but I want a report."

"With all due respect, sir, I'll let Regan do the departmental reports and I'll write my own." I tried to ignore Big M's 'shut up' glance. "As per my license, I have a confidentiality and responsibility agreement with my clients. However, I promise you I won't do anything to jeopardize your case."

"You are absolutely right about that."

I thought it better not to keep the conversation going. I knew I wasn't going to win—at least not on his turf. I turned towards Regan. "I'll see you tomorrow at seven."

"I'll be there—out front."

Big M took over the conversation. "Dan, I'll talk to you tomorrow."

Detective Wilson extended his hand first to me, then to Big M. "Be careful."

Chapter 64

Once inside his cruiser, Big M leaned back hard against the seat. "You've got yourself in much deeper than you should be. I feel responsible for that."

"You didn't know. Hell, neither did the O'Malleys. They're excited at the possibility their granddaughter might be alive. I believe my whole case is wrapped around who started the Sandwich fire. Elaine's murder proves that. My concern now is for Martin. We both know his life is in danger. The person behind the wheel of the Chevy knows something. Now my hands are tied. Detective Wilson's going to investigate. I need him to share whatever he finds."

"I don't think you'll have a problem with that as long as you assure him you won't go out on your own into a dangerous situation."

"I can't. I have a babysitter." I smiled.

"What are you doing for dinner?"

"Thought I might walk down to the North End."

"No, that's not going to work. Why don't we stop by the station, get your suitcase from your car, call Detective Mastro and see if he wants to meet us somewhere?"

"I know what you're doing. You want to fill him in on what happened today and tell him about the short leash your Dorchester detective friend thinks he has me on."

"Yep. That's exactly what I want to do. And what we're going to do." When Mike answered, Big M didn't mince words, just suggested we meet at Legal Seafood-Long Wharf on State Street. The conversation was short and sweet, ending with a nod.

"I assume we're having seafood tonight."

"We are," he said. "It's not far from the Towers."

"Close enough to visit Mike's Pastry for an after dinner cappuccino and a cannoli?"

Big M shook his head. "You're something else. A key player in a murder investigation, being followed by some unknown person and a familiar face at the Dorchester PD—the last two being the most concerning and you want to go for pastries."

"You're just like Sam. You both worry too much. I don't feel threatened."

"As long as you're in my neck of the woods, I'm going make sure you're not." He changed the subject. "Mike said he'd be at Legals in a half hour. We'll swing by Southie and get your suitcase, then head over to the restaurant and get a table."

"We're getting my suitcase before dinner, right?"

"Yep."

"Then why don't I follow you in my car to the Towers and park it in the garage?"

"Nope. Since you aren't going to need it tomorrow, we'll leave it in the lot. Besides, Detective Wilson has you riding with Officer Regan for the next few days."

"Hear me out. I'll leave it there tonight, but I'm picking it up sometime tomorrow afternoon. I'll park it at the Towers, but I want it near in case I have to make a quick get-away from you and Mike."

"Not funny."

"Not meant to be." I walked to the passenger side of Big M's unmarked and waited for him to unlock the door. "Tonight I'm going to put everything that's swimming around in my head down on paper. There are too many tentacles shooting out from the nucleus. Some are leading nowhere and have to be sealed off."

"Sounds like you're mixing a scene from *Twenty Thousand Leagues Under the Sea* with one from *Aliens*."

221

Chapter 65

Mike had put his name in with the hostess and was waiting for us at the bar. He raised his glass to get our attention. "Sam better be careful. The girl is starting to like Boston." He signaled the bartender. "Please give my friends a drink."

"I'll have a White Zin with a side of ice."

"It's been one of those days. I'll have a scotch on the rocks." Big M smiled.

"When did you get into town?" asked Mike.

"This morning, although it feels like I've been here for days."

"You're learning. Things around here don't move as fast as on the Island." Mike took a sip of his drink. "I'm sure I've got lots of table conversation coming my way. I heard about the murder of Elaine Gerber. You wouldn't be involved in that would you?"

"Involved? I wasn't there when she was murdered. Just because I was one of the last people to see her alive doesn't mean I was involved."

"Whoa. Don't be so touchy."

Big M raised his eyebrows, but didn't say a word.

The hostess tapped Mike on the shoulder. "Your table is ready."

We were led to a table away from the front of the restaurant. "Thank you."

We sat so that none of us had our back to the general population. It's a police thing I'd learned from Sam a long time ago.

"Perfect table to unwind at," said Big M. "To say we've had an eventful day is an understatement."

I raised my glass. "Thanks guys for being here for me."

"I'll agree to whatever you're saying, but I have no idea what's going on. Does anyone want to fill me in?" Mike took another drink.

I saw the waiter heading in our direction. "Let's order dinner first."

"One order of calamari, three plates and some extra marinara sauce please. We'll order our meals when you bring that out."

I looked at Mike. "You're a seasoned patron."

"It's the bachelor in me. If I'm not eating take out Chinese or pizza, I'm usually here or in the North End, but most of the time here, at the bar, eating calamari and a baked stuffed lobster sitting beside a stranger who has no idea what I do for a living. It keeps the conversation normal—if you know what I mean."

Big M sighed. "I certainly do."

"Now that we've got the first wave of food ordered, let's get down to the events of the day."

I could tell Mike was chomping at the bit to get briefed on what was going on, so I started by telling him my original reason for my trip to Boston. About half way through my story, our appetizer came.

Big M ordered another round of drinks, changing his to a glass of merlot.

"Have they found Martin yet?" Mike asked in between bites.

"The last we heard they haven't. Do you know Detective Wilson from the Dorchester PD?" I asked.

"I've heard of him, but have never met the man."

"We go way back. He's heading the investigation. I'm sure as soon as he hears something, he'll give me a call." Big M looked at me. "He's assigned an officer to be with Casey during the day. Wilson doesn't want her wandering around on her own. He feels she knows too much and is in danger. Frankly, I agree with him."

I leaned forward on the table. "I understand his concern. I have to admit that I share some of it. You know I believe my missing person case revolves around a murder that happened twenty-five years ago. Well, apparently so does someone else. The who is the key to both my case and the closed case that was originally deemed an accident. If only Raggedy Ann could talk, we wouldn't be sitting here eating calamari and waiting to order lobsters." I smiled. "Isn't that what we're ordering?"

Chapter 66

Big M pulled up in front of the Harbor Towers.

I patted my stomach. "Thanks for the cappuccino and cannoli. The perfect ending to a perfect meal."

Benny was standing in front of the gold framed glass doors leading to the Towers' lobby.

"Looks like I couldn't sneak away even if I wanted to." An unrehearsed yawn took over my mouth. "Don't worry. I'm not going anywhere. First thing I'm going to do is call Sam, then do paperwork."

Benny saw it was me getting out of the car. He scurried over, took my suitcase from the backseat and held open the Towers' door. "Good evening, Casey."

I gave Big M a wave and walked with Benny inside the building.

*****

I had the end of my key in my door lock when my cell phone rang. I fumbled around my purse until the caller hung up. Before I could check the caller ID, it rang again. Unknown lit up on the top of the screen.

"I was just about to call you." Nothing from the other end. "Sam, you still there?"

The call ended.

I punched in number one.

"Hey, Sherlock. I was wondering when I'd hear from you."

"Did you just call me?"

"No. I didn't. Why?"

"My cell rang and by the time I got it out of my purse, the call rang out. Then, two seconds later, it rang again. It said unknown, so I thought it was you. When I answered there wasn't anyone on the other end."

"Are you at the condo now?"

"Yes. I went to dinner with Big M and Mike. Big M just dropped me off and Benny walked me to the elevator."

Sam was silent for a few seconds. "I don't want you leaving the Towers tonight. You understand?"

"I have no reason to go out. I plan to do paperwork. It's been an exhausting day. Detective Wilson, from the Dorchester PD, has assigned an officer to work with me for the next couple days."

"Why did he assign an officer to you?"

"He thought it was a good idea, since I don't know the City that well. She's going to drive me around and stay with me." I knew Sam wouldn't buy my story, but he wouldn't approve of my staying in Boston if he knew what was actually going on.

"I want you to call me in the morning before you leave the condo. You hear me—before you leave the condo."

"I will." I tried to lighten the conversation. "How's Watson?"

"Misses you. Like I do."

"I miss my guys too. I'll be home Wednesday."

"Be careful."

"Always. Love you, Sam Summers."

"Love you too, Casey Quinby." He hesitated. "Talk to you in the morning."

The condo was quiet. I felt alone. Hell, I was alone. If I was going to get anything done, I had to get my head together and start reading. I put the television on just to have voices playing in the background, then headed for the kitchen to make a cup of coffee. It was going to be a long night.

It was one o'clock when I finally looked up from my reports. I'd read over the interviews I'd done with Brogan and Smalls and made a note to get back in touch with them. My meeting with Martin Gerber was short and definitely not sweet. He didn't say anything that could directly tie him to the Sandwich fire. I was sure he knew more than what he told me. Now he was missing. I didn't like the man, but I was sure he didn't kill his ex-wife. If he did know who did it, his life wasn't worth a hill of beans and he'd end up the same way. And Elaine—I couldn't help thinking how she was a victim—and not for the first time. She didn't realize she held the key to unlock a lot of information—information not only for my case, but to put the record straight regarding 18 Buzzy Lane. The person who set the fire and killed her brother and sister-in-law was known to her. This person had no idea what Elaine told me and couldn't take a chance on what I knew.

Chapter 67

Tuesday

The six a.m. light streaming through the windows made my surroundings friendlier. Regan was picking me up in an hour, but five snooze minutes wouldn't hurt. After spending the first three tossing and turning, it was time to head for the master bath. Standing under my very own raincloud and having water fall gracefully onto my face gave me a sense of tranquility and relaxation. If Sam will install one of these in my shower, it's a done deal.

I had to call Sam before I left the condo. I wrapped a towel around myself and another one around my head, then walked to the kitchen. The table was still covered with paperwork and my cell phone rested on top, acting as a paperweight. I speed dialed him.

"Mornin' sunshine."

"Reporting in as requested." I laughed.

"I'm impressed. You listened to what I said last night."

"I'm standing here wrapped in a couple towels. Regan's picking me up in twenty minutes, so I haven't got time to talk. Hopefully, we'll find something new today that gets me closer to Carleen." I still didn't want to tell him about Elaine and Martin. I wouldn't be lying if I told him one was dead, the other one missing and that's all I knew. He'd never believe me, so best I find out more today, then tell him tonight.

"That would be nice. I'd like to have my girl home. I like it better when you're running around the Cape, rather than terrorizing Boston."

"Do I hear a smile?" I walked into the bedroom to get dressed.

"You do."

"Let me get going and I'll give you a call later this afternoon. Oh, by the way, will you install a rainfall shower head in the bathroom?"

"What?"

"What you stood under to take a shower last Sunday."

I was down to fifteen minutes. Not enough time to dry my hair, so I pulled it back into a ponytail, then into a bun and secured it with a scrunchie. It was a jeans and jersey day, so I felt comfortable with the casual image staring back from the mirror.

I slipped the reports Detective Wilson wanted copied into my briefcase. Then, in another zippered section, I put my notes of things I wanted to do today.

It's only me, so I'll clean things up later.

Benny met me as I got out of the elevator. "I don't see luggage, so you're coming back tonight?"

"Yep. I'm here until Wednesday." I saw Regan pull up in front of the glass doors. "Can't talk now, I'll see you later."

"Have a good one, Miss Casey."

"I hope to."

Regan waited until I got to the car door before she unlocked it. "Good Morning."

I put my briefcase between my legs and secured the seatbelt. "Ready for take-off."

"Coffee and donuts, here we come." She pulled away from the curb into the far left lane so she could make a U-turn—an illegal one at that.

"You drive like me. We're going to get along just fine."

Regan pulled into a street space two up from Dunkin's front door.

"Maybe you driving me around is a good idea—you know, the 'it's okay for U-turns' and 'look the other way' parking tickets. We might be in an unmarked, but it's like that old TV show, *Cheers*, where everybody knows your name—Officer with a capital O."

"It sure cuts down on walking time."

229

"No kidding and, right about now, I need my French Vanilla."

We took our coffee and a donuts to the last unused table. The female yuppies dressed like they stepped out of Vogue Magazine with their Louis Vuitton backpacks and signature canvas Coach sneakers. The male models weren't much better, donning Armani suits with draped Burberry scarves, carrying the men's Vuitton briefcase and sporting red and black Air Jordans.

"My whole wardrobe doesn't cost as much as the outfit the girl ordering at the counter is wearing."

Regan laughed. "This is Boston. It's amazing what's important to some people. Me, I could be very happy dressing everyday like—." She traced the sides of her body with her hands from her shoulders to her knees and back again.

"You'd like Cape Cod." I finished the last bite of my powdered jelly and swigged it down with some coffee.

"Detective Wilson is expecting us. Do you have the reports he's looking for?"

"I have a stack ready for you to copy. A lot of it is general information. Today I'm hoping to get something more specific to go on."

"What've you got planned?"

"Getting more information from Detective Wilson on the person in the black Chevy Camaro."

"He'll have it for you."

"How long did you say you've been on the department?"

"It'll be four years next October."

"Always in Dorchester?"

"Yep."

"What do you think of Detective Wilson?"

"He's well respected with the guys." Regan's face wrinkled up. "Why do you ask?"

"No reason, just asking?" I knew Wilson was friends with Robert Cushing, but I didn't want to push the issue with Regan. Somebody within the department knew about or was involved in Cushing's extracurricular activities. My intuition could get me into

230

hot water, but I needed to satisfy my suspicions before I could dismiss them.

"We need to move. Detective Wilson will be waiting."

Regan was quiet on the ride to Dorchester.

I knew I had to clear the air before we met with her detective. Maybe a change of subject would help. "I should have asked you earlier. How's your mother doing?"

The pall lifted. "She was pretty good last night. But this morning was bad. I figure after we do the station check-in, we'll stop by to make sure she's all right. That okay with you?"

"Sure, and I'll check in with Sergeant Maloney. We may meet up with him later and fill him in."

"You're dancing with your words and talking in circles. When we leave the station, I want you to tell me what's going on. I'm not just your chauffeur. I'm supposed to be helping you."

"Deal. Until then, you're better off not knowing." I took a deep breath. "Bear with me. You'll understand."

Regan gave me a quick sideward glance. "I can't understand until you talk to me."

"Okay. Already. I get your point. We'll talk details over lunch."

Chapter 68

Detective Wilson was in his office. "Good morning, ladies."

After Regan said good morning back, I added, "Good morning, Detective Wilson."

"Did you get your reports together last night?"

I took out a folder and handed it to him. "They're all here."

"Officer Regan, please make a copy of them while I talk to Casey."

"Yes, sir." She left and closed the door behind her.

"Did you find out anything about Camaro guy for me?"

"You already had his name and address and that's all I have at this point. I called the Nantucket Police Department to check him out. They know of him. Apparently he comes from a well-to-do family, but the PD hasn't had any problems with him."

"Did they go by the house?"

"They're going to, then let me know if he's around."

I didn't want Detective Wilson to know, but my next move was to contact the Steamship Authority in and out of Hyannis, to and from Nantucket, to see if they have surveillance cameras. When Regan and I leave the station, I'll call Chief Lowe in Barnstable. If I ask, they'll brush me off, but if he asks, they'll give him answers.

"What are your plans today?"

"I'm going to swing by Martin's house again. Maybe he's back. My clients are expecting a call from me. Since that's who I'm working for, I'll probably do that first. Sergeant Maloney wanted me to let him know the place and time of the meeting so he could be there." The Big M reference let Wilson know I was in contact with the sergeant.

"I'd watch what you tell them."

"I'm sure they read the newspapers. The Gerber name is very familiar. There's nothing over and above what they read in the Globe or Herald."

Regan came back in carrying a set of copies. "Here you are, sir." She handed me back the originals.

Wilson put them on his desk. He was done with us—at least for the moment.

"If there's nothing else, I'd like to get going."

The detective directed his next cluster of words to Regan. "I want you to check in periodically."

"Yes, sir."

Once inside the car, Regan asked. "What was that all about? Did you and my boss have words?"

"More like an unspoken battle of minds."

"I don't understand."

"You will." I glanced back at the station.

Regan pulled onto the street. "Where to first?"

"After I make a call, we'll go to Martin Gerber's house. It's early. If he hasn't gone on a mini-vacation, he should be there. If he doesn't answer his door, maybe the nosey neighbor who saw him get into the black Camaro will tell us if he came home last night. That bit of information could move finding Martin to the top of the list."

"Do you think he was involved in Elaine's murder?"

"Not directly. If my timeline is correct, he was with me when she was murdered. Indirectly involved—in my opinion, yes. He knows who did it. We need to find him. He's a piece of shit. We know that. His knowledge and his mouth could get him killed. Frankly, I don't care except he's a key player in the 18 Buzzy Lane fire and I need to know what he's hiding."

I called Big M and asked if he would contact Patrick O'Malley to set up a meeting. He said he'd be free around two o'clock and suggested we meet at Jim Kelly's place. Since Boston Blackie's was located in Southie, it would be easy for them to get to and it wouldn't be crowded. That way we could talk. He told me he'd see me then, unless he had to change the time to fit Patrick's schedule. Regan listened to my side of the conversation.

"If my meeting happens, why don't you take an hour and go visit your mother. I'll ride in with Big M, then meet you back at the Southie station"

"That would work."

Traffic was heavy, but she knew backroads to get us to Alimeda Street. Except for a couple of kids walking with backpacks that could hold a full-sized watermelon, the streets were quiet. After several rights and a left, we pulled up in front of Martin's house. I saw the curtain in one of the first floor windows move to the side. When the person inside realized I was watching, they backed away and the material hung straight again.

I put my hand on the door handle. "Let's go wake Mr. Gerber."

We did a quick survey of the area before starting up the front walk. Regan had never been there before. The same junk was strewed beside the house and in front of the one car garage. Out of instinct, I did a three-sixty looking for the black Camaro.

Regan had already pushed the buzzer for Martin's apartment. There was no answer. She tried again, then stepped back far enough to get a clear view of his front windows. Martin's curtains didn't move, but the downstairs ones did.

"Stay there," I said to Regan. "I'm going to lean on this buzzer. If he's in there, it will annoy the hell out of him and I'm sure he'll answer." Thirty seconds later there was still no Martin.

"Casey, the first floor is very curious. We should talk to them."

"I'll work their buzzer. You have your badge ready to identify yourself when they peek out again."

When Regan pulled her badge from her pocket, her jacket opened just enough to reveal her Glock resting in its shoulder holster. It worked. The 'peeker' reacted to my efforts to make contact with them.

"Can I help you?" The female voice was soft and appeared frail.

Regan stepped up to the box. "I'm Officer Regan from the Dorchester Police Department. We'd like to talk to you."

The first floor door opened only as far as the security chain would allow and a partial face of an elderly lady stared out at us.

Regan held up her badge. "We need a few minutes of your time."

The door closed. I heard her fumble with the security chain. The door opened and a little old lady, in a flowered bathrobe and fluffy pink slippers gripping a three toed cane, invited us in.

She pointed to the couch in the living room. "Please, have a seat." She took the chair facing us. "I'm sorry I didn't answer my buzzer right away. These days you can't be too careful. Some horrible things happening out there."

I saw a copy of the Boston Globe on her coffee table and wondered if she'd read anything about Elaine Gerber's murder. From her timidity and her last comment, I was sure she had.

"My name is Casey Quinby and this is Officer Regan." I hadn't looked at the name on her mailbox. "We have a few questions about your upstairs neighbor, Martin Gerber."

"Since you've introduced yourself, let me tell you my name. I'm Elsie Tyler. I've been here for twenty years. My husband died six years ago. I've lived alone since then. It was right after my Henry died, Martin moved in. Funny man—too young to be retired, but I don't think he works—at least not steady. He keeps strange hours and doesn't have much company."

"Did you know his ex-wife, Elaine?"

"I knew who she was. She only came around a few times. Always had an envelope with her—one of those big tannish colored ones. One time he wasn't home, so she left it with me. I don't know what was in it. It was sealed and taped shut. I wouldn't have looked anyway." She kept fidgeting with her hands.

"Are you sure you don't know what was inside?"

Elsie sat up straight. "I wanted to open it, but you have to believe me, I didn't."

"I believe you. Do you remember talking to the police yesterday?

"They were also asking about Martin. I told them I saw him leave in a fancy black car."

"Have you read the paper or watched the news this morning?" I waited for a reply.

"No, I was just getting ready to make a coffee and some toast, then do some reading—the comics first, that's the only positive thing printed. The rest is mostly a waste of ink."

"Mostly. There's a story in this morning's Globe you're going to find disturbing." I didn't give her a chance to respond. "Elaine Gerber was murdered yesterday."

Elsie's eyes opened as round as quarters. She fell back against her chair. "And Martin? He didn't come home last night? I know that because he's very loud."

"You mean his voice is loud?" Since he didn't have many visitors, I wanted to see if he had a busy telephone life.

"His phone ringer must be turned up as loud as possible. I hear it every time it rings—and it rings plenty. In fact, it rang a bunch of times last night and again several times this morning, but he didn't answer. I would have known."

"How?" I asked.

"I said he was loud. You might think he weighed four hundred pounds. I could hear every footstep. Sometimes it was annoying. And, last night or this morning his television wasn't on. The man must be hard of hearing. I know what programs he listens to and when I was watching something else we'd clash. I hit the ceiling with my broom handle more than once. Finally, I just gave up."

I wanted to tell her, he was trying to make sure she couldn't hear his telephone conversations. His patterns convinced me that Robert Cushing's death fifteen years ago didn't stop the lieutenant's predecessor from keeping the doors open for business.

"I feel horrible about Elaine Gerber. I really didn't know the lady, but she was always very nice when she talked to me. They argued something fierce and she always stormed out of his apartment." Elsie put her hands over her face and slowly shook her head. "Should I be worried? You know I'm alone. I have no children and I'm the last sibling alive. I'm originally from Michigan, I moved here because of my husband's job. We're not a close family. Any relatives I have are still there."

I gave Regan the high sign and make a slight motion towards the door to indicate it was time to leave, then stood up. I reached into my pocket. "Elsie, don't worry. Here's one of my cards. If you think of anything else about Martin or have a problem, don't hesitate to call. My cell number is on the back. My office is a ways away from here, so if you need to reach somebody right away call Officer Regan." I held my hand out for one of her cards.

She wrote her cell number on the back and handed it to me. I gave it to Elsie. "Thank you for sharing. The information you gave us will be very helpful. If..." I hesitated. "When Martin comes home you need to make the call."

"I will."

We followed her to the front door. We weren't off the bottom step when the dead bolt snapped into place.

"One down."

Regan was about to drive off when her cell rang. Her expression turned somber when she looked at the caller ID. "Hi Mom. Is everything okay?"

I couldn't hear the conversation on the other end, but knew it wasn't good.

"We'll be there in ten minutes." She froze after she hit the end button.

"Regan, you okay?"

"No. My mother fell. The cancer has made her weak. She has a hard time getting around, but won't let me get her a visiting nurse during the day when Andrew and I are working. It's not the money.

She has insurance that will take care of it. She's stubborn." Regan looked at her watch.

"Don't worry about the time. Let's go see if she's all right. She's more important right now."

Chapter 69

I followed Regan into her mother's house. It was quiet except for Broadway tunes playing softly in a room down the hall.

"Sounds like my mother's in her room. She usually takes a nap in the afternoon, then stays up with us for a while after supper. Why don't you have a seat in the living room and I'll check on her." Regan pointed to the archway behind me.

"Let me know if you need help."

"I will."

I felt awkward—helpless. My father died of cancer. I knew the feeling Regan was experiencing. I looked around. The room was decorated like one you'd see on Cape Cod. There were white ruffled cape-style curtains framing the six over six windows. The couch and loveseat were covered with a navy and white striped fabric, decorated with hydrangea print throw pillows. The antique white coffee table sat on a blue, green and cream braided rug and the matching end tables were home to two navy-blue based lamps with white shades—Looked like ones from the Christmas Tree Shoppe. Across from the couch was the same antique white-colored TV stand, big enough to hold what looked like a fifty-five-inch television surrounded on both sides by lots of framed pictures. Except for one wall hanging of Adirondack chairs at a beach, the rest of the artwork didn't match the theme of the room. The wall farthest from me had a framed collage of what I presumed to be family pictures.

I glanced down the hallway. Regan was still in with her mother. The music was still playing softly. I didn't think it was the appropriate time to call Big M, so I busied myself by looking at the family photos. There were two white-framed wedding pictures. One of Regan and, I assumed, her husband and one of the wedding couple with their parents—in Regan's case, her mother. Those were the only two pictures to the right of the television. Most of the ones on the left side were in small single frames or two hinged frames that held two photos each. I picked up the hinged frame closest to me. It was Regan's graduation from high school on one side and her graduation from the Police Academy on the other. *That could be me.*

I bent down to study the smaller pictures. One was of a toddler in a posed picture with Santa. Most were of a younger person, maybe in her early twenties, with a small child either standing beside her or sitting in her lap. I guessed the young woman was Regan's mother, but if I remembered correctly, Regan said she was an only child. This child didn't resemble Regan at all.

I was concentrating so much on the pictures, I didn't hear Regan come into the room.

"I'm sorry I took so long. She's resting comfortably now. She said she'd like to meet you. I told her to relax for a few minutes, then I'd bring you in. I hope you don't mind."

"Absolutely not. I'd like to meet her."

"Thank you. Did you see my wedding pictures?"

"Handsome dude you've got there."

"He is. He's such a good man." Regan picked up the bride and groom picture and smiled. "The rest of these are old pictures of when I was a little kid, well not the graduation ones."

"Those are pictures of you?" I picked another one up—looked at Regan, then at the picture, then back to Regan.

"I know. No resemblance at all. How do you like the Bozo red hair?" She laughed. "I hated it. I've been coloring it ever since my junior year in high school."

A chilled feeling came over me. I stared back at the picture. "You're right—Bozo red."

Regan picked up an oval frame resting in the center of others. "This is my mom and my best friend." She grinned.

240

"There's only two of you in the picture?"

"Look down beside my left leg."

There it was—the Raggedy Ann doll that was left on the O'Malley's stoop.

"She went everywhere with me. I kept her on my bed until I got married, then I put her away so someday I could give her to my little girl."

"What's on her foot?"

"My initials. It was a baby gift when I was born. My mother's friend embroidered them so I'd always know it was my Raggedy Ann doll. I once told my mother I was going to change her hair color, but I never did."

"What were your initials?"

"CMD—Carla Mary Delaney."

I wasn't sure what to do next. Carleen Davis was standing two feet away from me and, at the moment, there was nothing I could do about it. Detective Wilson put her with me not for my safety, but so that he could keep us together. Elaine was murdered over whatever happened twenty-five years ago and now Regan's life was in danger.

"I'm going to check on my mother. If she's up to it, I'll make her a cup of tea and see if she'll sit with us for a few." Regan walked down the hallway and disappeared.

I took the opportunity to call Mike Mastro. It went to voice mail. "Mike, it's Casey. Listen to me. I need you to meet me at the Towers around five-thirty. My car is in Southie at the station. I'll pick it up, then head for the condo. I'm going to park in the garage and come through the lobby. When I get in your car, just drive away. See you then." I finished my call just as Regan emerged into the hallway with her mother holding onto her arm. I stood in a gesture to help.

"It's okay. I've got her. She's going to sit up for a while and have a tea." Regan smiled and her mother tried too.

I helped Regan get her mother settled and as comfortable as could be expected. It was obvious she was in a lot of pain.

"Mom, this is Casey Quinby. We're working a case together."

If she only knew how true that was.

I reached out and put my hands around hers. They were cold. I kept mine there while I talked to her. "Your daughter is one smart lady. The Dorchester Police Department is very lucky she chose to go into law enforcement."

Mrs. Delaney watched my face as I spoke. She was frail. I closed my eyes and saw my father and knew it was just a matter of time.

Regan was back before I wanted her to be. I knew her mother held the missing puzzle piece, but I had no idea how to get her to fit it in.

"Last week momma was up walking, not fast, but able to get around with a walker. And, two weeks before that, she was moving with a cane. She even took a taxi a couple times to go to the store. Andrew's job requires him to fly to New York for a few days every three months. Since my mother was doing so good, I took an extra shift at the station. When I got home Saturday morning, she was in bed, but her jacket was hanging on the back of one of the kitchen chairs. She heard me come in and got up. I kidded her about being out so early. She thought I was serious because she had been out. Said she took a taxi to the store because she wanted some raisin bread and didn't know what time I'd be home to get it for her."

That was when she visited the O'Malleys and left the doll. She knows she's dying and wants Regan to know who she really is. I felt so bad for Mrs. Delaney.

Regan turned to face me and whispered, "How can a person fail so quickly? The report she got yesterday said she may only have a few days. She told me she wants to die at home." Tears rolled down Regan's cheeks.

"Why don't you sit with her."

"Mom, want to look at pictures again?"

Her mother nodded and uttered a barely audible, "Yes."

"She loves the picture with Raggedy Ann."

Chapter 70

I planned on meeting with the O'Malleys at two, but thought it best to put it off at least until tomorrow. When Regan went back into her house to retrieve her cell phone she'd left on the coffee table, I called Big M to let him know we had to cancel and that I'd call him later.

Regan got back into the car just as I ended my call. "I was supposed to head back to the Cape, but things have changed and I'll probably be here until Friday. Whatever I wanted to do this afternoon will wait until tomorrow."

On the way to Southie, Regan pulled into a small neighborhood deli not far from her house. "Their roast beef, with Russian dressing and sliced sweet onions on a bulky roll are to die for. They copied it from the famous Jack and Marion's Deli that used to be in Brookline. And, while we enjoy lunch, you can talk. You told me you'd fill me in on your missing person case."

"Did I say that?"

"You did. And, I'm overdue calling Detective Wilson."

"He must not have missed us, 'cause he hasn't called us either."

Under different circumstances, lunch at Riley's would have been like dying and going to heaven. I had to tell Regan about my missing person case without giving her any specifics. I didn't know how much she already knew about her real family. I just knew that this wasn't the time to fill her in on what she didn't know. I basically told her that a couple from South Boston believed their granddaughter, who reportedly died in a fire twenty-five years ago, was alive. I used the confidentially clause attached to my license to plead the fifth. She said she understood, but I knew she didn't like it. She didn't react to my words. She was good. Someday she'd make a great detective.

"I have to bring the unmarked back when we're finished. The detective doesn't like us taking them home. I'll fill him in before I punch out. Before I do that, do you want me to follow you to the Towers?"

"Not necessary. It's not that far away and I'm going to pull into the garage. No one can follow me in without a pass card or code."

"All right, I'll pick you up in the morning. What time?"

"Same as today."

Regan pulled into the police parking lot in the back of Southie PD. My little green spider was waiting for me. I fished the keys from my purse and retrieved my briefcase from her back seat.

"Be careful. I'll see you in the morning."

I watched her pull away. It was four o'clock. If Mike got my message, he'd be at the Towers at five-thirty. That gave me time to gather my thoughts, run a cloth over my face and give Sam a call. If I told him what I discovered today, he'd tell me my job was done. But, it's not that easy. I hadn't told him about Elaine or Martin and I hadn't shared my suspicions about Detective Wilson. My suspicions were totally unwarranted. For now, I couldn't share them with anyone. Especially Sam and Big M.

The ride back to the Towers was uneventful. The guest parking space closest to the elevator was open. I pulled in, grabbed my stuff, inserted my room key in the slot to operate the elevator, then hustled inside when it opened. It seemed forever before the door closed, even though I pushed the button with the two arrows facing each other. The door opened onto the twelfth floor. Shamus' condo was half way down the corridor. Once inside, I felt safe.

Before I had a chance to give Sam a call, my cell rang.

It was Mike. "So we've got a date at five-thirty?"

"We do if you can make it."

"I'll be there. Where were you when you called? And, why were you whispering?"

"You'll find all that out later. Gotta go." I filled a glass with ice, then poured some wine before I called Sam. "Hi, I'm still amongst the living, sitting in a condo overlooking the harbor, sipping wine and talking to my honey." I tried to hide the anxiety in my voice.

"Since I'm not there, I have to take your word for it. You still planning on coming home tomorrow?"

I hesitated. "I'm not sure. I wasn't able to meet with the O'Malleys today, so Big M's setting up something for tomorrow. I'll talk to him later about the time."

"I don't buy it. Now for the real reason you're staying longer than expected."

I knew he was serious. Sam's one sentence directives could fill an entire page. The man could read me like a book.

"It's a long story and after I finish my wine, I'm meeting Mike for dinner."

"You're stalling. What are you and Mike going to talk about?"

"My timeline. I figure he's the best one to help me with it. He knows most of the players and, without having to do extensive background checks, that information is extremely helpful."

"Are you forgetting why you were hired?"

"Not at all." There was no need to say any more 'cause I wasn't going to win.

"Call me when you get home."

"Be sure to let Watson know I miss him."

"Trust me, he misses you."

"Later." I ended the call, finished my wine and got ready to meet Mike.

Chapter 71

"I'm glad you only wanted pizza. Officer Regan and I went to lunch at a place in Dorchester called Riley's Deli.

"Know the place well."

"If I don't get back to the Cape and stop all this eating out I'm going to turn into a beached whale."

"Never happen." Mike smiled. "I kept our conversation light at dinner, but I know you want to talk."

"I do. Why don't you come over to the Towers. The condo key gets you into the garage, so you don't have to worry about parking."

Mike rolled his eyes. "You think I worry about parking?"

I shrugged. "Oops, forgot who I was talking to."

"We'd probably get a lot more done there, than sitting in a crowded bar. I'd also feel better about not having to constantly look over my shoulder."

"Do you have any coffee there?"

"Are you kidding, I couldn't survive without my coffee. Shamus has a Keurig and I came prepared with a fresh box of K-cups."

"In that case, I'm going to have Manny pack me a to go bag of biscotti."

"Let me pick up the tab tonight?"

"Not allowed."

"I have an expense account on my contract."

"Yeah, so." Mike walked over to the register and after a minute, he came back carrying a bag of pastry that looked like enough for several days.

"Whales aren't pretty." I shook my head, picked up my purse and followed him to the front door of the pizzeria.

He stepped outside and looked around. "The coast is clear."

"You think I'm paranoid, don't you?"

"I didn't say that, but since you mentioned it, yes I do."

"Reserve your comments until you hear what I have to tell you." I walked away from him, towards his car.

*****

Mike could have parked on the street, but he opted for a spot in the garage a few away from mine. "If somebody is watching, there's no need to let them pinpoint our location."

We rode to the twelfth floor and walked the corridor to Shamus' condo. I had forgotten to pull the shades, so we were greeted with a memorable view of Boston Harbor at dusk.

"This is where you're staying?" Mike shook his fingers like he'd touched something hot. "Maybe I should consider changing professions."

"It belongs to a friend of Big M's. He works for the Globe and is on assignment overseas."

"This is what they call being in the right place at the right time."

I took the bag of pastry from Mike and set it on the kitchen table. "Want your coffee now?"

"That would be nice."

"Here's a plate and some napkins. Why don't you plate the pastries so we can get started as soon as the coffee's done."

I brought over the coffees, along with a small carton of cream, and sat in the chair across from Mike.

"You're dragging your feet. What happened today?"

"I found Carleen Davis."

"You what?" He stood up and threw his hands in the air. "Where—how—are you sure?"

"Yeah, I'm positive."

247

He sat back down and leaned in halfway across the table.

I didn't give him a chance to say anything else. "Carleen Davis is Carla Regan."

"Who is Carla Regan?"

"She's the officer assigned to babysit me while I'm in Boston." I took a deep breath, then took a big drink of coffee.

"Does she know who she really is?"

"I'm not sure, but she knows something. Putting her and me together on the streets is like sitting us on a shelf at an arcade shooting gallery. I don't think whoever is watching us will move against us until he finds out what and how much we know."

"You've skipped over how you know Regan is Carleen."

"Regan's mother is sick with cancer. We stopped at her house to check on her. It was sad. While Regan was in the bedroom with her mother, I was in the living room looking at family pictures. There's no father in Regan's life. I'm not sure what the story is there, but it's not relevant at the moment. Anyway, while I was looking at the pictures, Regan came back into the room. Most were of her and her mother. Then she picked up one that was in the middle of the rest. She laughed and made fun of her Bozo red hair. The Regan I know doesn't have red hair. It's a light brown now because she's colors it. She told me that. But I know, Carleen had Bozo red hair."

"What's this leading to?"

"Back to the picture. She said it was of her mother, her and her best friend. There were only two people in the picture. When I asked her what she meant. She pointed out the Raggedy Ann doll she was dangling by her side."

"Popular doll."

"She pointed out something on the foot of the doll. It was Regan's initials. It's the same doll that was delivered to the O'Malley's stoop a week and a half ago."

"Did you see it?"

"I didn't have to. She told me she kept it on her bed until she got married four months ago, then put it away to save for her daughter."

"Wow. Next step?"

"I'm meeting with Big M tomorrow before I meet with the O'Malleys. Regan will be with me. Frankly, I don't know what I'm going to do yet. All this brings me to another concern—Detective Wilson. He was the one who assigned Regan to me."

"That doesn't mean he knows Regan's real identity and the history behind it."

"There's other things. You know about the black Camaro. I told him I ran the plate number through the DMV and had the name and address of the person the car was registered to. He asked how I was able to search the DMV's data base. I told him I had my sources. I didn't tell him it was Sam. His whole demeanor changed. He also wanted Regan to write daily reports as to all our comings and goings. Call it woman's intuition, but that man's secret involves the missing puzzle pieces from the Sandwich fire and the deaths of Charlie and Megan Davis."

"You could be right, but you need more to go on before you make any accusations. Big M is going to be beside himself. Cops have a brotherhood, but it doesn't include the dirty ones. If Wilson's hands are muddy, then he needs to be taken down. Problem is, he may not be acting alone."

"That's my thinking. He didn't pull the trigger or start the fire, but, as far as I'm concerned, he's just as guilty."

"Do you want me to be there tomorrow?"

I took a deep breath, then slowly let it out. "You'd be the only impartial person at the meeting. Big M, Regan and me are liable to let our personal involvement tip the scales in our favor."

"That's why I said you need proof that can't be altered. Let me know what time you're going to be in Southie and I'll get there a half hour before. I'll chat with Big M first. That should soften the initial blow."

Chapter 72

Wednesday

Since Regan was picking me up at seven, I called Big M before he went into his morning briefing session. It was six-fifty-two. I took a chance he'd be at his desk. After the sixth ring I was ready to hang up when he answered.

"Sergeant Maloney, how may I help you?"

"It's me."

"Casey, what's wrong?"

"Can we set up a meeting for this morning?"

"I've got my briefing, then I'm free. How does nine sound?"

"We'll be there."

"We'll?"

"Regan and me."

"I forgot about her."

"Also, Detective Mastro will be joining us." I didn't elaborate.

Big M didn't say anything.

"See you in a little while." I still had a few minutes so I gave Mike a call.

He answered right away.

"Hi, just got off the phone with Big M. He's expecting us at nine. I told him you were joining us. He didn't ask why."

"I'll be there at eight-thirty. Gotta go."

He's as bad as Marnie with skipping the good-byes.

It was five past seven when I got off the elevator. Benny was at the front desk talking to another resident. He gave me a wave as I walked by. The traffic in front of the Towers wasn't bad. I looked around, but no Regan. I was only five minutes late, I can't imagine she'd leave and I know Benny wouldn't have shooed her away. I walked over and sat down at the empty bench beside the door. Seven-fifteen—no Regan. I checked my phone for messages. None. Maybe she hit traffic. It was just after seven-thirty when she pulled up.

I knew something was wrong the minute I got into the car. "Mornin'," I said. "It's overcast, what's with the sun glasses?"

"Rough night."

"Want to talk about it? We don't have to be in Southie until nine."

"There's a Dunkin's on West Broadway. Let's go there." She made her famous illegal U-turn.

The drive-thru was busy, but the tables inside weren't. I told her to sit down and I'd get the coffee and donuts. If her mother had taken a turn for the worse, then she would have called in for a personal.

"Thanks," she said in a shaky, quiet voice—her eyes looking anywhere but at me. "Casey, I'm not sure how to begin."

"Wherever you want to. We'll piece it together when you're done." I reached across the table and took her hands in mine. "Okay, partner?"

"The story I told you yesterday about my mother, it was just that, a story I made it up."

"Sometimes we do what we have to do."

"I'm Carleen Davis."

"I know that."

She looked up. Our eyes locked.

"I'm also all but certain it was you who put the Raggedy Ann doll on the O'Malley's stoop."

"My mother wanted me to know the truth before she died. She wanted me to know I had family. She told me about the O'Malleys."

"Did she tell you about your real parents? Or how she became your mother after they died in a fire?"

251

"She's tried several times, but stops before she starts—if you know what I mean."

"Has she mentioned any names, either familiar or unfamiliar to you?"

Regan wrapped her hands around her cup and moved it around enough to create a wave-like motion. "Robert Cushing. I don't ever remember meeting the man, but because of where I work, I know his reputation well."

"Did she ever refer to Detective Wilson?"

"His name came out once. She stopped talking the minute she said it—like the sound of it terrified her."

"Did she ever talk about the fire?"

"When I asked, she told me never to talk about it again, so I didn't. At least not to her. I've been trying find out something about it ever since she mentioned it."

"When was that?"

"About a month ago."

"Did you use the computers at the station?"

"I did, but was careful not to do it when anyone was around. That's why I took some extra shifts. They weren't street patrol, they were for desk coverage."

"Regan, did Wilson ever see you working the computer? Maybe he walked by and you suddenly changed the screen? Or maybe you left your desk for seconds and forgot to get out of the site you were researching?" I took a deep breath. "Somehow, he knows you know who you really are. Somehow, he's involved. And, somehow, he's going to stop you from finding out about your past."

"Casey, I'm scared."

"This morning we're going to meet with Big M and my friend, Detective Mike Mastro, from the Revere PD. Detective Mastro knows about you, but Big M just thinks you're an officer assigned to babysit me."

"Why is this Detective Mastro involved?"

"He's a friend of my significant other, Sam Summers, the head detective in the Bourne PD. He hooked me up with him to be my contact while I'm in Boston. I've done the interviews, but he was right behind me making sure the interviewees behaved themselves. I don't think Detective Wilson has any inkling Mike is involved and we have to keep it that way."

Chapter 73

Big M told the front desk to have somebody escort us to his office. From the look on his face, I knew Mike had informed him of my findings, but I couldn't decipher what he was thinking.

They stood to greet us. I introduced Mike to Regan, then Big M motioned us toward the two chairs across from his desk. Mike pulled another one over to the side and Big M took his seat. The game was about to start.

"Regan, twenty-five years of your life have been taken from you. But, you wouldn't have had those twenty-five years if someone hadn't taken you out of the house on 18 Buzzy Lane in Sandwich before it was destroyed in a fire. Your real parents were either murdered and the person or persons used the fire as a cover-up or they died as a result of the fire. At the time of the investigation, nothing was found to indicate a cover-up, so it was deemed an accident and the case was closed. Your real grandparents, Patrick and Mary O'Malley came to me a week ago last Saturday with information to indicate you were still alive."

Regan eyes dropped. Her hands locked together so tight, her nails dug into her palms. "I put the Raggedy Ann doll on their stoop. I took the coward's way out, but I was afraid what might happen if I gave it to them in person."

"How did you find out?" asked Big M.

"My mother. She has cancer. We've been told she won't be with us much longer." Regan started to cry.

Big M took a box of tissues from his desk drawer. "Did she tell you anything else?"

Regan retold her story.

"Here's the problem. Both of you are in danger because you know too much. The thing is, we know how much you know, but whoever is watching you doesn't. We're banking on the person or persons to keep you safe until they find out. We're not going to let them find out."

Mike leaned forward, resting his forearms on the desk. "I fully believe there's a problem within the Dorchester Police Department. Regan, you're going to have to be very careful what you say and what you do. If Detective Wilson asks you questions, you have to play dumb. Although, his questions will be vague, he's hoping you'll buy into them and offer up information. He might create a fictitious case and ask what you'd do or what you thought about it. I've done it, so I know it works. Be careful."

"Do you really think Detective Wilson knows something?" asked Regan.

Big M spoke up. "I've known the guy over thirty years. Our families have been involved in law enforcement for generations. We've played on the same team and against each other in all levels. His father was tight with Cushing. Actually, the two families were tight."

"Then Wilson knew Charlie well?" I waited for Big M to answer.

"Yep. Charlie, Elaine and the other three siblings. In fact, he dated Elaine for a short time until Martin came into the picture." Big M sighed. "I'll give you history on Wilson, but we're up against a wall until we find out who else is involved—like the person in the black Camaro."

"Yesterday, when I talked to Wilson, he said he called the Nantucket PD to check out Camaro man. They said he came from a well-to-do family and they've never had a problem with him. I had to ask if they'd gone by his house to see it he was around. Supposedly, they were going to and get back to him." I shook my head. "I don't think any of that happened. After I left Wilson's office, I called Chief Lowe at Barnstable PD and asked if he'd do

255

some checking for surveillance cameras at the Steamship Authority. He'll get answers faster than me and I'll get a call as soon as he has information."

"Good job." Mike nodded.

"We know he was in Boston on Monday when Elaine was murdered. What we don't know is what time he got here. If we luck out and there are surveillance cameras, we'll be able to determine approximately what time he got to Boston. Until then, we can make all the speculations we want, but can't prove anything one way or the other." I checked my cell to make sure I didn't miss a call.

Big M rocked in his chair creating a hypnotizing squeak as he leaned back. "Regan, did you know about the fire?"

"I knew there was a fire, but no details. My mother wouldn't talk about it."

"Could you ask her again? This time tell her you know the fire was started and it would be much easier if she'd tell her side of the story. Tell her you've been doing research, but have hit a brick wall. If you let her know that you could be in danger, she may talk." Big M stopped rocking and rested his arms on the desk.

"I'll try. My husband is out of town on business for a few days." Regan looked at me. "I know I've said that before, but this time it's the truth. When I get home, I'll sit with her and explain what's going on." Before Regan could say anything else her cell rang. It was Carney Hospital. She stood up and walked to the far corner of the office. "Yes, I'll be right there."

I stood and moved toward her. "What's wrong?"

"I have to go. My mother was just taken to Carney. A friend of hers was at the house. Mabel must have called the ambulance."

"I'm going with you."

Big M and Mike stood up and walked us to the door.

Mike put his hand on my back. "Stay close to her."

Chapter 74

Mrs. Delaney was in one of the emergency room cubicles. Her friend, Mabel, was in the waiting room standing by the front door watching for Regan.

"Your mother kept drifting in and out of consciousness. She's done it before, but this time she drifted away and her breathing slowed. Something was wrong, so I called 9-1-1. I gave the EMTs your cell number. They came out and told me the hospital gave you a call and you were on your way here."

Mabel, stooped with age, only came up to Regan's shoulders. She shook when she reached out to take Regan's hands, tears trickled down her cheeks and her eyes conveyed an understandable sadness. Regan gathered her in her arms. "It's okay, Mabel. You sit here with my friend, Casey. I'm going back to Mom's room."

There were a few chairs open at the far end of the waiting room, closest to the door leading to the emergency cubicles.

"Ginny is my best friend. We grew up together. I don't know what I'll do if I lose her."

I knew how bad Ginny was, but tried to soothe Mabel. "She's in good hands here. And, Regan is with her."

"That girl is a godsend. I remember when she was born. Well, not born. Ginny wasn't actually there when the little one came into this world. But, she might as well have been. Carla, you know that's Regan real name, was only a month old when she came to live with Ginny. It was one of those private adoptions. You know, no questions asked."

My head was spinning.

"Ginny's fiancé got killed in an automobile accident. I didn't much like him. Always thought he was into drugs, but she loved him. It wasn't but a couple days after David died, Carla appeared. I'll never forget how excited she was. It was truly a gift from God."

"Was David from Dorchester?"

"Oh sure. His father was on the Dorchester Police Department."

Now I knew too much. There was no way Regan was staying alone at her house tonight with Andrew out of town. We could swing by her house, pick up some clothes and she could stay at the Towers. I was ready to resume my conversation with Mabel when my cell rang.

"Hello."

"Casey, Chief Lowe here."

I cupped my cell and told Mabel I'd be right back.

"I just heard back from the Steamship Authority. They do have cameras that record all the cars coming from and going to Nantucket. The Camaro in question is a frequent flyer. They emailed me a copy of the dates and times for the last two months. Said they could go back further if needed to, but I told them to hold off until they heard from me. I'll email you what I've got. In the meantime, you specifically asked about last Monday. He left the island at nine-fifteen and arrived in Hyannis at eleven."

"Perfect. Thanks Chief. I'll get back to you later." Things were moving fast. The twenty-five-year time warp was about to be closed. My math skills were never very good, especially without using a pencil and paper. But, if it took him ten minutes to get his car, then an hour and thirty minutes in medium traffic, that would get him to Boston at twelve-forty-five the earliest. Elaine was murdered at approximately twelve-thirty. Blake Myers would have still been en route. He didn't kill Elaine. So, if it wasn't Martin or it wasn't Camaro man, we're back to square one.

I walked to where Mabel was sitting. Her eyes were puffy and red. She dabbed them as I sat down beside her. Her best friend was dying and she knew it. The only comfort she had was to talk about the good times.

"You doing okay?"

"Not really. Could I get a glass of water?"

I looked around. There was a vending machine by the front door. "I'll be right back."

I loosened the top and handed Mabel a bottle of Zephyrhills.

"We were talking about Ginny's fiancé before I got a call. You said his name was David?"

"David Wilson."

I almost choked on my saliva. "What was his father's name?"

"Let me see. It was Henry … or was it Daniel. No Daniel was his brother. I'm sure it was Henry."

My head shifted into overdrive. "Mabel, I have to make a call. I'll be right back." This time I walked outside to call Mike.

"Casey, you okay?"

"Guess you look at your caller ID. We're still at the hospital. I've been keeping Regan's mother's friend, Mabel, company while Regan is in with her mother and the doctor. I haven't heard what the prognosis is, but Mabel hasn't stopped talking since we sat down."

"Do you want to clarify that?"

I explained the lifelong friendship between the two, then went on to tell him about David Wilson and my call from Chief Lowe. "Regan is going to stay with me tonight at the Towers. I don't know what time we'll be leaving here, but I'll let you know when we do. It would be a good idea to get everything in order before we expose Detective Wilson."

"Casey, there's no we. You've finished your case. You're not a cop. Big M and I will take it from here."

"Wait a minute. I may have found Carleen, but that doesn't mean my case is over. As far as I'm concerned the O'Malleys, Carleen and I aren't exactly surrounded by an iron curtain. Until I'm sure the three aforementioned parties are safe, I'm not done. Besides, Regan is a cop."

"We'll talk tonight."

259

"Regan's coming back. Later." I ended the call.

"They've got her stabilized and are moving her to a room. She's sleeping, which is a good thing." Regan turned to Mabel and gave her a hug. "We'll give you a ride home. When I hear something more I'll call."

Mabel got into the backseat behind me. "I'm all strapped in. Did you know you get fined if you don't wear your seatbelt?" She shook her head with every word. "I read an article about it in the Globe."

Regan's head moved slightly to the right. "You have something in the fridge for supper?"

"Oh sure, I made mac and cheese last night and there's plenty left over. I might even have a little glass of wine. And tonight's my TV night. I watch *The Mysteries of Laura*, then *Law and Order: SUV* and, if I stay awake long enough, I love *Chicago PD*."

I couldn't help but laugh. "A girl after my own heart."

"I haven't been called a girl for years. Regan, this friend is a keeper." She reached forward and patted my shoulder.

Regan made a left onto a street just wide enough for two cars to pass, then four houses down she pulled into a driveway beside a small, well maintained white bungalow with forest-green shutters and trim. "Here we are. I'll give you a call in the morning. If Mom's able to have visitors, I'll come get you. Okay?"

"I'd like that."

Regan and I got out of the car. As I helped Mabel out, she crooked her finger and motioned me closer. "Take care of Ginny's baby girl."

We waited until she was inside before we drove away.

"Mabel's quite the talker."

"She sure is." I figured I'd fill Regan in later when we weren't riding through Boston traffic. "I talked to Detective Mastro while you were in with your mother. He wanted me to give him a call when we left the hospital." We hadn't eaten anything since morning. "It's been a tough day. You feel like getting something to eat? He's going to ask if we'd like to go out to dinner."

"That would work, but before we do, I have to call Andrew to let him know about my mother."

"You can make that call when we stop at your house to get some clothes."

"Clothes for what?"

"Because you're staying at Harbor Towers with me tonight."

"I'll be fine at home."

"I'm not fine with that. There's too much happening around us. The Towers has tight security, so that's where we're going to stay."

I punched in Mike's number. "We just left the hospital and we're hungry. We're making a quick stop at Regan's house, then we'll meet you."

Regan smiled for the first time today.

"How about Pagliuca's? I could go for an antipasto and some eggplant parm." If we're being followed, Pagliuca's is small and there are no hidden tables. I really wanted to tell Regan about my talk with Mabel without anyone else listening, but Mike wasn't going to let that happen.

"I'll meet you there at six. Does that give you two enough time?"

Chapter 75

We lucked out with a parking space on Hanover Street. Of course, it was a permit parking only spot. Cruisers have the permits invisibly tattooed on their windows, so we were okay. There was already a line formed outside the restaurant door.

"Six o'clock on a Wednesday night. Guess that comes with good food." My cell rang. The list of people who shared the name unknown on my caller ID was growing. I cautiously said, "Hello."

"Good thing I don't hold my breath waiting for you to call."

"Sorry. It's been an eventful day. We started with donuts this morning and haven't stopped until now."

"Where are you?" Sam wasn't using his happy voice.

"Just got to Pagliuca's. Regan and I are meeting Mike for dinner."

"Have your dinner and call me when you get back to the condo."

"Kisses to you and the boy."

He hung up before I could say anything else.

"Wait here, Mike's probably already inside." I made my way through the crowd blocking the entryway and looked around the restaurant. We saw each other at the same time. Mike waved. I held up a 'wait a minute' finger and went back outside to get Regan.

"There were already two glasses of White Zin and a glass of ice on the table. I know that's Casey's choice, hope it's yours."

"Thanks, it'll do just fine. With the day we've had, anything with an alcohol content is perfect."

I held my glass up and proposed a toast to Mabel.

"Who's Mabel."

"Ginny Delaney's best friend. The one I told you about in my phone call."

Mike shook his head. "Right."

We all took a sip, then set our drinks down when the antipasto came.

"Hope you don't mind. I took the liberty to order an antipasto."

"What a guy. You listen well. How come you haven't been snatched up?"

"Been there…done that." He nodded. "Tell me about your day and, dare I say, Mabel."

I looked around the restaurant for any ears straining to be part of our conversation. "First of all, Regan's mother is resting comfortably at Carney Hospital. Not sure how long they're going to keep her, but while I'm in Boston, Regan will be staying with me at the Towers."

"Aren't you married?"

"Andrew is out of town on business. I'd be fine at home, but Casey seems to think there's power in numbers, even if it is only two."

"Agreed," said Mike.

I contemplated leaving out my Mabel story until I was alone with Regan, but then thought Mike should hear what I had to say. "Regan doesn't know about any of my conversation with Mabel. I gave you some of it when I talked to you earlier, so bear with me if I repeat myself."

Regan looked at Mike, then leaned forward to listen to me.

"I told you Regan's mother was engaged to David Wilson—Detective Dan Wilson's brother."

Regan's face went blank.

"He was killed in an automobile accident a couple days before you came to live with Ginny Delaney. Mabel said she thought he was into drugs, but didn't know for sure."

Mike took a deep breath. "David Wilson could have been one of the juveniles that ran with Charlie Davis. His name never came up, but I'm not surprised. It must have been pulled before it ever got processed."

"I tried to research my real family. Since my mother wouldn't tell me anything, I didn't have much to go on. I knew about a fire, but that's all—a fire. After our meeting this morning, I was going to try to get her to tell me. I never had the chance."

"You told me you found out, but you didn't tell me the whole story, did you?" I asked.

"After Andrew and I moved into her house, we had to pack up the bedroom we were going to use, to make space for our stuff. One day, when Andrew was at work and I was making room in the attic, I came across a trunk and several boxes stuck way back in a corner. The trunk was only half full—no clothes, just papers. I knew my mother's maiden name was Delaney, so I assumed she was a single mother. You know what I mean. I never questioned her. She was, is, a great mom." Regan stopped to wipe her eyes.

We finished the antipasto and ordered our meals, along with another drink.

Regan took a deep breath. "I found a birth certificate for Carleen Mary Davis clipped to a copy of mine. I was totally confused, but because my mother was having a bad time, I didn't want to upset her with questions. That's when I started doing my own research. Not long before you came to Boston, I found out my real parents were Charlie and Megan Davis from Sandwich. When I worked up the nerve to talk to my mother, she told me about the O'Malleys. I wanted to meet them, but was scared. Scared for me, for them, but most of all for my mother." She leaned on the table and cradled her face in her hands.

"Okay, you knew your parents were Charlie and Megan Davis and your grandparents were the O'Malleys. Did you know Charlie's stepfather was Lieutenant Robert Cushing?" I asked.

"I know now I'm Lieutenant Cushing's step granddaughter."

264

Mike and I both nodded.

"Detective Wilson's brother, David, might have been the one who killed my real parents, either before or as a result of the fire."

"I don't think he acted alone. I believe the Lieutenant and, possibly, Detective Wilson's father, Harry, were running a very successful drug business. I have to find out when and where David's fatal car crash occurred. If it was the day of the Sandwich fire and somewhere en route back to Boston, then it could very well have been planned. There were several individuals in the pool, but only one was the planner. One thing I'm sure of, it was the planner who took you from your crib that night."

"Casey, how much of this have you shared with Sam?"

"Not much. Until today all I had were assumptions, except Elaine's murder and Martin's disappearance. I'll give him a call tonight."

Our food came, we ate, but our conversation didn't stop.

"Regan, you need to stay away from the station tomorrow. When you and Casey leave the Towers, go directly to the hospital. Get there around eight. Call Detective Wilson and tell him you need to stay with your mother and you'll contact him after you've talked to her doctor. I don't think he'd be stupid enough to approach either one of you in such a public place. I'll go into my office early and do some checking on the David Wilson accident and whatever else I can find on him, then meet you at the hospital around nine."

Regan looked first at Detective Mastro, then to me. "I enjoyed dinner. I just wish it was under better circumstances."

"Next time it will be. And, we'll add Sam and Andrew to the invitation." Mike forced a smile. His mind wasn't in the moment.

Chapter 76

"I'm so full I don't feel like a Mike's pastry. A coffee isn't even calling my name. But, I'm sure another White Zin isn't out of the picture once we're comfortably settled in for the night."

Regan agreed. "With some ice on the side."

Regan pulled up in front of the Towers. Benny was standing just inside the door and came out to greet me. He had a puzzled look on his face.

"You okay?" I asked.

"Yeah, yeah. I'm fine. Long day."

"My driver forgot she was staying the night. Thanks for the greeting, but we're going to make a U-turn and park in the garage. If you're on in the morning, we'll see you then." I gave him a two finger salute as I closed the window.

Regan slid the parking card through the reader and I instructed her to the guest parking for the twelfth floor. There was a space beside my car. Before we had a chance to get our gear from the truck, I noticed Benny coming through the door.

"Was I supposed to register my guest?"

His reply was short and directed over our shoulders rather than at us. "No."

Before I realized what was happening, Benny had Regan on the ground and was securing her hands behind her back with disposable cuffs. I took one step forward in her direction and was grabbed from behind. I couldn't see my assailant, but from the way I was being restrained, I was sure it was a male. Two seconds later, I found myself in the same predicament as Regan.

Before I had a chance to respond, she let out a cry, "Detective Wilson."

It was the last thing said before we were gagged, bound, then put into the back of the detective's car and rendered unconscious with something sweet smelling like chloroform .

Chapter 77

I didn't know how much time had passed since Regan and I had been bound and gagged. It was dark out when we were abducted and even darker now. The disposable cuffs had been replaced with rope pulled so tight they cut into my skin. We were still in the back of the car with gags firmly in place. I was groggy, but Regan was still out from whatever it was we were given.

I knew we weren't in the Towers garage anymore because I couldn't see any of the lights that lined the walls. I could hear distant traffic noise, but nothing in the immediate area was recognizable. There wasn't anyone in the driver's side, but Benny was sitting sideways in the passenger seat. The once friendly expression I'd come to trust was gone. He had morphed into a Whitey Bulger-type henchman. I kept quiet. I didn't want him to know I was somewhat alert.

The click of the driver's side door handle was deafening. It was Detective Wilson. I made sure my eyes were closed, but retained the narrowest of slits to view my surroundings.

Stay calm.

Wilson gave us the once over, then turned toward Benny. "Has there been any movement from either one of them?"

"Nope. I've been watching. They're still out."

"Any cars ride by?"

"Only one—a pick-up truck. Didn't slow down, just kept going."

"That's good. The side door to the building is open. We have to move fast. Take the cop first. Put her inside, then come back for the PI. I'll secure the car."

"How long this building been closed?"

"Must be fifteen years now. Used to be a fur warehouse. There's not much to fuel a fire on the first two floors. But it will smolder and that's what we want. It will take a while before anyone sees the smoke. We'll put some accelerant along the edges of the first floor walls. The wood in the walls is so old, when it catches, the fire will travel up to where these two will be." Detective Wilson turned again to check us out. "When they find them, it'll take a while before they'll be identified."

"Even if the fire department gets here before they burn up, they won't find any ID's in their pockets. I took the cop's gun, badge, cell phone and anything that was in the cruiser to the condo. All the PI's identification must have been in her briefcase or purse because she didn't have anything on her."

"Good work." Wilson got out of the car, looked around, and gave Benny the thumbs up. He watched as Benny carried Regan, then me down the alley. Once we were both inside and the door closed, Benny stood watch until Wilson joined him.

There was something familiar about the outside of the building, but I couldn't put my finger on it and I didn't want to take a chance of moving my head to take a better look. I couldn't understand why Regan was still out of it, but figured it was probably a good thing. The detective had a gun. I saw it back at the Towers' garage. If they thought either one of us heard our impending fate, two quick shots would erase it. I did wonder why Wilson didn't just shoot us, but figured he only had his police issued Glock that could possibly be traced.

"You take the cop. I'll take the PI. Follow me to the third floor. Don't sweat there's no electricity. I got my flashlight. While we're in the stairwell, the flashlight won't be an issue, but once we're in the actual warehouse, it could be. I'm going to run the light along the floor, so stay close. Upstairs there's a room full of old boxes and packing paper. It will make good tinder once the fire reaches them."

My mind was semi-alert, but my body was limp. I wanted to grab Wilson's gun, but it was in his shoulder holster and the rope around my wrists held me captive. As we turned a corner and went into the stairwell, I saw Regan's lifeless body slung like a bag of potatoes over Benny's shoulder. I had to play dumb if we stood any chance of walking out of here alive.

Detective Wilson stopped in front of the third floor entry door. He moved the flashlight down, then faced the beam to highlight a path ending behind a pile of boxes and bales of discolored and curled packing paper. "This shipping material will create a wall long enough for us to get these two situated. Once we're out of here there's no light source to create any shadows that might be spotted by an outside observer."

Per the detective's instructions, Benny moved Regan about ten feet away from where Wilson had dumped me. I was face first against a pile of dusty, moldy old boxes. I could feel the pressure building in my nose. A sneeze would be deadly. I closed my eyes tight and prayed.

"The chloroform is going to wear off soon."

I knew it was chloroform.

"We'll pretzel them so they can't walk. Tie their wrists and ankles together with the same rope. I'll do the PI. You take the cop."

Benny nodded. "Whatdaya got to fuel the fire?"

"Damn, I left the lighter fluid in the trunk."

"Lighter fluid?"

"Trust me, lighter fluid is very effective. I want this building to burn. I don't want to destroy a whole block. And, I want to be sitting in Boston Blackies having a beer and talking to friends while the fire department is doing their thing."

Ten minutes later, Detective Wilson and Benny made their way from the third floor stairwell, down to first floor of the warehouse. "Wait here, I'll get the stuff from the car."

Chapter 78

I didn't know what was happening in the rest of the building, but I had to make a move. I maneuvered my body away from the boxes and rocked until I turned over. A low groan froze my movement. "Regan, Regan." I didn't have time to wait. I rolled back on my hands and legs. The pain in my bad leg let me know I was still alive. I used the dirt on the floor to inch-slide my body in her direction, quietly calling her name.

Finally, a response. "Casey, where are you?" Where are we?"

"I'm working my way over to you. We're in an old building. I don't know where. But, I do know we have to get out of here fast."

"I can't move."

"Stay still. I'll be there in a minute." Hearing her voice gave me a shot of adrenalin. I rolled over to my other side so I'd be working with a good leg. As I did, I felt something hard push into my thigh. My cell phone. Benny never checked my cargo pocket hidden by a zippered flap.

"Regan, talk to me."

"You're close."

"They didn't find my cell. It's in my cargo pocket. We've got to untie each other so I can get to it and call someone. You stay put and I'll slide up behind you." I made a few more moves, then bumped into Regan's feet. When I rolled over to figure out our next move, I was facing her back. "It's so dark I can't see how the ropes are tied."

"I smell smoke. Oh my God. They're burning us. Oh. God."

Her voice trembled. "We've got to get free."

271

"I'm going to flip so we're back-to-back. Let me untie you first." I found the center of the rope and pulled us as close as possible, then, still holding on, dragged myself closer to her feet. "I've got it."

"What?"

"The knot. I've got the end."

"The smoke … it's getting worse."

"Don't breathe deep. Stay still and let me work on the knot." If we didn't get out of there soon, the rising smoke would kill us before the flames. "I've loosened it. Try to wiggle your feet to release some of the tension, then I'll be able to pull off one of your shoes. Keep your foot still. Got it."

Regan slid her foot through the loosened loop. "My feet are free, but my hands aren't."

I shimmied up to her hands and repeated the process. "Pull them out. Don't stand up. Get the ropes holding my hands free first." I tried to squeeze them together to release the tension. It worked.

"I'm going to pull down. You pull up." I felt Regan's hand guide the rope over my knuckles.

"Stay still." The smoke was getting thicker. The heat was increasing. The fire was feasting on the old warehouse. The flames adding some light, eerie orange light. Dancing. Jabbing. Moving like Fred Astaire or Mohammed Ali. Another minute and I had the ropes off my ankles. I tore at the zipper and jerked up the cargo flap. I had it. My cell phone. We had a chance now.

When we were brought to the third floor, I tried to create a map in my mind. I counted Wilson's footsteps—thirty. I imagined them to be shorter than normal due to the fact he was carrying extra weight. There was some kind of logo painted on the floor, but without a flashlight I couldn't see anything.

Regan came to me. She grabbed my arm. "The flashlight on your cell—use it."

I held my phone out in front of me and Regan grabbed my hand. We stayed low along the wall of boxes. Through the smoke we could see the door. We were getting closer. Then I saw the faded logo. I stopped.

"What's wrong?"

"I saw this. I saw it." I pointed at the logo on the floor.

"You were drugged."

"I was groggy."

"That's not going to get us out of here. Let's go." Regan started to pull away from me.

"Stop. I heard Wilson tell Benny this building used to be a fur warehouse. I can't read the whole name, but the second line says fur."

"So what?"

I didn't want us to get separated so I grabbed Regan's hand. We dashed for the door. I picked up a torn piece of cardboard and used it to fan the thickening smoke. "We're going to make it girl."

My hand grasped the knob. My adrenaline surged. I burst into the door. It was warm against my shoulder. It flew open and slammed into the metal railing on the stairway landing. The echo cut through the fog. If Wilson was still out there, hopefully he'd guess the building was starting to collapse.

Once inside the stairwell, I pulled the door shut behind us. I punched speed dial on my cell. "Come on Sam, answer your phone." It went to message. "Help...we're in an abandoned fur warehouse building in the North End. It's on fire. Call Marnie ... say James Cagney door ... she'll tell you the location."

"What was that?"

I ignored Regan and punched the number two button.

"I'm unable to answer. Please leave a message and I'll get back to you as soon as possible." Marnie's voice wasn't comforting.

I screamed into the phone. "Help ... fire ... fur warehouse in North End next to James Cagney door ... help. Call Big M." I wanted to call Detective Mastro, but the smoke was seeping under the door. "Grab the railing and let's go."

Neither of us were steady on our feet. Two flights of stairs down. If the structure stayed up just that many more stairs, we could breathe fresh air. My chest hurt. I couldn't control my coughing. I wiped the soot laden sweat from my forehead back into my hair.

Regan gasped. "I can't breathe."

"Hold on." I grabbed her arm and tried to hold the railing and my cell with the other. It didn't work. My cell slipped out of my hand, fell the full two stories and crashed on the cement floor directly under us. Our communication from inside the building to the outside world was closed. What light we had was gone. It was pitch black. We stayed together and, without taking our hands off the railing, slowly crept down until we reached the first floor.

"Don't move. I'm going to try to find my cell." I slithered down the wall and carefully hand-walked the surface. "Ouch," I yelled without knowing if someone might be listening. I knew I'd cut my hand, but at the moment it wasn't important. "The screen's shattered and the phone's dead."

"Benny carried me through a side door into the warehouse. I'm pretty certain this stairwell door comes into the back corner of the first floor. If we hug the wall we'll be okay."

When we opened the door, I smelled something odd. I guessed accelerant. A flickering light pinpointed the concentration of the fire.

Regan stopped to get her bearings. "It's not as smoky here. We need a door. You look one way and I'll look the other."

I pointed across the room. "Windows—that's the front of the building. They'll be a door to the right. The one they brought us in through. Let's go." I stepped in front of Regan.

She grasped the bottom of my shirt to keep up with me.

"The door." I reached for the handle. It didn't move. It was locked. I slammed into it. It didn't budge. "Son of a bitch." The windows are in the front. The fire was concentrated in the back. Whatever was fueling it was a slow burn, otherwise the flames would be out of control, the third floor paper goods would be fully engulfed and we'd be dead.

We ran to the windows. "Take your other shoe off and get up on my shoulders. Break that damn glass."

274

I bent down. Regan used the wall to steady herself as she climbed onto my shoulders. She kept her hands against the wall as I stood up.

Perfect height.

"Start banging."

Chapter 79

I opened my eyes. Regan was lying beside me. Her eyes closed. Her body lifeless. I tried to roll over, but couldn't. I didn't smell smoke. I did see fire. Was I dead? Tears streaked my gritty face.

"Casey, it's Mike. You're going to be okay. Talk to me—talk to me." He got down on his knees and cradled me in his arms.

I could hear sirens in the distance. Flashing lights from the cruisers blinded my vision. "Regan, is she okay?"

"She is. There's an ambulance on the way."

I looked at Mike. My vision wasn't clear, but I was safe. "We need to go to Southie. We need to go now."

"Not going to happen." Mike laid me back down when a uniform came over to talk to him. He stepped back. I couldn't hear his conversation.

Fire trucks and an ambulance pulled up across the street in front of the fur warehouse. I wanted to stand up, but my legs wouldn't let me.

"You told me we were going to make it." Regan whispered. "I didn't die in a fire twenty-five years ago and I didn't intend to die in a fire today." She closed her eyes again.

The uniform left and Mike came back to stay with us.

I sat up.

Big M came running from across the street. "What happened?"

"The short version is Regan and I were kidnapped by Detective Wilson and Benny, the doorman at the Towers. They used chloroform and brought us here, then set the building on fire. The chloroform affected Regan more than me. I played dumb. They thought I was out, I was drowsy, but heard everything they said."

Big M knelt down beside me. "Why do you want to go to Southie?"

"Detective Wilson is sitting at Boston Blackies. That's his alibi. I don't think Benny is with him. He may have pulled a shift at the Towers. I don't care as much about him. He was just a pawn on Wilson's chess board. Get him alone and he'll sing like a canary."

"Marnie called me, then Sam. He's on his way up. He's going to call me when he gets close."

"I'll call him now, otherwise he'll drive a hundred-twenty miles an hour with lights blaring." I reached into my pocket, then shook my head. "I need your cell. Mine's destroyed."

Big M stood up and walked over to talk to Regan while I made my call. I joined them after I assured Sam everything was fine, even though it wouldn't be until I was in his arms.

Big M left Regan and me alone to talk and walked over to where Mike was standing with several uniforms. He was on his cell when he came back. "I've got two unmarks meeting us at Boston Blackies. It's against my better judgement, but they'll wait for us before they go in. Afterwards, I'm taking both of you to the North End Station to make a report and answer questions."

Mike put his cell back in his pocket. "That was Detective Conti. They picked up Martin Gerber and Blake Myers an hour ago riding around State Street. They claim they know nothing about the fire, but haven't stopped talking since they got to the station. There was enough coke in the car to keep them under wraps for awhile, even if they make bail. Druggies yes, but kidnapping and attempted murder—no. They also sent a cruiser to Harbor Towers, but Benny wasn't working. They got his home address and paid him a visit. He appeared shocked when he opened the door to two uniformed officers. They said the television was on, there were three empty and one half full beer bottles on the end table and a heavy stench of marijuana. The mention of kidnapping, attempted murder and arson, coupled with the beer and a psychoactive drug made Benny a spirited squealer.

"Casey, you and Regan come with me. Mike's going to follow us."

I noticed the two unmarks parked about thirty feet from the bar. As we pulled in front of them, Sam's car turned onto East 8th Street and parked a few car lengths away from Blackies. It was a scene from a movie set—five unmarked black Impalas all equipped with police interceptor packages carrying a total of five police officers and two detectives and me, waiting for the signal to make a move on an unsuspecting bar patron.

Big M turned to Regan in the back seat. "You ready for this?"

"Right behind you, sir."

"Let's go."

The rest of the officers followed Big M, Detective Mastro, Officer Regan, myself and Sam into Boston Blackies. Jim Kelley recognized what was going to happen and stepped back when he saw us come through the door. Detective Wilson's back was toward us. His attention was divided between the television above the bar and some guy sitting beside him. The few people standing nearby quickly scattered.

Big M gave Mike and two of his officers the high sign to move in. They moved fast. Big M cuffed Wilson's arms behind him and spun him around to face Officer Regan and myself. One of the Southie officers retrieved Wilson's service revolver while another officer frisked him for additional weapons.

"What do you think you're doing?"

Regan stepped forward. Her eyes focused. Her voice strong. "You have the right to remain silent. Anything you say can and will be used against you in a court of law. You have the right to speak to an attorney, and to have an attorney present during any questioning. If you cannot afford a lawyer, one will be provided for you at government expense."

Big M held Wilson's arms tight. "Kidnapping, attempted murder, attempted murder of a police officer, arson and, when we're done with Martin Gerber and Blake Myers, drug trafficking."

Mike leaned forward. "Think about all those guys you sent to Walpole. I'm sure they'll be glad to see you. You can have a permanent reunion because you're never going to see the light of day again."

Wilson's face dropped. It was over.

Chapter 80

Detective Mastro and a uniform from Southie escorted Detective Daniel Wilson to the North End precinct. One of the unmarked from the South End followed.

Sam pulled me close and held me tight against his body. I felt his heartbeat bang against the inside of his chest. He said nothing. Sometimes words are overrated.

Big M had his arm around Regan. "You okay?"

"Shook up, but okay."

"Sam, meet Carleen Mary Davis."

Regan held out her hand.

He took one of his off my back. "You don't know how glad I am to meet you."

I turned. Tears formed in my eyes. Regan and I came together as one.

"Thank you, Casey. Thank you for giving me my life back. I thought it was my fate to die in a fire, but it wasn't—not then and not now."

Big M stepped forward. "Unfortunately, we have to go to the North End to file reports. After that we've got a lot to talk about."

"Regan, you need to stay with us at Harbor Towers tonight. Andrew isn't home and your mom is in the hospital."

"Okay. I'd like that."

I walked over to Big M. "Can you come by for a while? We all need some tea and conversation."

"Speaking of conversation. You better call Marnie. She's the one who figured out where you were." He smiled. "I have a question. What's a James Cagney door?"

Chapter 81

Thursday

Regan, Sam and I spent the night at Harbor Towers.

Morning came far too quickly. It was nine-thirty when Sam's cell started buzzing.

"Hello."

"Big M here. Sorry to wake you, but I've already had a call this morning from the O'Malleys. They saw the story about the fire in the Globe and heard it on Channel 5 News. They didn't know—still don't—who Regan really is, but they heard Casey's name. I told them she was all right, but wanted to meet with them sometime today. Actually, I took the liberty to say we'd meet them for lunch at one o'clock at JJ's."

"We'll be there."

I rolled over and wrapped my arms around Sam. "Who was that?"

"Big M."

"What did he want?"

"It's a message for you and Regan. I'll tell you both at the same time." He slapped my butt. "We might as well get up."

Regan was already up, sitting in the overstuffed chair overlooking the harbor. "Morning."

I walked over and gave her a hug. "Coffee?"

"Definitely."

"Sam?"

"Of course." He took a seat on the couch. "Big M called. The O'Malleys want to meet with Casey and Big M today. They don't know me and have no idea who Officer Regan really is. Big M set up a luncheon date for one o'clock at JJ's. He wants us all to be there. Regan, do you know where that is?"

"I do." Her voice quivered. "First, I have to go to the hospital to be with my mother."

I brought Sam and Regan their coffee. "We'll go with you. I want to say 'hi' to her, then I'll join Sam in the lobby. Are you ready for this?"

"I am."

*****

Two hours later we pulled in front of JJ's Bar and Grille.

"We're early, let's go inside to wait." I looked around and saw Big M giving us the high sign.

"Morning girls and Sam." Big M looked at Regan. "I didn't say anything to the O'Malleys about you, so I'm sure this is going to be an emotional, but happy meeting." He stood up. "They're here."

Regan took a deep breath. "Once I found out I was adopted, I hoped for this day."

The four of us stood as the O'Malleys approached the table.

Big M motioned for me to step forward. I took Regan's hand and held it out for the O'Malleys. "Patrick and Mary O'Malley, I'd like you to meet your granddaughter, Carleen Mary Davis Regan.

Mary O'Malley reached out. Tears rolled down her cheeks. "Welcome home."

Patrick turned to me and smiled, then embraced both his wife and granddaughter wrapping them together as one. He repeated his wife's words. "Welcome home, baby girl. Welcome home."

The rest of the story.....

Martin Gerber and Blake Myers were sentenced to twenty years for drug trafficking, but were given ten years off their sentences for testifying against Dorchester Detective Daniel Wilson. Martin Gerber received an additional five years for withholding evidence regarding the fire at 18 Buzzy Lane in Sandwich. Both Gerber and Myers were found innocent in connection with the fire at the fur warehouse in the North End.

Prison life won't be pretty for Detective Daniel Wilson who was found guilty of kidnapping, attempted murder on me, attempted murder on a police officer, arson and the murder of Elaine Davis. He received life without parole for Elaine's murder. His other four sentences will run concurrent. He now resides at Souza-Baranowski Correctional Center in Lancaster, Massachusetts—fifty miles from Boston. Charges related to the Buzzy Lane fire are pending in the court.

As for Benny, he gets to spend the next twenty years sharing a six by eight foot cubicle with bubba. His Boston Harbor Towers' days are over.

Officer Carla Regan remained on the Dorchester Police Department and was given a commendation for her part in the prosecution of Detective Wilson. She buried her mother two weeks after meeting her grandparents, Patrick and Mary O'Malley. Regan kept the name she grew up with, but added Davis before Delaney— Carla Davis Delaney Regan. Sam and I have met up with Regan and Andrew several times and I'm happy to report, they're expecting their first child in seven months.

I sent thank-you cards to Detective Mike Mastro and Shamus Flannigan—one for saving my life and one for sharing a slice of the Boston high life.

Sam, me and Watson are back in Hyannisport—well, Sam's there most of the time. Who knows what will happen next.

If you enjoyed, **18 BUZZY LANE**, the fifth book in the Casey Quinby Mystery Series, please post a reader's review on Amazon.com.

I can be reached by email at judiciance@gmail.com or visit me at my website, judiciance.com. And, don't forget to sign up to follow me and receive my newsletter.

Made in the USA
San Bernardino, CA
06 October 2016